The Girl in Peckham & Kowloon

YOLANDA CHRISTIAN

Yolanda Christian

eyeofanartist.blogspot.com

This book is a work of fiction

However, Cheeki dos Remédios and Barto dos Santos are real
people, although the events and dialogue that occur are of the
author's imagination. Any resemblance to any other person,
living or dead, is coincidental

Thank you: David Wong, The Hong Kong Records Office, Dr. Roy
Eric Xavier & www.fareastcurrents.com, Horatio Ozorio who tells
it *The Way It Was*, Freddie Hyndman, Mary Michaels, Mark,
Brenda, Charlie, Zan, Victoria, the Westminster writing group
and many people I've met along the way

She often dreamt she was black, or her mother was a deep black, and the whitest of white skin she'd been born with always surprised her.

—a familiar landmark, what with lurking shadows turning parking meters into vibrant guitar-shapes, red brick walls bouncing back the chilly sun, and blue office windows full of grime and emptiness masking industrial activity; Peckham was a part of her.

It was obvious by the two eyes drilling into her backside that Bert was at his bay window rubbing sleep out of his eyes and lighting up a fag.

The plane climbed down, curved over tin shacks and mammoth tenements, and dipped for Kai Tak Airport. It lowered its wheels onto a single strip jutting out into a bay and halted at the water's edge, in front of sampans, boats, ferries and skyscrapers.

Peckham High Street

CATCHING THE TRAIN to Euston Station is no easy feat. It's one of those rites of passage you make if you want to be a successful artist. But first of all, you think you'll lose your train ticket or at least part of it—and then you'll be stranded in the big bad city. And if that doesn't happen it's because the train has already left without you. There again, you could be walking along the platform, it's waiting for you, solid and still, and your heart goes pitter-patter, pitter-patter, *Please don't leave without me!* and your foot slips between the platform and the train. You've seen it happen. Now you're minus a limb. Oh, Jolienta—she stared at the reflection in the window . . . white forehead, black hair, red lips waiting for that one kiss—if that doesn't happen, you get on the train, sit down, make yourself comfortable, the train pulls away, and you ask yourself: AM I ON THE RIGHT TRAIN? You twist your neck searching for someone to extinguish your fear. You feel hysterical. You smile. You order coffee. It tastes awful. The train builds momentum, chugs along, and brings with it a sense of adventure. You add a dab of romance and watch hedges, trees and bridges fly by. The train cradles you with its movement and mechanical hum. You are on the brink of life. You are speeding towards London. You are on the brink of all hopes and dreams.

Jolienta dos Remédios told herself to relax.

I'm on the brink!

Jolienta dos Remédios told herself to sit back.

I'm on the brink!

Jolienta dos Remédios closed her eyes.

The train screeched into Euston Station. She grabbed her coat and pulled out the ticket. A purposeful crowd carried her towards the ticket collector. The gates where the station guards were, the tannoy system, the rush of people, the taxis at the side— everything magnified, more insistent, more dangerous . . . people scurrying in all directions; some descending by escalator, heads vanishing into the ground. She put the ticket back and smoothed her pocket down; she had never used the Underground before, had never taken a bus into the depths of London.

*   *   *

For a moment, she was dazzled—Peckham High Street was a huddle of shops topped off with green canopies, way beyond her expectations. And he, of all people, was everywhere. He was in the cornices of buildings, in the lampposts that tilted, in the shop façades that sparkled, in the social interactions of cafés, and in the sharp contrast of light and dark. All she had to do was to get Tom to say Yes, and Peckham High Street, and Hopper, would be hers. She had dressed for the occasion too, on Tuesday the fifteenth of June nineteen eighty-two, a day of solid sunshine. She was wearing her favorite black dress with flute sleeves, a necklace of Indian beads, oyster-drop earrings and a thin black vintage coat.

What shall I do now? Jolienta thought, looking up and down the high street. Margo said Tom was precise. He might not like it if I turn up early.

A pigeon flew across the sky. She watched it settle on Welch's Florist & Greengrocer. A man in trilby and trench coat emerged from Bellenden Grove; his shadow spread across the words 'Flowers for All Occasions' and obscured the letter S. In the window, weighing scales pulsated like an all-seeing-eye over oranges and lemons. A scene of pure Edward Hopper. Images were waiting to be captured up and down the high street. She flexed her fingers. What if I can't find Tom's address and then I'm late?

She scraped gum off the sole of her shoe and tried to think. A trail of stubs stopped outside a nearby taxi office, and behind her, Melon Road stretched into a narrow corridor of brick wall and barbed wire. On the street, the windows of the Paris Café dripped with steam and oily brown kebab smells blew out over street-urine. In the doorway of 8 Tracks & Tapes, a sign said The Bouncing Ball Reggae Club, and had an arrow pointing upwards. 8 Tracks & Tapes itself was all ripped hood with second-hand goods dangling over pavement; pots and pans glinting in the sun. A fur coat and a clump of electrics added to the collection.

How can anyone earn a living inside this gloomy pit?

She peered through the doorway, stepped into darkness, tightened her eyes. There were wall clocks with pendulums, tarnished jewellery in glass cases, layers of dust, transistor radios, Constable reproductions in nasty frames, and at one end of the counter, the white face of a woman with peroxide-hair was beginning to form. She had an Alsatian dog sprawled over her feet, and as far as Jolienta could see, the woman was about as responsive as a jar of pickled cabbage. Only the dog responded by panting, his tongue heaving in and out.

Nothing going on here then. Perhaps it's a secret gambling den. When night arrives, ol' Cabbage Face comes alive, fed on a diet of nicotine, vodka and dice. That club upstairs, The Bouncing Ball Reggae Club. That's where it all happens.

The dog yawned and stretched out his paws.

She left the shop, glad to be outside again. The High Street continued. An off-licence. A secondhand car showroom. Manze's Eel, Pie & Mash Shop dominated the corner at the junction of Queen Street and Old Kent Road. Its tiles reflected car bumpers and traffic lights. Its nameplate shone, a mass of green and gold.

Eleven fifty? Better get back. Don't worry, Tom and I are bound to get on. Look. There's The Alliance pub Margo told me about.

Here it is. SUMNER ROAD ESTATE, LONDON BOROUGH OF SOUTHWARK, where Tom lives. Under the archway. Into the courtyard. Which way now?

The nearest staircase was to the left. Three flights. Number Thirty-three was in the corner, had a brown door, a peephole, a letterbox and a doorbell. A cable had been tied between pipes to make a washing line. There was no washing on it. She took a deep breath. The doorbell cried.

"Hello? Jolienta? I'm Tom."

He was slender, slight even and was eyeing her with curiosity. She fingered her necklace.

My, what a girly white face he has. A peach or a baby's bottom comes to mind. That heavy fringe over dark glasses. His chin juts out. "Hello, Tom. I'm early. I hope that's all right."

"Of course, Jolienta. Do come in. Lunch is ready. Let me take your coat."

Tom bowed slightly and waited.

"Margo speaks highly of you," he added.

Oh, you can tell he's been to Oxford, can't you? Jolienta thought. His voice is full of privilege and learning. His diction is perfect, while I sound so northern. My voice is up and down, lacks weight and purpose. Listen to the singsong of my voice—"Pleased to meet you, Tom. I'm looking forward to lunch. Your sister, Margo? Yes, she's a good friend of mine."—Why, I sound pathetic.

Tom smiled, ushered her into the living room and pointed at a polished table surrounded by chairs.

The interview had begun.

"I'll serve lunch, Jolienta. We'll discuss the rent and so on."

Tom disappeared. Seconds later, he was leaning over with a tea towel draped on an arm, laying down ivory dishes. As they landed on the table, Jolienta saw a network of cracks in the porcelain.

"I've made a cheese soufflé, a salad and a strawberry meringue for dessert," Tom said. "As you can see, the soufflé didn't sink. The meringue is my best one yet."

All she could do was stare. She had never eaten a soufflé in the whole of her life and had never met a man who could make one, and make a meringue too. The crisp white pudding with red blobs was perfect.

Tom nudged a tub dish towards her. She shifted uncomfortably in her seat.

Oh, my childhood, she thought. Unhappy meal times of Spam and fatty meat that made me gag. A kitchen out of bounds too damp for shelves. Everything piled onto one Formica table ready to topple. Now I'm here with a soufflé.

Tom pointed at a glass bottle resting in the middle of the table. "Would you like some vinaigrette? I used walnut oil."

"Vinaigrette? Walnut oil?"

"Yes."

What's a *vinaigrette*?

"Yes, please, Tom," she replied, traversing into the unknown. Images of home barricaded the way: no fridge, the oven roof collapsed the one time I tried to bake. Everything was tinned. Tinned peas, tinned peaches, tinned milk. Maybe now and then we'd have a slice of cucumber and a tomato. What do I do with the soufflé? Eat it in the dish or spoon it out next to the salad?

Jolienta poured a trickle of golden vinaigrette onto the salad, grasped a large spoon and dug into the soufflé.

"It didn't sink," Tom said with a chortle.

She tapped the spoon. The dollop slid onto the plate.

"I'm impressed. You went to so much trouble."

"It's a pleasure, Jolienta."

It was hot, soft and cheesy and melted in her mouth.

"Delicious."

She nibbled some lettuce. The vinaigrette burst into sweet and sour. She told herself not to dribble or spill and kept an eye on Tom. He was helping himself to potato salad with red onion, tomato sprinkled with fresh "oregano", and was pouring the walnut liquid over the lot.

Twenty minutes elapsed. Tom put his plate aside in readiness for dessert. To her shame, she found she was begrudging him the fresh strawberries, while he radiated nothing more than goodwill. She looked at him again. This time, she saw his sister, Margo, who fretted about everything and was far from precise.

They're opposites, aren't they? But they do have the same zebra-long eyelashes. Both are pretty with strong chins. They have the same angular bones too. He's probably six or seven years older than she is. Mind you, the resemblance must be coincidental; they were adopted from separate families and hate each other. I met the parents over a cup of tea in St Albans. That is, I went flying across their polished floor. Mrs Benedict was furious, because Margo had got a 2:2. Poor Margo, she just sat there, crushed, while her mother demolished her. I tried to gloss over the put down, but the insult had done its job.

What was it Margo said about Tom? What was it? Well, whatever it was, accommodation in London's hard to find so I will have to put up with it, whatever 'it' is.

"Jolienta . . . Margo tells me you follow Edward Hopper, the American painter."

Tom sliced into the meringue and handed her a small plate. "I went to his retrospective at the Hayward; I felt like I was being submerged into the nineteen-forties. He's very much the graphic designer, don't you think?"

"Tom, to me, he's priceless. A unique artist. He's the nearest I have to a mentor. Unfortunately, he's dead in the ground. Nineteen sixty-seven was the year. I'll never get to meet him."

Tom frowned.

"I can't believe you made this, Tom. It looks and tastes as though it came from an expensive shop."

"You are kind." Tom wrinkled his nose. "Coffee? It's Colombian."

He held out a coffee pot, a shiny cylindrical thing. It didn't have a plug attached to it. She cleared her throat; she didn't know what 'Colombian' was.

"Yes, please, Tom."

"Cream or milk?"

"Whatever's easiest."

"Which?"

"Cream. Thank you."

He poured the coffee out and dripped a thread of cream into two white China cups. "I hear you aspire to John Berger's writings, Jolienta?"

"Er, yes . . . I've read most of his books . . . Did Margo tell you about that? I met him in Northampton, you know. I believe in The Role of the Artist in Society, Tom, which is what he writes about, and I've embarked on a body of work in relation to the vernacular."

"How interesting. I too, believe in The Artist in Society. I'm a fan of his."

"But you're a musician."

"Yes, Jolienta, but I support the Labour Party, therefore, I believe in community. Would you like some cheese and biscuits?"

"No thanks. I'm stuffed."

"I hear you've been offered a place at The Slade School of Art?"

"Yes. Can't wait. Scared though."

"Surely not. Anyway, what's this about your work in relation to the vernacular? What exactly do you mean? I'd like to hear more."

Jolienta took a moment to compose herself.

He wants to hear about my nights spent drawing telephone kiosks in the dark as strangers dialled up their loved ones, and he wants to hear about my days spent painting the town square and other buildings, with an easel planted in the middle of a dual carriageway. She sipped some coffee. It tasted good.

"It's about capturing our heritage, Tom. There's a bond between people and places. And you, Tom, what do you do exactly?"

"A pianist and composer. I teach mathematics in Westminster, part time. Kris is a reporter at the Beeb. He's away at the moment, back in a couple of weeks. He's been commissioned to write a biography on behalf of a member of the Royal Family. Ghost-write it, that is."

He giggled. A high-pitched titter.

"If he tells you about the book, Jolienta, I haven't mentioned it. He can be a touchy individual.

"I'll write to you to let you know my decision about you moving in. I might ask Kris. I might not. The tenancy is in my name. It's my decision.

"He can be a peculiar fellow at times, Kris. If you were to have a problem with him . . . well, it would be best to come and tell me."

"A problem with Kris, Tom? What do you mean?"

"Oh, you'll see. Anyway, let me show you which room is available. The rent is four pounds a week. Would you like to see my piano?"

*   *   *

Jolienta gazed at the tenements of Southampton Way. Plane trees dotted the pavements and disappeared behind a lamppost. It was a tidy, but disconcerting view.

How quickly it all happened, she thought. Margo calling Tom, him suggesting lunch, him writing to say, Yes, move in . . . then Margo hired a van from the Student's Union and drove me all the way here. Just like that. "I mean, that ramshackle van. The tarmac flashed by under me. I could see it roar past my feet. The gears rattled, screeched and banged all the way along the M1 and the wind blew around my thighs as if nothing was sacred."

She kicked a box out of the way, unfolded a stepladder, loaded a roller with white paint and climbed to reach the top of the bedroom wall.

A figure in the hallway? Would that be Kris then?

The man strode in and planted his legs on the bedroom floor.

Oh, very macho. Anyone would think he was going to shake me off the ladder.

"Hello," the man said. "I'm Kris."

His deep voice filled the room. Aryan blondness illuminated the walls, blue eyes pierced gold-rimmed glasses, and a sarcastic face left pink lips wrapped around a bent roll-up. He was clean-shaven, handsome, about the same age as Tom, was broader, and wore a grey suit with a shirt open at the collar. No tie. She had to look away. She put the roller back in its tray.

"You've moved in. 'Jolienta', isn't it?" he said grinning. "Thought I'd let you know, I like to smoke," he sucked on his roll-up, "drink gin and tonic and play Ry Cooder. What's more, I won't wash my dishes for weeks on end, and there's nothing you can do about it. Tom's piano practice gets on my nerves. I defy you to say it won't get on yours." He wagged a finger. "It will get on your nerves."

He inhaled, exhaled, took his time. The bedroom vibrated.

He speaks beautifully. Sounds like a BBC presenter. Not an upper class toff like Tom then. Is he sizing me up? 'Not impressed,' his face seems to be saying, 'roundish face with no make-up, short dark hair no style, shapeless T-shirt, tracksuit bottoms, no waistline'. Bloody cheek.

"Do *you* have any annoying habits, Jolienta?" A leer spread across his face.

"Er, oil painting in the bedroom. The smell of turpentine can be overwhelming at times. But, I'll be sure to keep the door shut."

She steadied herself on the ladder and pushed the roller up. It hissed then stuck to the wall.

"Are you glad to be back in London, Kris?"

"Actually, Jolienta . . ."

He stared at her, drilled into her soul. It was deliberate.

"I was bored. Not much to do in the evenings. Yes, I'm glad to be back and to meet you."

Her insides flipped.

"And I was recently commissioned to ghost-write a biography for a member of the Royal Family."

They both realized Tom was in the hallway, hopping from side to side. "Everything all right chaps? Anyone for sherry?" Tom said.

*   *   *

Jolienta emptied a shopping bag and stacked tins inside the cupboard space she'd been allotted. Hardboard nailed over the window blotted out a balcony landing of rubbish chutes and decay. The kitchen was a dingy space—something she was used to, except it contained two objects of fascination—the cylindrical coffee pot and a black telephone. Both belonged to Tom. The coffee pot, inert on the stove, posed many questions—What is 'Columbian'? It can't be instant. How do I open it? Dare I even use it? What if I break it? And the beautiful telephone with the black curly cord beckoned without a need for coins.

She didn't know anyone who owned a telephone, and contented herself with its presence: black, bold, clean and shiny. There was the luxury of a fridge too and a cooker that promised not to disintegrate. All courtesy of Tom. Yes, her new home was a luxury and had a bathroom. No more having to wash feet in the kitchen sink or having to trek through the yard to use the toilet. Who would have guessed the council flat was so lovely inside!

The living room contained a sturdy puce three-piece suite and a Persian carpet. A large oval mirror in a mahogany frame sat over the drinks cabinet, where Kris' gin and tonic bottles vied with Tom's sherry decanter. In the corner, next to the cabinet, a cheese plant languished in darkness, because the curtains and dining table blocked out most of the natural light. On inspection, the drawers of the table were full of tobacco, cannabis, cigarette papers and foil-wrapped chocolate teddy bears. She had been interviewed in that room at the start of summer, and had been submerged into, or perhaps subdued by, Tom and Kris' world.

The next room along was Tom's, the most pleasing room in the flat, a near square in shape, and when Tom opened his bedroom door it almost touched his grand piano, which in turn prodded the bed. She was surprised by that bed—straight out of a school dormitory with white sheets and old woollen blankets. The piano was the real deal though with three pedals, ivory and ebony keys, an oak-veneered case and laminated beech bridges. On the desk was a sunburst design with an inscription, THE AEOLIAN COMPANY LTD, LONDON, 1922. Next to the pedals were slippers, not prim and exacting like their owner, but squat and irregular like cowpats. The one time he had invited her in, the record player had been open with an album inside, and the name on the label had been his—Thomas Benedict. His walls were stark suggesting someone with a lack of visual awareness. A small comfort.

The narrow hallway led to two more bedrooms. On the left side, the main feature inside Kris' room was a long pole jammed between two walls straining under a row of white shirts. His double mattress was on the floor and his window gave an enviable view of The Alliance pub.

Her room was the smallest. Of course. There was a futon mattress on the floor, a dark-wood wardrobe courtesy of Tom, and blank canvases were stacked next to portfolios. One box contained a 'Made in Hong Kong' black angora jumper. Another stored documents; obscure ones attesting to the past.

Out on the balcony landing, if she wanted to, and it felt good when she did, she surveyed the whole of the Sumner Road Estate and Peckham High Street. Neighbours still talked about the arrival of "that bleedin' piano" and about a giant removal van driving into the courtyard, where a crane had hoisted it to the third landing, and it was then squeezed in on its side while "some skinny bloke got excited".

If she wanted to and she often did, she watched traffic trundle towards Peckham Rye or flow the other way to Camberwell Green. Life was moving forward, she was in command of it and nothing was going to get in her way.

Sumner Road Estate

DAYLIGHT STREAMED INTO THE LIVING ROOM, joined the overhead electric light, bounced off the oval mirror and reduced Tom to a swaying skeleton. As usual, the cheese plant was in darkness and a ray of light tickled the drinks cabinet. Gordon's Gin, Martini, whisky, vodka, amontillado sherry, champagne; they sparked and fizzed with a life of their own.

"Bloody Kris still won't say which member of the Royal Family he's ghost-writing for, but surely the book cover will reveal all, eh, Kris?"

Tom, he had such a commanding voice and was laughing and gyrating in front of the window, casting shadows on the mantelpiece. She held onto her newspaper. Kris was glued to the TV. Or pretending to be.

"He refuses to say who it is," Tom continued, his chin jutting out aging his peachy white face. "Princess Margaret, eh? What do you say to that, Kris?"

She looked up and met his gaze. She had to. Tom was the landlord. His signature was on the tenancy agreement. Tom, glaring at her from across the room, he had found an advert in The Evening Standard inviting Londoners to apply for a council flat on a first-come-first-served basis. Apparently, no one wanted to live on the Peckham council estate. Crazy. So he spent the whole day on the phone, dialing and re-dialing, until he got onto the housing list. In return, he was to fill each bedroom as soon as possible—hence Kris, hence herself. When she paid rent to him, she always forgot that the real landlord was London Borough of Southwark.

Her eyes met Tom's.

"Yes, I do. I do refuse," Kris said, suddenly aware of the conversation around him. "I would never renege on a contractual agreement. The member of the Royal Family will remain confidential." He jabbed the air with a finger, sat back and drew on his roll up. His brow was furrowed setting off wavy blond hair, making him every inch the Hollywood star. Shreds of tobacco sprinkled across his thighs. He blew smoke at Tom, goading him, rattled ice cubes in his glass. Now he was thinking.

Tom moved away from the smoke, which was threading its way up to the ceiling. "You and your bloody smoking. What about us? We don't smoke. You and your bloody smoking, drinking and bloody Ry Cooder. Played over and over. Tobacco everywhere. You seem to think the drawers of *my* table are designed to house your grimy little habits. Now, what's the latest? You've put an advert in the Lonely Hearts column of Cosmopolitan just so you can ventilate your perverse delights and writer's research on unsuspecting ladies!" He thrust his loins in and out, faster and faster, a sex machine gaining velocity and screeched, "You sick bastard!"

The paper fell into her lap. Her lips clamped shut. Most days, she avoided the living room, because the men made her feel stupid, but this was hilarious.

"Yes, Jolienta, it's true. I have." Kris locked eyes with her.

How dare he, she gasped. How dare he talk to me and look at me like that? How dare he? After that first encounter in my room, he has ignored me every single day. He's ignored me in the hallway as our bodies brush against each other, ignored me in the living room as he pours himself a gin and tonic or nibbles a chocolate teddy, ignored me outside the bathroom—never leaving behind the faintest hint of bodily functions. Of course. And somehow, somehow, he manages to ignore me even when we bump into each other in the high street. He's never given me a clue as to why he behaves this way. And now he speaks to me as if nothing has ever happened. How dare he?

Tom grinned.

Kris grinned. His amber twig glowed as he inhaled. He raised an eyebrow. "Yep, I placed an ad in Cosmo. Could be fun. That's if I can hear myself think over the fucking piano."

She rubbed her legs. The settee had a habit of making her itch.

What have I gotten myself into, she wondered. Look at Tom rocking back and forth like a mental health patient. He's the one equipped to compose classical music and dissect the Theory of Relativity. And Kris? He's a BBC reporter, golden yet cruel; too much testosterone for one man.

I'm in awe of them. Afraid of them. Proud of them. Yet they always, always, fail to acknowledge me and anything about me. For a start, they both know I'm exhibiting at the ICA—The New Contemporaries no less, but have they ever said, 'Congratulations on your achievement. What are you painting now? Can I have a look?' No, they bloody well haven't. And Kris continues to play games with me. One minute, he'll speak to me. Then the next, I will be sent back to pleb-land.

I should move out. That's what I should do. But where would I go? The papers are full of horror stories.

I must stay calm. After all, I'm here for one reason—to make it to the top. And how many people get to live in the big city, in luxury, for a rent of four pounds a week?

Didn't I swear I'd become a famous artist?

That's all that matters.

I. Me. The one with buckteeth, pop-belly, slitty eyes, surrounded by well-dressed kids at school, who all had nice parents. Well, I harnessed my intelligence. That's what I did. I knew some day, somehow, I'd overcome the humiliations of flapping shoes and pass-me-downs, overcome my squabbling unkind sisters, overcome my mother's harsh ways.

I dreamt about giving pain to that woman. I said to myself when I was alone in bed at night, miserable, crying, alone—I said I'll make it. I'll find freedom. And then everything else will fall into place . . . love, family, success. Happiness.

At nine years of age, I won a painting competition thanks to a matchstick. Imagine the pride I felt when the teacher announced to the whole class, 'Jolienta, you've won a prize: a giant box of watercolours. Congratulations, my dear.'

I saw my name in print for the first time in that magazine. No doubt, Tom and Kris would find that funny.

No paintbrush? Why use fingers, use card, use rags. Use a matchstick. Anything's possible if you put your mind to it.

At ten years of age, I dreamt about going to the Slade School of Art. Oh, to bask in the glow of Wyndham Lewis, Gertler, Nash and Spencer.

At eleven years of age, I discovered Arthur Rimbaud, the French poet. I'd better not end up like him I tell you—arms dealer on horseback in Abyssinia, riddled with disease and injury, both legs amputated, dead at thirty-seven.

And then I triumphed.

I beat off competition from all over the country and was offered a place at the Slade School of Art. OK, I didn't get in for painting. It was for printmaking. But in the early days, it was Hopper's etchings that got him noticed and got him on the right track.

Huh. Kris and his dating plan. With a bit of luck he'll end up catching something. You never know. Or his ex-girlfriend will track him down—the one who rings and rings, getting on our nerves. That phone, it never stops.

Kris: sex on the brain. OK, good sex is desirable, but I've

never had it, only heard about it. Besides, I'm only twenty. I don't see what the fuss is about. Don't see what the hurry is. And Tom's recovering from a disaster with a frigid violinist. That's what he said.

Jolienta put the paper down and got up for the hallway. Tom and Kris laughed. She got to her room and closed the door. She lay down. The window brought in the sound of a car horn, a crunch of metal, a police radio and silence.

*   *   *

Sunshine licked the tenements of Southampton Way into a dour orange. The pavements below were deserted. Tom was practicing scales next door as per usual. Jolienta pulled at the pockets of her jeans and let them fall to the floor, fumbled through her diary, double-checked the dates, re-counted the weeks and shook her shoulders loose. Four weeks to go. Four weeks until the Slade opened its doors. Four weeks to paint more of Peckham High Street without any distraction.

Welch's Florist stared back—a riveting green canvas, where the owner was described in a series of brushstrokes within a dark interior. The man in the trench coat and trilby was unresolved. Another canvas, Carlos & The Paris Café, rendered in burnt sienna and umber, hung next to Welch's. Its dejected men drank cups of tea and were more in the style of James Ensor than Edward Hopper.

The waiting around's awful, Jolienta decided. I'm so glad I met some of the neighbours on the estate. They were a revelation. The French woman said Tom and Kris were *distant* and *superior* and asked me, *How do you suffer them?* You know, if it wasn't for her and her husband . . . And the man downstairs examined my paintings the other day and wanted to know, *Lovely. Really lovely, but, Olienta, why's everything wonky?*

I was touched. I tried to explain that I paint reality. I said to him, *Can't you see that?* The thing is, Manze's Eel, Pie & Mash Shop leans to the right at the junction of the high street and Queen Street. It really does. The lamppost in front of it leans to the left. Everything leans one way or another if you observe the directions long enough, and to sample the shop's meat pie swimming in liquor as bright green as the shop façade, well, that's a treat, even if it tastes of nothing in particular.

Tom's piano-practice stopped. Jolienta heard movement in the hallway. The front door clicked shut.

"Sometimes, the flat's empty," she said aloud. "Sometimes it isn't. It's hard to know. Tom's a slender man and moves about, in and out, quietly. It's only when Kris is in and what with his tendency to be brash and noisy, or if Tom is playing the piano, that I know someone is actually in."

*   *   *

The sun shone on Peckham High Street and she was ready to explore. The Crown leant to the right teasing spectators with strong shadows on creamy walls. Its windows refused to reveal any occupant to the outside world. She crossed over to The Hounditch of Peckham, a corner departmental store with a well-stocked perfume counter, glided past the mysterious Prestos supermarket and continued to Peckham Rye.

It's not especially inviting, she thought, stopping at the entrance of Peckham Rye in-door market, but all of the best things are tucked away, covered in grime, waiting to be discovered.

She wandered through the entrance and was immediately surprised by a pet store. Stacked to the ceiling and at the very top, a painted Scottie dog wagged its tail, *Spratts 'builds-up' a dog!* Budgerigars flew across decorative panels, *Budgerigar Mixture at Keenest Prices.* The main sign declared, *Peckham Corn Store's Pre-War Quality! Pure Nut Oil FIRST for 14 YEARS, Housewife's Frying Oil,*

DELIVERED FREE *by Harry Otto.*

After that, the interior wasn't that interesting. There were two exits. One for the railway station, where a canopy sheltered a Polish delicatessen, a tailor's shop called FOX and a barber's. The other exit led to Choumert Road and an outdoor market, ripe with the smell of plantain and mango. Someone had left a Simple Simon out in the road. He wore a hat, scarf and striped pantaloons, and was steadying himself on a menu of 'Pie & Mash, Stewed & Jellied Eels'. Broccoli cost forty pence. Courgettes seventy pence. Carrots as thick as rolling pins were twelve. A man opened a bag. Potatoes tumbled in. Pineapples, in crates stamped 'Holland', caught the dipping light, their leaves sprouted out in surprise. Shadows and light transformed the human figure.

After lunch in the Paris Café, Jolienta found a tree anchored in the centre of a church garden. Its branches stretched out like the omnipotent hand of God, but every time she tried to sit down to capture it in charcoal, a white dog advanced, snarling. At Camberwell Green, an old man in rags was on his knees begging. Life was ready to leave his body.

*   *   *

Jolienta turned over and faced the trickle of silvery notes.

Ha, that will annoy Kris. Tom's playing drives him nuts. The thing is, I never get tired of it. Whether it's scales or the whole caboodle. To me it's like . . . like I have my own resident pianist in my home of luxury! What's more, his notes have inspired a new theory, an infallible one at that.

She pushed the pillow into the nape of her neck and followed the repetitious notes, up and down, up and down. The scales stopped. She heard Tom pick up his bicycle and leave the flat.

Tom taught mathematics part-time and he'd be in shirt and tie. Kris was probably dead to the world, back from his night shift at the Beeb. Tom was a force to reckon with, but Kris dominated the flat, because his masculinity peppered everything into submission.

When she thought it through, and it kept nagging at her, bothering her, Kris managed to get away with all kinds of mischief, while she spent most of her time scampering around like a hamster. The facts were—any disruption to his daytime sleep and all hell would break out, but when *he* came home in the early hours, he did exactly as he pleased—played Van Morrison blah blah, and too loudly, flicked chocolate wrappers into the air, stank the place out with cigarettes. Much to Tom's annoyance. Such a nuisance . . . drawers full of tobacco, bits migrating to the carpet, piling up. Oh, how he loves to pile dishes in the sink, especially if Tom's about to make a culinary delight such as Shish Kebab with Lemon & Chilli Garlic Sauce followed by Baked Alaska for one.

Her own routine evolved around the high street and Peckham. She was always on the look out for a shadow, a scene of desolation, a sort of beauty or disconnection between people.

"Who cares that Tom and Kris like to ignore me as I carry my paintings in and out, and it is difficult doing this along the narrow hallway without getting clothes soiled. They both refuse to acknowledge the neighbours as well—neighbours who are happy to examine the latest version of The Bouncing Ball Reggae Club or some other work-in-progress.

"Well, I might not have Tom and Kris' swagger or income, but I'm doing just fine, and the local activists have agreed to put on an exhibition of mine. I'm going to have my first solo exhibition in the high street, three shops away from Welch's! One of the Peckham Action Group, the posh one with big lips, the one who wears an army coat . . . thanks to him The South London Press are to write an article about my portrayals of Peckham, and some guy called Jules, who looks remarkably like Kris, except he's small and giggles, is to take a photo of me next to Manze's Eel, Pie and Mash Shop. I'll wear my black angora sunflower jumper. Impress him. When I wear that jumper, I'm invincible. It really is the most beautiful item of clothing."

She pushed the pillow away, annoyed for staying in bed and dwelling on Tom and Kris. They weren't worth it. She brushed her teeth and pretended the face staring back was happy.

"Have I ever given them ammunition to criticize me?"

She turned the tap off.

"I store used teabags on top of the fridge, drink instant coffee instead of freshly ground coffee beans. I reheat vegetable curries until the pan burns. Kris calls them compost heaps. Cheek. I'm not articulate. Well not around them anyway. I'm not worldly. I'm naff—and you know what—I never knew that until I moved in here.

*   *   *

One of the drawings, 'Hubble Factory', showed a building leaning drastically to the right with a crane in front of it leaning dramatically to the left. The factory's cavernous windows were illuminated by bright sunlight emphasizing the building's emptiness, and the façade displayed the word 'H U B B L E' in a vertical formation. Each letter cast a long diagonal shadow across tangerine brick. After much hesitation—because everything in the flat belonged to Tom, including the wall—she had hung it to the side of the drinks cabinet just before lack of light shrank the room. Tom hadn't expressed any opinion about its appearance on the wall—like or dislike. Maybe he hadn't seen it. Kris hadn't commented either.

One of the men came in and poured out a drink. She didn't need to look up to know who it was.

"Jol!"

She jolted upright.

"How much for the drawing? It would make a good present."

Her heart thudded; Kris had a booming voice. A stick of

charcoal dropped onto the man in trilby and raincoat striding past Welch's Florist.

Tomorrow, he will blank me as usual, she thought.

Jolienta steeled herself. Her voice came out calm, "I haven't really thought about selling it, Kris."

He jabbed his cigarette at the drawing and began to talk about "brilliant oranges, deep blacks and extreme contrasts of light, which overall convey an unsteady yet solid edifice."

He turned around and faced her. "I love it."

He had his back to her again.

"I'm sure Brian will like it. My best friend. Is it Manchester, Jol? Is it still standing? How about forty quid? He's getting married soon, Jol."

She stopped herself from replying. She was way too polite for her own good. Anyway, does he deserve to own any of my work? she thought. Has Tom ever even looked at it? I hate them when they treat me this way.

I do need the money.

She glanced at the drawing over the drinks cabinet, close to the cheese plant, the plant that struggled each day for daylight. The plant bowed towards the floor and submitted to darkness.

"I'll let you know."

The charcoal stick dug into the drawing and emphasized the man pushing his hand down into his pocket. It defined the folds of his raincoat on that sunny day, that first sunny day in Peckham. His hat obscured the letter S in 'Florist'. He was pure Hopper.

"Just about to wash his bloody dishes," Tom hollered.

Tom wanted to bake pumpkin au gratin and said he was "exasperated by the irascible Kris" blah blah—one of his favorite expressions.

"By the way, Jolienta, he's gone on another assignment."

"Kris? Gone?"

"Yes."

"I was just talking to him a moment ago. He said he wanted to buy one of my drawings."

"Good Lord. Oh, well, you know what he's like."

Tom placed the pumpkin in the oven and closed the oven door.

No goodbye from Kris then? How exhausting. Those blue eyes. That manner of his.

The next day, she scrapped her palette clean and prepared it. The view from the bedroom window was the same—tenements, trees, a bent lamppost. Brush strokes flowed onto canvas before the sun moved on changing every shadow along the way. Movement of light set off a chain reaction of differing hues and contrast, meaning that no exact portrayal could ever be achieved with speed of hand alone, unless the work commenced at exactly the same time each day, in the same exact location, and as long as the weather conditions were the same too, and remained that way. The window of opportunity was very fleeting.

Jolienta used pigments she'd never used before, expensive, obscure pigments like lapis lazuli, and tried to superimpose her mind's eye on the compositions—something she wasn't good at.

She reverted to what was natural: her version of Hopper. The room became dense with the smell of turpentine, spattered with flecks of viridian green, and sometimes she painted a T-shirt by accident or dipped a brush into a cup of tea before she'd had a chance to drink it. Other times, while developing an image or adding layers of paint to an established one, she would open the window to let the fumes out and graze idly on the pavements below. Southampton Way was devoid of anything other than rectangular tenements.

*　　*　　*

A knock resounded through the flat.

"I'll go, Tom."

Jolienta walked past Tom's door. A small woman, pasty-white, with strawberry blonde hair woven into plaits and wearing a floral dress, was standing on the balcony landing. The woman was grinning a big toothy smile.

"Hi. I'm Rita. I live at Number Thirty-five."

Rita gestured to the right. "I thought it was time I said 'Hi'."

Rita had a lisp. Her voice was squeaky. A high-pitched mouse? and what with her creamy complexion and fair hair, she invoked edelweiss and Swiss cowbells.

Rita giggled, scrunched up her shoulders and waited. Jolienta invited her into the living room and brought in cups of tea. The neighbour explained that she was originally from Somerset and now shared the flat next door with three male photographers.

"I got dwrunk in The Grove one night, fell in love with James at firtht sight—one of the photogwaphers—the tallest, the handthomest. I weally did. Ha, ha. And when the pub called for last orders, I made thure I got an invitation to go back with them . . . to their flat, the one along the balcony. I pwetended to fall asleep in an armchair, I waited an hour or two, made thure everyone was in bed. I couldn't hear a sound, and then, tee hee hee, I swlipped *into* his bed."

She scrunched up her shoulders.

"He didn't waise any objection. Well, he did waise something! After that, I called round every night, each time with a new exthuse, until he caved in and loved me back. I've been living there ever thince. That was eight months ago." She scrunched up her shoulders and grinned a massive grin.

Wow, if I ever feel that strongly about anyone, Jolienta thought, if it ever happens to me, will I be able to act with the same conviction? A shiver ran up her spine.

Surely it will happen one day, the whole caboodle: children around the table eating dinner, fresh flowers in a vase, husband in the bath waiting for his back to be scrubbed.

"You share your flat with two men, don't you, Jo-*lien*-ter?" Rita squeaked.

"Yeah. Tom and Kris."

"Which one is the blond one?"

"Oh, that'll be Kris."

"He's stwange. None of us can get him to thay 'hello'. The others are weally put out."

"I'm not surprised to hear you say this. I tell you . . . some of the stories . . . some of the incidents that take place. You'd never believe it. Kris thinks we're all plebs anyway. Especially me."

"Oh? Naughty, naughty Kwis. Tom says hello though. Poth, isn't he?"

"If you like."

"What's he do?"

"He's a composer, a pianist. Teaches mathematics too. Yes, it's true," Jolienta confirmed with a nod. "He's got a first in both subjects and has a grand piano in his bedroom."

"Tee hee hee. Must tell the others that. Jo-*lien*-ter, when you come wound, you'll meet a guy with a head of curls like a Bwillo Pad, another one who spends most of his time getting stoned, and you'll meet James, the handsome, yummy James, my darling."

Rita wriggled and giggled. Her eyes were a clear blue, surrounded by straw-yellow lashes. She really was a fresh-faced country girl. "That sounds like fun, Rita. I could do with some of that. Tell me, d'you all eat together, because everything's done separately in this flat. Except for the toilet rolls, that is."

"Oh yes, we all take turns cooking, but Bwillo hates the fact that I don't like salt and pepwer. He gets weally worked up about it. And the other one gets cwoss, because I bleach my undies in a bucket. He hates the smell. Anyway, Jo-*lien*-ter," Rita said, "I have to get up early tomowow for teacher-twaining. Come round for coffee some evening, meet the guys. You'll find them very diffwent to Tom and Kris."

"Ha ha. Thanks. I will."

Her neighbour grinned, happy to expose a network of laughter-lines and turned left on the balcony.

"I don't like her, that Rita-woman," Tom said, appearing in the hallway.

"What? Rita? You don't like Rita. Why?"

"I don't know. Yes, I do. I think she's funny. Funny peculiar." His nose was a screwed up old turnip.

"You mean she makes you cringe because she's so sweet? Is that what you mean?"

"Yes. That's right."

"Well, I like to think I get on with most people, Tom." She glared at the wall above his head.

"That's because you're a chameleon."

"What?" Her chin stuck out.

"It's true. I've seen you. You change according to the person with whom you are talking. I've watched you."

He smiled an apology and disappeared into his room. Seconds later, he returned wearing a suit jacket and a leather bag over his shoulder. "Jolienta, I'm off to do some leafleting for The Labour Party. Oh, something I've been meaning to bring up—you should join me in The Peckham Action Shop sometime. Meet the steering group. They're lobbying against a six-lane motorway aimed at tearing out the heart of Peckham High Street."

He hurried onto the balcony ready to take on the world. Jolienta remained inert. She saw him in her mind's eye springing down the flights of steps, a brazen colt, and she tried to reconcile that, at times, she resembled a green lizard with protruding eyes.

Kris Stanton

THE FRONT DOOR FLEW OPEN, Kris darted into the living room, his camel coat flapping at his sides. Jolienta caught sight of a piece of sky before the door slammed to. She heard the sound of alcohol being poured out and Kris releasing himself into Tom's armchair. She grinned at Tom; Kris had been away for a month and now he was back.

"Tom! Jol! I've got replies back from Cosmopolitan!"

He gulped back a gin and tonic in one and waved a pink envelope at them.

"God, she's written on Snoopy paper. Ha, ha. Snoopy paper. Hilarious. She must be the naïve type. Not up for a shag, eh? I'll give that one a miss. What's in this one?" He chuckled and tore at the gummed seal of another envelope. "This one's enclosed a photograph. She looks OK. I'll drop her a line."

Kris studied her face for a moment and then studied Tom's, smirked and began to open another envelope.

"Hmm, an Asian chick. Nah. Take too long. My God, this one says she's an art student, introduces herself and writes *Can I suck your cock?* Jesus. I'm giving that one a miss."

"Ha, ha! Scared are we, Kris?" Tom shrieked and banged his leg against the table. "Ouch." He rubbed his leg and laughed. "Not up for the challenge, eh Kris?"

The letter and a photograph floated to the floor. Kris' feet padded softly down the hallway. There was something satisfying about that—watching him flee—him being outdone by a girl. An art student too. His stereo went on. The volume increased three times.

*　　*　　*

Kris leaned in and looked at the canvases on the wall.

"Kris. Try knocking next time." Why I could have been naked. Cheek. Nosy bastard. Now he's looking at the clutter on my bed. I suppose he'd like to be in it, humping up and down.

"Kris, what do you want?"

"Jolienta, I've finished the last chapter for Princess . . . Not that I'm offering it to you to read you understand; that would be a breach of confidentiality. The last few pages were difficult. How to be erudite, faithful to my Royal client. Keep it readable. Avoid clichés. It's been a challenge. To tell you the truth, I'm completely shagged out."

"Well done, Kris. Perhaps I'll read it when it's published then."

"Ugh."

Kris vanished from the doorway.

Typical. Typical. I wonder what he's up to now?

Jolienta heard him enter Tom's room without knocking.

Nothing new there then.

Peals of laughter spilled out.

Nothing new there either.

Her mind's eye homed in on Tom sitting at his piano in striped pyjamas and dressing gown, slippers spread over the floor, chandelier brightly blanking out a few stars over Southampton Way and the back of the council estate quiet except for the shriek of a fox. She continued to listen. She continued to watch with her eye: her mind's eye.

Kris sat down before Tom could object.

'I shouldn't think this bed's seen much action,' Kris thought, bouncing up and down on the bed. 'You know, ho ho, there's something quite virginal about ol' Tom. I wonder if he is?'

"Tom, why did you ask Jolienta to move in?" he blurted.

His gold-rimmed spectacles slipped a fraction down his beautiful nose.

"Everything was fine with just the two of us, wasn't it? Why did you change that? You didn't ask me for my opinion, did you? That accent of hers, for Christ's sake, it's like John Lennon meets Minnie Mouse. She . . . she gets on my nerves. I want her out."

Tom cleared his throat; his flat-mate took a long time to adapt to new people and was an awkward bugger at the best of times. "Actually, I enjoy having her live here," he growled. "It beats living alone with you, you bastard." He sighed. 'That's the way to handle him.'

They began to whisper. The banter started up again. The volume rose.

"She's painting images of Peckham for God's sake. Why would anyone want to do that?" Kris wailed.

"I know." Tom waggled his toes on the piano pedals. "What do you make of her art? Not my thing at all. Yak." He pulled his tongue out and pretended to vomit.

"Tom, the buildings lean all over the place! Nothing's straight."

The men giggled.

"Do you think she's a bit touched in the head?"

Squeals and grunts escaped the men.

'Mind you, to be fair,' Kris thought, 'Tom would prefer it if Jolienta was a throwback to the Pre-Raphaelite era. I mean, he's not exactly avant-garde, is he?' He fiddled with Tom's top blanket.

"I'm a Wallace-Collection man myself," Tom said. "What about you?" 'How strange he and I have never discussed the fine arts before.' Tom tightened the cord of his gown and reminded himself to be patient with Kris. 'Anyway, his neuroses keep me on my toes, exercise my brain.'

"I'm more of a . . . Andy Warhol man," Kris said finally.

Jolienta tiptoed back to her room. How she hated it when so-called friends were mean. It was an unhappy talent she had—seeing and hearing with her mind's eye. The worst part was she could be talking to any person, at any time, and their thoughts would often flash up on their foreheads like subtitles. As a result, she'd be exposed to untold embarrassment, hurt, and insults. The insults might even be directed at her, because . . . because . . . people hated her sense of conviction and they wanted her to drift away on some great big ocean.

Kris was an impossible character though. Those blue eyes of his. That head was like a closed vault. Maybe the fact he'd been sitting next door and not directly in front of her had helped her read his thoughts for the first time? But no, another time, one evening, one of his friends had been in the living room, a hulk of a man bursting out of his shirt. "Hello, how are you?" I said while brushing my teeth, and before I knew it he had the hots for me. Subtitles exploded across Kris' brow that time. *Don't tell me you actually fancy her? I'll sort you out later.* Then, he more or less manhandled the guy out of the flat. Bloody Kris! Kick him in the goolies. That's what I say!

Anyway, two weeks to go until the Slade opens up. Two weeks of Tom bitching and Kris dominating the flat. Two weeks of Kris' indifference and the pair of them laughing about Rita, about how she makes them cringe, makes them feel like they're sucking lemons. The weirdest thing of all, Kris *is* going to buy my Hubble Factory drawing. How weird is that?

Two weeks to go. They will fade into the background.

*   *   *

According to the irascible Kris Stanton, each woman who had replied to his ad, excluding the art student of course, was to be treated to a chicken dinner washed down with Liebfraumilch, a few puffs of a joint to American music, followed by bed, "for clinical sex, not lovemaking. I'm a young buck and I'll write about it." Kris—so self-absorbed, so inside himself—he didn't notice I'd finished the sentence for him.

I wonder how he'd react if I introduced him to my new boyfriend? Shame he won't be around tomorrow.

Jolienta crawled into bed, pulled the cover over and began to imagine what it would be like to make love to Polish Stan. They were discovering each other with tentative kisses and nibbles, holding hands coyly, pressing their bodies together, setting each other on fire.

He's very handsome. That's for sure. Long eyelashes. Longer than a giraffe's. The frame of an ardent warrior and a five o' clock shadow always on his pretty chin.

The next morning she woke up, butterflies in her stomach and tried to make the day go by quickly. Evening arrived. She hurried towards the clattering letterbox. Their eyes locked. She was lost, spinning around in his irises, growing warm and pink, flipping upside down and swelling with desire.

Stanislaus kissed her on the lips, slipped an arm around her and patted her on the bottom.

"Hi there, come on in," she gurgled.

They stumbled into the living room.

"Tom, this is Stanislaus."

"Excuse me, Stanislaus, if I carry on eating, won't you?"

Tom was in the middle of "suppering" on aubergine pickle, lamb chops in coriander and spinach in butter, and was holding a glass of champagne. He refrained from taking another sip and gave them both a fake smile.

Jolienta pulled Stanislaus to the settee, pressed him close, as close as humanly possible. The men looked as though they were getting ready for a fight. She rubbed the tip of her nose up and down Stan's neck.

"How sweet," Tom said.

Stanislaus disentangled himself. "Did you say something?"

Somehow, Tom managed to initiate a discussion on the Theory of Relativity, while inviting Stanislaus to join him at the table. Oh Stan, you don't know any better, allowing yourself to get involved like that!

The men sparred to and fro. She didn't know anything about astrology and remained silent. Eventually, the jousting ended and when it did, she was full of pride. Polish Stan had held his own. She handed him a bottle of wine to uncork and whispered into his ear. They got up, holding on to each other.

"How sweet!"

Undeterred, she led Stanislaus to her room. They pulled and pushed, kissed and sucked, stroked and tickled, but it was only for Stanislaus to discover his manhood was too big.

*　　*　　*

Kris loosened his tie and reached into his pocket. "Jol, here's the cheque. Forty quid. That's what we said."

He put it on the table and poured himself a drink.

"By the way, Woman-Number-One is coming around this evening. You know, Cosmopolitan . . .? Maybe you and Tom could make yourselves scarce."

"I might go next door."

"Join the plebs?"

"No, I think I'll stay in and see what Woman-Number-One is like."

"You're funny. You should be a comedienne."

Tom walked in and glanced at Kris.

"I'm expecting company in an hour or so, Tom."

"Wo*ohoo*, you filthy bastard."

"Shit. She's early."

Kris hurried to the door.

A woman came into the living room. Kris hovered about her.

Not quite what I expected, Jolienta thought. Woman-Number-One was slim, tall, with short wavy fair hair. The hairstyle and clothing were on the conservative side—grey jumper over a maroon skirt, which ended below the knees, black shoes with a small heel. Her bra was loose and she wore little make-up.

He sat the woman down and poured out two glasses of wine.

"Won't be long. Dinner on its way," he said, a gleam in his eye.

Kris slipped into the kitchen and returned holding an oven tray brimming with a golden-brown chicken surrounded by crispy potatoes and well-done parsnips.

"Phoorh, you'd make a good house-husband," Woman-Number-One announced.

Funny. Very funny.

Tom emerged from the bathroom and gave the woman a grin. She wanted to warn the woman. Tom probably did too, but it wasn't any of their business. There was nothing to do except get out of the way, avoid the smells of a roast dinner and let Kris make his next move.

Tom excused himself. "I'm going to edit music sheets."

She was glad to follow him. "I'm going to tidy my room up."

Her bedroom was in a state of flux. Paintbrushes and jars everywhere. Jules was due the next day at ten-thirty. She hadn't bothered to ask why he needed more photographs, because every time she spoke, he tittered, which killed off any attraction. It was late. She was tired. And she didn't need any introduction to the Peckham Action Group from Tom either. She had discovered them for herself. And they had appreciated her.

What an eclectic bunch they were too—the Peckham Action Group. Mainly middle-class, except for one woman of working class stock at the helm together with a disinherited millionaire. The group was fighting to save Peckham High Street from being torn apart by a six-lane motorway. The motorway would destroy the Paris Café, Welch's Florist and many other shops and venues.

How would removing these pockets of humanity help Peckham? What about the many evocations of Edward Hopper that still needed to be done?

She woke up, sweat on her brow.

What's that noise? What's that thumping?

Jolienta shook her head in confusion.

"OOOOooooH!" Woman-Number-One called out.

*   *   *

Jolienta leapt out of bed and pulled on a green dressing gown. Kris flung his door open—how unusual—slammed it behind him—how unusual—and raced into the hall ahead of her. His chest was bare, shoulders-square, physique lean, pyjama bottoms loosely-tied and she saw a tuft of blond hair sprouting out from below his navel.

Kris reached Tom's door and began to jerk his hands up and down in a 'V' sign in time to Chopin's Piano Concerto Number One. Jolienta yawned, waited for him to get out of the way, and put the kettle on.

What? Someone in the kitchen? Can't be. Kris is running a bath. Can't be him. Tom is playing Chopin. Hang on. It's a woman. Another woman. A short stocky woman in office clothes. Woman-Number-Two? How did he slip this one in? Woman-Number-Two?

She pushed bread into the toaster and nodded at the stranger. Kris appeared and began to talk to the woman in a low voice. She scrutinized them watching for signs of intimacy. Kris peered into the fridge, pretended to look inside.

The woman is short. She's fat. Hairy chin. Does it get any better than this? You can tell they've had sex. Clinical sex. What's the point of that? What is the point of that? I'll leave them to it, whatever it is they are up to. Jolienta dressed and ran down the flights of steps and into the courtyard. She swung her bag to and fro, a string cosh-shaped thing, a giant hairnet really. A group of teenagers were kicking a football. The goalkeeper ran the wrong way and the ball banged against the wall narrowly missing a coffee-coloured toddler clinging to his brother's leg.

Rubbish was overflowing from the central disposal unit and sent an acrid smell past her nose. Up on the third landing, someone was hanging out washing in the far corner. She didn't know his name—some biker always clad in leather who liked to drink milk, only milk, and lived with other bikers. Someone said they ran a bike club for local teenagers. Rita and the others were friendly with them, so only a matter of time.

What to cook for dinner today then?

She paced up and down the aisles of Prestos supermarket and hurried home, hungry. In the courtyard, Kris and Woman-Number-Two were dodging a row of bed sheets.

Oh, what bad luck. What am I going to say to them? My mind's blank. Well, at least he's taking her home. That's something. That really is something.

Kris and Woman-Number-Two advanced. They were almost level. Jolienta put on a polite smile. The woman gave her a stab to the retina and the subtitles sprang out, *What's your story, living in the same flat as this blond hunk?*

She wanted to shout back, "No chance. Not in a million years!" but swept by with a fixed smile. She charged up the stairs and emptied out the shopping. "Hey Tom, good entertainment, don't you think?"

Tom giggled and disappeared.

Toast, two fried eggs, a toast-sandwich. A cup of tea.

*   *   *

Purdey's the Fishmonger was taking shape and what a nice man he was in his straw boater and full-length apron. Out went the used white spirit and rags. Jolienta wiped the windowsill, tidied the bed and filled a laundry bag.

I wonder what Edward Hopper would say about Purdey's if he was alive and next to me now? His wife was always frustrated with him, longing for conversation, but he was a man of few words and enigmatic to the end.

I'm hungry. What shall I eat?

Jolienta looked inside the small cupboard, her territory in the kitchen. Beans? His wife, Jo, didn't care much for cooking. She was happy to get by with tinned food. In fact, Hopper had to beg or pretend to be the pet cat in order to get a square meal. I suppose Jo had to get her own back somehow. She was always sidelined by his fame. Funny he made no attempt to cook, I mean, I enjoy cooking.

Kris squeezed past and peered into his cupboard.

"So Kris, did you have a good time last night then?" She was taking a chance; she knew that. She held her breath and waited.

"No, Jol, the woman was a dog!"

He glowered at her.

"What d'you mean?"

He flung his spoon into the sink. It span round clitter-clatter clitter-clatter. His face was scarlet. "She farted. She bloody well farted."

*   *   *

Oh, Tom, you look about eighteen years old with rosebud cheeks. A solitary hair is sprouting out of your chin and your fringe is standing up in a wave where the outside breeze left it. Now, you're in a hurry to speak to me. How odd. You're insistent. Normally, your eyes shine out a warning that if any person dare approach you, impinge upon your time, cross you, then years of public school will come out batting. The delivery will be without mercy. I'm always ready for some sort of backlash, you know. A hard ball in the eye.

Tom leant his bicycle against the wall not wanting to scuff the white paint. "You'll never guess who I saw at Paddington Station."

"Go on then. The suspense is killing me."

"Woman-Number-One. Tall with short fair hair and do you remember what she said that night?" Tom mocked the woman's please-take-advantage-of-me voice: *"Oh Kris, you'd make a good house-husband!* Ha. I was getting off at Paddington Station when I caught sight of her and of course I said Hello. She took one look at me and ran. I swear. Teetering in Stiletto shoes! She nearly fell over. I'm not exaggerating." His eyes sank into folds of mirth.

"Oh, no, really? Kris, he's such a rat."

Jolienta promised herself there and then to erase the woman's cries of passion from memory. That was the least she could do.

There were other women in Kris' life too, thanks to Cosmopolitan. Once, she caught the back view of an unknown woman leaving the flat. Another time, she heard muffled noises coming from his room, and then there was the day when he actually complained, *For Christ's sake, she was having a period. I said, "Eeouw, no thanks"*.

The most intriguing time of all was when she had just got back from the Slade and had gone to open the living room door, but the doorknob wouldn't budge. After numerous attempts to wrestle with it, turn it, she realized he was hanging on the other side for dear life while his latest put her knickers back on.

The very last woman she ever saw in relation to his dating campaign, cut an intriguing figure—dark-hair peeping out from under a silk headscarf, handsome, almost aristocratic, bright red lipstick—the kind that never smudges—black cigarette-holder, expensive hand-tailored overcoat, red suede shoes. This woman slapped Kris across the face and stormed off.

Kris. Such a conundrum. Polish Stan: an enigma. So many strange people. So many difficult people in the big bad city. At least, she and the Pole were in love. To be sure, they were mad about each other, and she had grown to love everything that was Polish and what's more, Polish Stan was on his way. She had better prepare a nice meal. Polish sausage? Pickled red cabbage? Creamy potatoes. She must paint her toenails too.

The Alliance Pub

TOM AND KRIS ARE OUT. The sky is clear. Southampton Way stands with its blocks of flats glaring at me, impervious, unyielding.

Jolienta scowled at fibres sticking out of the settee's armrest and scratched an elbow. A marble trickled overhead from one end of the ceiling to the other and young feet ran after it.

Shame on Tom. Every time the boy's marble rolls across, he scowls at it as if it's a major infringement on his civil liberties. He actually went up and complained to the French woman about it, and blow me, the woman was left speechless by his lofty manner. I mean, I wonder how she feels about his piano scales wafting through her floorboards each day?

The marble bounced into clumsy evolutions and stopped. Jolienta saw the children she'd grown up with, racing up and down the street, chalking the pavement, skipping, chanting, skimming the tarmac with roller-skates. A gang was at the bottom of the street, a cul-de-sac of high walls. "Chinky!" they shouted. They were quick on their feet. She was quick too. She never got caught, and the sturdy leader—a handsome lad, encouraged the gang to bang on the front door and ask annoying questions.

What cun-tree is yer mudder from? they asked.

She never knew how to reply, because she didn't know the answer.

Does yer mudder wear false eyelashes? Is she ec-cen-trik?

Sometimes, they accosted her with, *Do you 'ave a dad?* Again, she had no answer. Her father was a mystery. Sometimes, she tried to conjure him—tall, very white, large nose, dark hair, drove a bubble car. One day, outside of the adjacent nursery school, he stopped and asked her to get in. The seat next to him was shiny and smelt nice, and she'd felt compelled to ask—*Are you my daddy?*

Mother and the Man, the man who was my father. He wore a string vest. He tickled me in bed. Mother came in. Everything changed. Someone said he was dead. I called out to the empty fire-grate, *But when was the phew-ner-ral?* Needless to say, the grate didn't reply.

Why d'you 'ave two-inch nails stickin' out yer front door? the kids chanted. That was what Mother did to stop them banging on the door.

Does she eat Pid-gion Pie? they cried.

Every two weeks a man in uniform called, pulled a pigeon out of a cage and wrung its neck, hence the rumour they ate Pigeon Pie at Number twenty-four. The cull was carried out from the top of the bay window in order to save roof tiles from being dislodged, but tiles only fell off the roof in high winds, scattering across the pavements, splintering and jagged. Repairmen came and went. Tinkered about. They couldn't have fixed the roof properly, because buckets and pans continued to play out a tune in the living room and kitchen.

No one would believe it. I could go on and on. The paraffin heater billowed fumes when it wanted to, blackened the walls and curtains, and I found my sister, one afternoon, soot caked around the nostrils about to draw her last breath. I shook her, refused to give up, and for fun, I held a mirror to her face and shrieked with laughter. That woke her up. Those days. Blue airmail letters made out of onionskin. Parcels from the USA and Canada. They cut through the gloom and reduced us to screaming brats. There were trays of apricots, dates, prunes, nuts, slices of lemon, chewy and sweet, jumpers with stiff zips to fight over, jackets to shriek about, stiff handkerchiefs to scratch your nose on and sometimes, a crisp dollar bill to admire.

One day, a Chinese trunk was delivered to the house. Its carved lid released a strange smell, not unpleasant. It contained rugs embroidered with birds and dragons, a padded gown, silk sarongs, lace tablecloths, jars of Tiger Balm, and a black angora jumper with a sunflower design constructed out of tiny glass beads. Made in Hong Kong. Somehow, I held on to that one.

"Hey, she's a bit of a doll!" Kris cried.

Jolienta gasped. How did Kris come in and switch the TV on without me knowing?

She put a letter back into its envelope. It had made her laugh out loud and then cry and then reminisce.

A women's tennis match was on. Helena Sukova was sending a backhand lob down an inside tram line. "She . . . she looks a bit like your ex, Kris."

"Huh?" Kris turned and frowned. "Who's that letter from?"

"My mother. Must be the only tourist on the planet to step off a plane wearing a ginormous sombrero. She wasn't in Mexico either. She was in North Africa, on holiday in Tangiers."

"I'd like to read that letter."

"Where she gets the money from I don't know. Probably, the house is left to rot, the roof to cave in. Why not, I say. It's her life."

Kris reached over and took the letter. A photograph of a small oriental woman with false eyelashes, straddling a camel in the desert and wearing a large sombrero, edged its way out of the envelope. He studied the photograph, read the letter.

"Hey Jol, she writes a good letter. What's this?"

"Oh yes, shorthand. Must have got in accidentally. As a young woman, she worked as a stenographer in the Hong Kong courts.

At least, that's what I believe to be true."

"What nationality is she?"

"Born in Hong Kong. Technically, she's Portuguese. It's confusing. I've been trying to figure it out. She never talks about the past."

"Interesting woman."

"All I've have to go on is a certificate with a Hong Kong stamp on it. It's tucked away in one of my boxes. You know, Kris, one day I'm going to China, in search of my roots. Don't know how I'll get there, but I will.

"I discovered Han Suyin, the writer. She's mixed culture too, part-Chinese part-Belgian. I've got this great aunt, Cheeki dos Remédios, who lives in L.A. She's the only one left who might remember what happened, why the family dispersed all over the world. I've got lots of relatives you know, but I don't know who they are or where they are. My mother won't talk about the past."

She waited to hear him snigger.

"Jol, after China, you should go visit this Cheeki. I wish I knew more about my roots."

He continued, "My father died when I was six. I was enraged. Fucking enraged." Words began to form on his forehead. *My mother never talks about him! My sister never talks about him! They never talk about him.*

Kris exposing his feelings to me?

She wanted to touch him. "Kris, I'm putting an exhibition on in The Peckham Action Shop. I'm planning a private view on . . ."

"I'll be in Edinburgh, Jol."

He sipped his drink. He increased the volume and sat back.

*　　*　　*

The Alliance at night would make a stunning painting. It would also be a chance to experiment with different kinds of blacks. Kris need never know. How outrageous her act of trespass would be—

48

painting the view from his window. Ha! *Nighthawks* was the inspiration, Hopper's famous painting of figures hunched over a counter in an American diner. It was a hypnotic image and she wanted something of it. That painting made her feel outright jealous. That one, and the one of the pulsating petrol pump station. And the one with the sun setting over Manhattan Bridge and not a person in sight.

Oh, I suppose I'd better run it past Tom.

She paused at Tom's door and listened.

He must be reading.

I better had run it past him, in case Kris is allergic to turpentine residue or something. Or maybe he booby-traps his room. He thinks he's that important.

Tom's über-white face greeted her. "Best to ring him and ask for permission, Jolienta. He'll probably find it intrusive. Here's the number. Try to sound confident. Good luck."

Jolienta forced herself to go into the kitchen and pick up the shiny black receiver with the curly cord. She dialled the long-distance number.

"Hello, Kris Stanton here. Can I help you?"

Oh, that was quick. No time to steady my nerves then.

"Jolienta?"

She heard the disbelief in his voice. His thoughts travelled up the curly cord—'What the fuck does Minnie Mouse want? What the fuck does she want? Jolienta calling *me*?'

"What d'you want?" Kris said.

Oooh, he'd make a good Gestapo agent. Oooh, I do hate him.

"I'm calling to ask for your permission to paint the view from your bedroom window. Your window provides an excellent view of The Alliance. The perspective is distorted. The activity at night changes colour and mood. I promise not to leave a mess behind."

"You want to paint The Alliance from my bedroom window?"

"Yes. At night. The composition from that vantage point is

49

unusual, and I want to explore using different types of black to describe the night. You won't even know I've been there. I won't touch a thing."

"How do you know about the view? Have you been in my room?"

"No. When Tom interviewed me, he gave me a tour of the flat. I've got a good memory. I've always wanted to paint that view. If you let me do this, I won't be snooping around looking at your personal possessions."

Jolienta told herself to expect the inevitable.

"I forbid you to enter my room under any circumstances."

She ended the conversation quickly. Better than hearing him click off mid-sentence.

Evening arrived. Tom was out leafleting the streets of Peckham. She slipped into Kris' room. The window gave a bird's eye view of The Alliance. It rose from the ground, a sturdy cream-coloured edifice, illuminated, beckoning, teasing. The windows shone brightly, framed by red drapes with golden ties, as joyful as a party in full swing. Its flat roof ended in layers of creamy concrete invoking a wedding cake. Trees swayed with volume and hints of blue. A basketball court faded into darkness. Shadows flew off the walls transforming The Alliance into a madhouse.

I'm going to paint it whether he likes it or not.

A few shirts on the pole jutted out of sequence. She half-expected Kris to burst in, and shook with fear. She eyed his bed, flinched, smelt the smell of his sheets.

"What the hell," she said, breaking the silence. "I'm going to paint The Alliance whether he likes it or not."

She switched on the light, unfolded a portable table, tucked her legs in, took a piece of chalk and drew around each foot. "He's got the same nasty carpet as me, I see."

Jolienta squeezed oil paint onto a well-scrapped palette, arranged pigments into groups of warm and cold, and lined up brushes—sable and hog hair in varying sizes. Distilled turpentine and white spirit were poured into separate jars. Rags were ready. Everything was ready.

Pine tickled her nostrils. Distilled turpentine was a powerful scent reeking of history: Rembrandt, Goya, Van Gogh, Hopper. She opened her eyes and looked at the window. Her reflection stared back, white and morose, blocking the view of The Alliance.

What shall I do? Switch the light off? Many artists have painted night scenes, but have any of them painted those scenes in the dark?

It'll go down well at The Slade. *She paints in the dark.*

I don't think so.

Stop being negative.

Why, when you've been held back the way I have, you let nothing stand in your way.

Jolienta memorized the colours on the palette and switched off the overhead light. The Alliance mushroomed towards her. She examined the structure of the building, examined the contrasts of light, depth of hue and followed the contours generated by street lamps, and scrutinized shadows and shapes. She agreed to relinquish control to the darkness, agreed to allow the unexpected to take place and began to paint an outline in viridian green. The Alliance loomed, tantalized, beckoned. She breathed in and out. She disengaged. Her body floated out of the window and down to Sumner Road. The pub sign creaked overhead. The saloon doors swung open. Noise spilled out. A woman lifted up a pint of beer and drank. Parked cars resembled slumbering rodents.

Inside Kris' room, the canvas accepted layers of paint. Vermillion reds and viridian greens became shadow and night.

"There are many types of black," Jolienta said to the room, "adding a dab of Prussian blue to my mix kills the black, but if I add cadmium red, the black becomes velvety and warm. What happens if I add pale green from that new tube?"

The Alliance closed its doors. The lights went out. She re-entered her body, stepped out of the chalk marks and fell into bed. In the morning, her room was consumed with a white light. She scrambled into the hallway.

Kris will be furious if I've got paint on his carpet. Tom's door is shut. Quick. Open the door . . . Rags and brushes are heaped on the table . . . The carpet's OK. Phew. I'm not going to look at the painting until it's finished. I will go back to his room every evening until it's complete.

Evening arrived. Tom left the flat with his shoulder bag full of leaflets. Jolienta put on overalls and hurried to Kris' room. Moonlight picked out the chalk marks. She stepped into them, sat down, grasped the most relevant brushes, the ones that she felt most at home with, the ones that settled into her hands as if they belonged, the ones loaded with moist paint and breathed in deeply. She floated down to The Alliance Pub of Sumner Road. Stripped of earthly energy, rags and brushes fell wherever gravity took them. Eventually, she came back to her body and staggered to her room. Sleep was instantaneous.

On the seventh night, the painting refused to accept more paint. Her chest shuddered with excitement. *I'm on the brink.*

Morning. Jolienta carried the painting to her window, careful not to disturb oil paint hanging over the edges. She dared to look.

The colours were a revelation. The pub's walls were an unexpected emerald green. Pale blue and lavender described the black of the night better than any manufactured tube of black paint. Brushstrokes buzzed with movement. Layers of pigment sang. The perspective was odd, cartoon-like.

She tried to figure out what it all meant.

The lack of control, the lack of light in the room . . . she gulped back coffee, swallowed beans on toast. True creativity had emerged. Something else too. Something lurking. Something confounding. She drained her cup dry and went to Kris' room. In daylight, the view presented an ordinary pub like any other. Its angle of vision was of slight interest; it was only when night fell that The Alliance was transformed beyond recognition.

I think, what's confounding me is . . . Hopper sets up a tension between a man and a woman, say, in an office encounter, or in a painting like *Nighthawks* and the viewer became an observer to an encounter, and it's almost always an isolated setting. Hopper hypnotizes us with the human condition. It's poignant. And what have I done? I've done the opposite. My painting portrays people discretely enjoying themselves; instead, the observer is invited to witness the aloneness of the artist. You know, I never intended that.

*   *   *

"Coming round for a bite this evening, Oventa? It's my turn."

"Oh, thanks. What time?"

"Seven-thirty."

"That'll be great. I'll look forward to that."

"D'you like sprats?"

"I don't know what they are to be honest."

"They're small fish. You deep-fry them, give them a squeeze of lemon and eat them with a buttered baguette. They're tasty. I'm expecting a few people round. Rita and James aren't joining us. They're going through a lovey-dovey phase. Huh, they're always having a lovey-dovey, you know what. Just as well if you ask me, because with Rita not around, I get to use salt and pepper."

"See you later then. I'll bring some booze. I mean alcohol, er, wine."

The man with the Brillo Pad of hair smiled, ran his eyes over her chest and continued down the steps to the courtyard.

I hope he didn't find my accent off-putting, Jolienta thought. He's quite a dish really. That hair.

Seven-thirty.

Jolienta looked in the mirror, practiced a smile, pulled out a bottle of Blue Nun and went out onto the landing. An air vent in a small window next to Number Thirty-five's door whirred around and round, releasing giggles onto the balcony. Through the bubbled glass window, Jolienta saw two figures splashing water.

Someone's having fun.

She turned and looked back at the flat. Garbage was bursting out of a rubbish chute. The bricks above it were charred too.

"Hey, far out man. It's that artist-chick from next door. Cool. Come on in, Polenta, we're having a joint. The Boom Town Rats are on."

Whoever he was, his ponytail bobbed up and down. She gulped—the living room was full of smoke, the TV was huge and next to a vast complicated stereo system. Several men were sprawled over a platform covered in rugs, cushions, beanbags and camera equipment.

"Jolly, come in here and say hello," a male voice called out.

Sounds like James in the bathroom.

"Jolly, come on in," two voices said from the other side of the flat.

She was outside the bathroom. "Come in? While you're both in the bath?"

"Jolly, come on in and take a look," James said. "Rita looks really cute. Ha, ha, ha."

Oh, do I have to.

"You want me to come in? Are you both naked?" Jolienta said.

"Hurry up before the soapy foam dies away. Hurry up, Jolly!"

"Jol-ly, Jol-ly!" the two voices chanted.

Jolienta heard water slop against the side of the bath and splash onto the floor.

"Tee, hee, hee," Rita said.

She gripped the handle and prised the door open. Rita was covered in soapsuds. Her blonde locks were loosely gathered into

54

a bun at the top, and she was scrunching up her shoulders as if she had clothes on and was having a cup of tea. "Tee, hee, hee."

James, delectable James, whose noble head touched the ceiling, had his sleeves rolled up and was holding a large yellow sponge, which was dripping over the floor.

"Jolly, doesn't she look adorable? Isn't she the cutest thing you ever did see? Go on . . . go on . . . Tell me. Go on. Ha, ha, ha."

*   *   *

The bus turned at The Green, drove parallel to an overhead rail track, passed East Street Market and trundled along the tarmac. It slowed down by a giant pink elephant and shopping complex, an ugly part of London, a swipe at hopes and dreams. How did people feel about living around here? she wondered.

The traffic stopped and started, confining the bus' progress for a good thirty minutes, and started up again with humming engines, lane-jostlers, and went on in the summer heat to St George's Circus, a more sedate area, where trees towered over Italian cafés and furniture shops.

The bus reached the Houses of Parliament and Downing Street and halted at a zebra crossing. On the upper deck, sunlight reflected back a ghostly white face—her face. She often dreamt she was black, or her mother was a deep black, and the whitest of white skin she'd been born with always surprised her.

Time to get off.

Blue sky. Nelson's column. Pigeons. Visitors. Police cars. Ice-cream vans. Black shiny cabs. Fountains spraying diamonds into the air. Big Ben. Trafalgar Square. Gower Street.

A porter's lodge marked the entrance to the Slade School of Art and the university campus.

The sight of the grounds made her knees weaken. She had waited for this moment. Ten years to be exact.

Euston Station bleated out its mechanical messages.

The next day was not a rehearsal.

Jolienta strode past the iron gate, nodded at the porter, and took a left turn into the Pearson Building. The etching studio at the top was already packed with students. She spoke to an American with a head of black curls, obviously well practiced in the skill of networking, and she noticed a tall Swedish woman with long blond hair. There were several elegant Indian women there too—one from Manchester called Geeta. There was an Iranian with an unmistakable moustache and a small group of English people, including a man called Dave and a punk called Fig. Fig had a Mohican haircut and wore a kilt.

It rained, snowed and rained again

IT WAS EASY TO IMAGINE ETCHINGS OF PECKHAM High Street hanging from the print racks. The Rochat presses were ready to go, and so were the griddles and Bunsen burners. A cupboard, covered in mucky fingerprints, was stocked with mezzotint rockers, roulettes, leather daubers and humble items such as the spatula. A roll of scrim was attached to the wall.

Fresh scrim on a dispenser? Can't be. Jolienta stared at the roll invigorated that the future offered less-struggle when it came to wiping an etching plate. No more having to go through studio bins and use tacky leftovers. But, and there is always a 'but' she told herself; the etching technician was standing guard, arms folded, a prison warden with blue-white skin and orange hair. Yes, there is always a 'but'. What a frosty face. What a stony expression. I must tread carefully with this one.

Barto dos Santos, the Head of Department, emerged from the swing doors to greet his new arrivals. His black hair was tipped with silver. He wore a medallion on his chest. As he spoke, it was a Portuguese accent that came forth, plus one nostril curled up.

That nostril doesn't do him any favours, Jolienta thought. What a strange voice. Kind of nasal. He has a cold, or something is stuck up his noddle. Full of food and wine, no doubt. Full of the Mediterranean. His apron's stiff from years of ink, resin and chemical splashes. Impressive. Now, the atmosphere is heating up. It has never occurred to me before; everybody wants what I want. And with the same intensity. We all want to 'make it' in the art world.

Barto ended his introductions, patted his belly and sent his frame hurtling through the slide doors. His absence triggered a scramble for studio space. When territories were established, the students commenced work. The American was bent over a copper plate, burnishing the edges with fury. Dave was in and out and settled on a litho plate in the lithography studio. The Swedish woman had a plate balanced on a leather cushion and was gouging at it. Omar put his plate inside the aquatint box in the corridor. In a series of nervous actions, her hand stung and bled. She covered the wound with masking tape. Nobody noticed.

Stop trying so hard, she told herself.

"Break-time," someone said. "Shall we try the coffee bar? The one in the Cloisters?"

No one moved.

"The studios are run by Euan Uglow, aren't they?"

"He's the one who spent seven years on one pose," someone else said, and with that, everyone piled into the corridor.

Each studio along the corridor opened up to a place of relentless-looking and describing. Jolienta had to admit she'd never seen anything like it in her life. Plumb lines and horizontal lengths of string formed a mass between rafters, wooden floor and walls, dicing up an absent composition into accessible portions. Observations of naked bodies had been recorded with nicks of umber or burnt sienna, culminating in mottled walls. Faded outlines of where a foot had been, or strips of tape, recorded past objects and the human form.

Suddenly, she wanted to know if she'd measure up.

Am I going to fall on my face? Am I out of my depth? I have never seen anything like this before. Nothing is left to chance.

The students clambered down a spiral staircase. The nearest

entrance to the Cloisters was in a corner of the main block of the university building, facing the lawn, trees and astronomy domes. The students found the coffee bar, a Dickensian place of wooden panelling.

*   *   *

Once a month, Barto liked to take first and second year students to a private room in the British Museum, where staff arranged a display of original prints into desk easels. On this occasion, his selection consisted of Piranesi's prisons of staircases and figures without hope, and one of Goya's etchings from the *Los Desastres de la Guerra* series, which showed a man about to behead a soldier. A Whistler etching was on display too—a scene of Venice. Jolienta was struck by the use of line and the way Whistler had inked the plate. Not that she was forgetting Edward Hopper. God forbid. It was just that 8 Tracks & Tapes needed a delicate line with a wispy residue of surface ink.

Lunchtime. Tottenham Court Road. People going up and down, searching for things to buy. Things to eat. Things to take home.

Jolienta wondered what the other students were doing and started back to the porter's lodge.

She was ready, apron on.

Barto peered over her shoulder. His right nostril made that funny shape again. "Eed has not changed since ze days of Rembrandt, you know," he said, and pointed at the singed bellows above her head by way of explanation.

Eager to establish a rapport, Jolienta nodded, put the plate facedown into the lips of the bellows and ran a taper under the plate, keeping the flame steady. The smell of hard ground being sealed brought Sunday Mass to mind. Not a bad memory; sitting in a polished pew, the smell of incense weaving through the air.

Barto checked the plate and moved on to the next student.

When the plate was cool, a traced drawing was pressed down

onto the hard ground and served as an image transfer. She selected a needle to scratch along the shiny imprint. The next stage involved acid. Etching was a leap of faith not unlike painting; you could go to a lot of effort and still wind up with a mess.

Jolienta made a note of the time on the acid room clock. Bird feathers lay immobile in pools of coppery fluid. She slid the plate into the acid solution. The extractor fan started up. Balls of gas bubbled along the exposed lines to reveal pots and pans, suspended fur coats and the bric-à-brac of 8 Tracks & Tapes.

*   *   *

The caretaker began to lock up. The night sky heaved; she tightened her scarf, pulled on gloves and was glad to see a bus heading towards to her. She climbed up to the upper deck. The bus trembled and lurched along Gower Street. Hot air blew over her legs. She rocked with the bus. Wind and rain lashed against the windows. Forest Hill hurtled by. A street lamp illuminated a signpost for the Horniman Museum.

Damn!

She shook herself awake.

Tom and Kris—they've taught me to expect the unexpected all right, and here I am—fool, drifting off to sleep and going right past Peckham High Street. What's the point of being warm and snug one minute and then drenched in bitter wind and rain the next?

She rang the bell, clutched her coat below the last button to stop the sides from flying open, and braced herself against the twists and turns of the storm. The rain stopped, but trees entrenched between lampposts waved and thrashed. She bowed her head into the wind. An icy gust swept by. Jolienta stumbled. A side entrance to the Sumner Road Estate, which she'd never used before—it cut through a piece of land mainly used by dogs—

appeared out of nowhere. She reached the top of a slope, slipped with a thud, slipped onto mud again, tried to regain balance in the dark and resorted to crawling on hands and knees on remaining grassland.

Thank God for guiding me home on such a night.

In went the key. The door crashed against the hall wall.

His coat was on a hook. Central heating blasted into her face.

"Hey, Kris, how's it going then?" He's back in time for Christmas and the weather forecast is severe frost. Did he hear me call out?

She wiped her ankles clean and saw his angst-brow. She sponged mud off her shoes and saw his blond wavy hair. She washed each foot in the sink and saw his eyes: blue, aloof, unyielding.

"I'm-all-right-J-O-L," Kris yelled from the hallway. "I-slept-well. I'm-about-to-cook-dinner-expecting-someone-then-it's-work-for-me. Eleven-thirty-shift. The-dining-table's-mine-tonight."

Why's he speaking to me like a robot?

"You're both welcome to have some of mine," Jolienta called out. "I made it yesterday."

She scowled in the bathroom mirror. That was way too acquiescent.

"No-thank-you-I'm-not-into-compost-heaps."

"You cheeky b - - - - - -!"

"Huh? Ha. He's-my-best-friend. He is."

Jolienta patted her hair dry with a towel and glanced in the mirror. The bell rang. She slipped into the kitchen. Kris and his friend fell over Tom's bicycle. She kept her back to them and ladled food into a bowl. Her cheeks were red-hot.

Well, that can't be helped, she decided, but I'm sitting down at that table with him and his friend, whether he likes it or not.

She sat down at the table.

Southampton Way is peaceful under moonlight and if I twist

my neck, I can just about see snowflakes flying through the air.

She started to eat, head over bowl.

"Jolienta, meet Brian."

How unusual. He's introducing me to his friend. An introduction was the last thing I expected. I was going to sit here and simply eat. Well, I only have myself to blame if I'm intimidated. I must try to relax.

"Hello Brian. Congratulations by the way. You were married recently I hear."

"Yes. The wedding was fantastic. We went to Madeira."

Brian was wearing a thick brown suit-jacket, a green and brown tie, spectacles, and he had a clipped beard of ginger and grey. He looked like a biology teacher. He didn't look like the type of person Kris would have as a best friend.

"Jolienta, tell me, how are you getting on in London?" Brian said. "Have you come across 'Campaign' yet?" He folded his arms and sat back.

"Campaign? Never heard of it. What is it?"

"It's a newspaper full of the latest vacancies. You should find a job and move out. Kris doesn't like you."

He slid the newspaper towards her.

She glanced at Kris. He was pouring white wine into two glasses. Not three. There you go. You see, I was right to expect the unexpected. I was right.

Down went the last piece of red pepper in the bowl.

"Thanks Brian, but I don't have any reason to look for a job. I'm committed, you know, to Peckham . . . to the Slade School of Art. Not everyone gets in to do a postgraduate course there, you know. I'm settled, and I'm busy." She waved her hand in the direction of Number Thirty-five. "Also, I've got friends here. On the estate, you know."

Kris! she simmered inside. He doesn't have friends in Peckham! He doesn't care about the six-lane motorway set to plough its way through the high street. He hasn't connected with Peckham, not in the way I have, exploring every shop, road, and street; getting to know the people, capturing people and places on canvas and in print. Why should I be the one to move out?

Her stomach turned over.

It's the same flip, day in and day out, right from the first day we met and he strode on in like a bull on heat. I thought he was going to knock me off the ladder that day.

The audacity of it. Getting his friend to do his dirty work.

Kris' gravy boat landed on the table.

"You mean that motley crew next door?" Kris said, burying his face in chicken, peas and potatoes. "Bunch of wankers."

The side of his neck was covered in goose bumps.

Enough. I have had enough. Tom said Kris' book was out and that *It will sink into oblivion*. Where is it? I will rub his nose in it.

She got up, went to Tom's armchair and began to search under cushions. She found it. She held it up. It had a grey cover with no illustration, nothing to single it out or save it from anyone's bin. Who cares which member of the Royal family it was written for? No one will read it.

"Well done, Kris."

She waited for his reaction.

'The bastards fucked up the cover,' the subtitles said flickering across his forehead, 'and they used toilet paper to print the damn thing on.'

Brian stood up as if on cue. "Oh Jolienta, that factory drawing of yours . . . not my cup of tea. Never mind. Bye." He stuck his hand out, which was another way of telling her to leave the room. She grasped it firmly, and gathered up her bowl and spoon.

I did quite well, she thought, except my shoulders are shaking.

She was safe inside her room again. She slipped off her damp clothes, put on a brown top with padded shoulders and stepped into fresh trousers. The waist button wouldn't do up. She looked for a safety pin and for lipstick.

Polish Stan's on his way. Not long now, she whispered. Not long now.

*   *   *

Stanislaus listened patiently to a breakdown of the latest incident and suggested she drown her sorrows in some of his dad's vodka. Without waiting, he produced a bottle from his rucksack and poured from a large bottle into two plastic tumblers. He ambled around the room, examined her paintings, sipped and smiled, and stopped to kiss her. "It's as if you know a secret, darling," he declared with a wide smile and a dimple in his chin.

"What d'you mean?"

"I can't explain it. It's as if you know something we don't."

His arms enveloped her. He slipped his hand under her top and undid the bra. She had to lick his chest—smooth, lean, smelling of soap. Their lips met. Their tongues twisted into a knot. Their bodies tipped onto the mattress. Their legs wove together.

He undid the safety pin and reached inside. "Delicious," he said, and began to explore the folds of skin.

"Mieou." She was pretending to be a cat.

He yanked off her trousers and breathed in deeply. His face was very red. He unzipped himself with difficulty. He pushed forward, again, and again, but no. His manhood. They sank onto the mattress.

The flat was silent.

Jolienta turned onto her side and kissed him on the cheek. His body was warm. His arm was draped over her waist and he was nuzzling her shoulder.

"I'm sorry," he muttered.

Jolienta drifted along Peckham High Street and floated along Manhattan Bridge Loop, the inspiration for Hubble Factory.

"What the?" Stanislaus pushed the cover away and glowered at the wall.

Jolienta sat up, rubbed her eyes, tried to think. "It's Kris . . . his stereo . . . he's got it on full blast." Her throat was hoarse. "He knows you're in my bed."

*   *   *

"Tom. Dinner. Friday evening. You too, Jolienta." Kris nodded to confirm that she was included.

She watched him squash his roll-up into the bottom of his mug.

"Will it be the chicken roast or the fish pie, Kris?" Tom said.

"I'm inviting a friend along. Not one of my exploits, you'll be pleased to hear. Someone from University days. A classically-trained singer. Her name's Veronica."

"I see."

"And Shepherd's Pie will be on the menu."

"Woo*hoo*. We accept your invitation, don't we, Jolienta? Shepherd's Pie? I confess, I'm intrigued . . . What I mean is, you're actually going to cook for someone other than yourself. Not to be missed."

*   *   *

The doorbell uttered its tinny cry. Jolienta stayed where she was. Kris strode to the door and invited a woman in, took her coat and chatted to her in the hallway.

Taking her coat? Kris—chivalrous? Huh?

Kris laughed.

He and his woman friend were certainly amused to see each other and were behaving like old buddies.

If he's capable of having a female friend, then why is he always giving me such a hard time?

Kris gave the woman a large glass of red wine, which she accepted with an eager and pretty Irish lilt.

"Hello. Veronica?"

"Hello. And you are?"

"Tom. Kris tells me you're a classical singer. I'm a composer. Tell me. What are your ultimate aspirations?"

"Steady on, Tom," Veronica said. She made herself comfortable by the gas fire and pulled down the hem of her dress.

"Your repertoire?" Tom continued.

Kris came in holding the Shepherd's Pie thanks to thick oven gloves. They gathered around the table, gazed at the steaming heavy gravy leaking over the crust.

They ate with relish and gulped back warm aromatic red wine. Jolienta stared at the guest. How could any woman be a friend to Kris? She investigated Veronica's face. Small oval shape, short feathery hair, eyelashes longer than Polish Stan's. They flicked over and touched the upper lids. And, it has to be said, Veronica had an ability to laugh at Kris and Tom's jokes with uncanny precision.

Kris cleared the table and brought in Marks & Sparks chocolate mousse with raspberries and double cream. Delicious and unexpected. They were about to finish with Tom's Columbian coffee and Fortnum & Mason's chocolate mints, when Tom offered to play the piano.

Kris and Veronica both said Yes and got up.

What? We're *all* going into Tom's bedroom?

Jolienta followed them out and looked for a place to sit.

I'll have to perch on the edge of the bed then.

She tried to compress her body into a compact shape. Veronica was already confortable—lying diagonally across the bed like Lady Godiva. She saw Veronica wriggle at Tom. Kris was on the floor leaning against the radiator, knees bent, legs apart, furrowed brow, glass-in-hand, cigarette sticking out of his mouth.

Tom began to waggle his toes in preparation.

Oh, it has been a challenge, Jolienta sighed inwardly. Maybe I should pinch myself—sitting in Tom's room like this, and Kris too, sitting at my feet. The situation has finally improved. We are a trio. At long last. To be honest, I love them. Both of them. If you share a home, well, you end up being like family, don't you? Besides, we have a lot in common: Tom adopted at birth, Kris lost his dad when he was six, and my father died or disappeared before I was four. The three of us have no knowledge of our past.

Tom flexed his fingers and began to knead the keyboard.

It must have been the effect of the alcohol, because when he had finished playing no one commented on what was supposed to have been part of his latest composition. He asked Veronica for a request. She suggested one of Chopin's Nocturnes in E-flat.

The melody and its arpeggios flowed from his piano and filled the room with emotion. The high notes and trills pretty well summed Tom up—elegant, precise, earnest. The melody conjured up a fresh morning in the countryside with dappled sunlight on trees, and a sparkling river in a Seurat painting. Above all, Jolienta heard the sound of a woman being wooed. From the corner of her eye, she spied on Veronica and noted that Veronica was spying on Tom. The nocturne ended. Veronica stood up.

"It's bin absolutely *marv*ellous, but my taxi's waitin' in the court*yard*".

"I'll come down with you, Ronnie. See you off." Kris held out her coat. "Here you are."

They disappeared onto the balcony.

What a lovely lovely evening, Jolienta thought. How unexpected. Kris including me! Us all together. Tom playing his piano like that. Wow! What a lovely lovely evening.

Kris came rushing back into the living room. "OK, Tom." He rubbed his hands by the fire. "What did you think of *that*?"

"What do you mean?"

Kris ran round the space between the settee and the gas fire, jogged on the spot and pretended to have ice in his underpants.

"Come on, Tom. She's an attractive lady. What did you think of that?"

The window rattled and the cheese plant trembled.

"Er?" Tom said, finger on chin. "Yeeees, she was quite nice, I suppose. What was her name again?" and he began to stack up plates and cutlery to take to the kitchen.

"There has to be more, Jolienta," Tom said, turning to her. "There just has to be more. What do you mean by *pedestrian point of view*? How can you apply such a word to aesthetics? What do you mean? I'm fed up with hearing the same old arguments. I want to hear something new."

Kris scratched the stubble on his chin and lit a roll-up. He sucked on it and blew at the drinks cabinet. He was thinking.

Jolienta sighed. Again. She had to be alert at all times. Tom was harking back to a conversation from two weeks ago, and as usual she'd been out of her depth, unable to deflect his academic forays. Funny though—it seems he hadn't noticed Veronica. Poor Kris. He was obviously trying to hatch a plot and it wasn't working. Tom was impervious to Veronica.

The Slade School of Art

A COLD TWILIGHT DESCENDED OVER THE UNIVERSITY FORECOURT. Black coat over black dress, Jolienta glanced over the grounds and saw the porter. He was ready to lock the iron-gate. He waved.

Slade students congregated in the semi-circle during the summer, squashed into two wooden benches. As a rule, she only sat in this spot if she'd arranged to meet someone. Even then, she was always ready for some kind of ambush.

Time to go home. Jolienta stepped onto the lawn. Her oyster earrings, which made her lobes bulge and itch, and which helped the dimensions of her face—or so she thought, were absent. One had lost a piece of shell, the other, its clasp. These days, she didn't recognize herself anyway what with unruly hair and lines around the eyes. Exactly why her face kept changing was a question she didn't like to ask. Her leather-clad feet strode towards the gate. Right . . . left . . . right . . . left.

"Chimp!"

She stopped, heard the sound again and looked up into a canopy of trees.

Where is the chirp coming from?

"Chimp! Tsip!"

She looked up and down and scoured the ground.

"Chimp!"

It looked perfect standing there by itself in the gravel pathway.

The sparrow had a soft round raw umber crown, zinc white crest and nape, which contrasted against black orbital feathers and jet-black eyes. His wings and tail appeared undamaged. His feet were balanced evenly on the ground. However, the bird wouldn't move. It stayed where it was.

"Chimp, chimp! Tsip, tsip," the sparrow said. "Chimp. Tsip!"

Jolienta knelt down and gazed at it. His breast and flank fluffed out and then he hopped into the palm of her hand.

"Eeee, a've seen everything now," the Porter said, behind her.

"I'd better get a taxi."

The Porter shook his head and strolled back. Jolienta scooped the bird up. Opposite the Porter's lodge, the Cruciform Building, a huddle of red and pink brickwork with a turret in the middle, and home to the Medical School, cast a cold shadow across Gower Street. Jolienta stopped and tried to think. It was cold and getting late. A black cab slowed down. A man with a brief case got out, and without saying a word, he took her by the elbow and helped her in.

"Thank you. Very kind."

The man closed the taxi door behind her and smiled.

"All righ' lav?" the driver said, peering into his mirror.

"Yes, thanks. Peckham High Street, please."

She prized her hands apart. A large black eye glared back.

The driver checked his side mirror. The meter started up. The taxi glided along the street, joined Charing Cross Road and sped over Trafalgar Square, beating the lights. The driver turned into Waterloo Bridge Road. The meter said seven pounds. The numbers clattered up faster and faster. She felt tense; there was a limited amount of cash in her bag. The bird didn't move or make a sound.

He can live in my bedroom until he's ready to face the world. "Driver, turn left into Sumner Road. Left again for the courtyard."

The driver swung into the estate.

"Will you do me a favour, mister? When I get out, will you reach into my bag and pay yourself?"

"Whart yer got there, darlin'?"

"A sparrow."

"Blah-dy 'ell."

Jolienta climbed the stairs and banged her foot against the door.

"Forgotten your key, Jolienta?"

"Sorry, Tom. Hands full."

"Good Lord. What are you doing?"

"I've got a sick sparrow in my hands."

"Oh, you are *sweet*. It'll never survive. It will be dead by morning."

There he goes again.

"We will see, Tom."

She closed the bedroom door, knelt on the floor and opened her hands. The bird refused to move. His beady eyes stared back. She put him under the window inside a nest of soft clothing.

"Now don't let your heart give out."

That should calm him down. What next?

She gathered milk, water, bread, sunflower seeds, a box of matches, and impaled a soggy piece of bread with a matchstick. Jolienta pushed the stick at the bird. The bird blinked and opened his beak.

"Chimp."

Rain tapped against the window. Off came the shoes. Off came the socks. She rubbed the soles of her feet. The phone rang. Tom answered. "No. He's not in Alison. In fact, he's away until the fourteenth."

"Oh, he's away until the fourteenth? Did you hear that, sparrow? I hope he doesn't tell Kris about you. I'll never hear the last of it."

"Chimp."

The bird flapped, relaxed his wings and moved.

He seemed to drink a little water and pecked at a seed. Jolienta yawned, stretched out and rubbed the heel of her foot on the carpet. No one could accuse her of not working hard or trying her best, she thought, and yawned again. She did her best. Every day. She pulled the duvet over. Pulled at it and covered her body.

Don't worry, Mr Sparrow, I'll get there one day. I will make it to the top. Fame. Glory. It will all be there. I will be among the great artists of all time. I will command big prices. Not forty quid for Hubble Factory, a drawing of oranges, reds and cavernous shadows. And when I'm rich, I'll pay for the best vet available!

Oh no, I've been asleep all night long!

The sparrow darted across the room, spun a flurry of shadows across the walls and landed on the roof of the wardrobe.

"Chirr ch cha, cherr ch, cha cha, cha cha, chu cha, churrr cha ca chu cha cha ca chrrrppp. Chi che cha, ch ch, cha cha, cha cha, chu cha, chu cha ca chu cha cha ca chirrip. Chi che cha, ch chrrrrr, cha cha, cha cha, chu cha, chu cha ca chu cha cha ca chrrrrpp!"

She hurried to the window. The bird hopped onto the ledge, eyeballed her with his black eye, sang his morning song and soared into the sky. She watched his progress until there was nothing left to see. His nest of clothing under the window didn't show the presence or absence of any living thing. She tied her dressing gown at the waist and tried to figure out what it meant.

Tom was outside the bathroom and his eyes sought hers.

"'Morning, Tom."

"Well, is it dead, then? What happened, then?" Tom said.

"He flew away then, Tom."

*   *   *

At last, the lithography tutor was able to instruct her on how to prepare a stone. Out of all of the printmaking staff, he was the quietest, the most industrious—more reserved than shy—and very much the Englishman in the traditional sense of the word. He was a gentleman of lily-white skin, untouched by the sun's rays, ready to impart knowledge in a methodical and trustworthy manner. He liked to wear a pinstriped apron and took great store in his wife's packed sandwiches and flask of tea.

"First of all, Jolienta," the tutor said, "There is the physical effort of carrying the stone to the sink and not trapping fingers beneath it. A stone like this one requires two people to lift it. It *is* possible to drop it and break a foot. Take heed. It has been known."

Jolienta picked up the Portland stone resting on the trolley and placed it inside the industrial sink.

The tutor raised an eyebrow. "Yes, Jolienta. Very unwise and I strongly advise you to listen to me in future."

'Goodness me,' he thought, 'she's a health and safety risk.'

"Next, the stone has to be washed down to remove the previous drawing."

He rubbed the stone with turpentine and aimed a jet of water at it, dispersing grey fluid into the sink. 'I hope she's listening.'

"Sprinkle sand over it. Here, from this pot. Then, take the smaller lighter stone—this one will do—and place it on top. Move it over the larger one in a continuous figure of eight movement. Like this."

He demonstrated. She watched.

"Both stones should be kept wet at all times."

'She is a funny one,' he thought, 'staring at me like that as if each word is of paramount importance.'

"Apply the figure of eight to each of the four corners or you will end up with an uneven surface, which will result in a patchy drawing. Continue this process for about ten minutes. Gradually change from sand to finer grade of carborundum. Forty minutes should do it." He stepped off the wooden platform, which creaked and rose slightly. "I'll leave you to it, Jolienta. A dab of ink to test for residual grease, just like I showed Geeta the other day, and leave the stones to dry."

He put on his tweed overcoat.

"I'm off to Curwen. I'll show you how to sensitize the stones when I get back." 'Assuming she hasn't broken a foot or had some other disaster while I'm gone.'

"Thanks, Ronald. I'm really grateful."

Jolienta doused the stones with water and sand, and began to initiate the figure of eight. As the top stone moved over the large stone, the sound of the sea emerged, much like a seashell being held up to the ear. Shoulder and calf muscles began to ache. After thirty minutes, Jolienta rinsed the stones and smudged ink across the surfaces. The ink didn't stick. The stones washed clear.

"Jolienta, there's a call for you in the etching studio."

It was the tall Swede with perfect hair and make up.

"The phone," the blonde woman said, "over there."

"For me?"

The Swede tossed her hair and disappeared.

Telephone boxes and their occupants made excellent visual material, but actually using a telephone was another matter altogether, especially, if the person on the other end was Kris.

Who the hell do I know who has a phone?

Jolienta eyed the phone with suspicion.

"Hello?"

"It's Margo."

"Margo? What a surprise. It's been ages."

"Jol . . . er, maybe, er maybe, I haven't always been a good friend to you."

"What a strange thing to say."

"How are you getting on with my brother, the great composer?"

"To be honest, we're getting on quite well at the moment. I suppose you know he has a girlfriend. A classical singer."

"No, I didn't. He doesn't communicate with me. I hope the

girlfriend survives the experience. The drive down to Peckham was the last time I spoke to him, and that was only because you were there. Anyway, I just wanted to say thank you for sticking by me when we went to visit my parents last year."

"Oh, come on. You introduced me to Tom and drove me all the way here. Thanks to you, I live in luxury, in London, for four pounds a week! Don't think I'm not grateful."

"Jola, we've gotta get a move on. Barto's goin' mad out there."

"Hang on, Dave. No need to bounce up and down. Margo, I'm right in the middle. I'll write soon."

"Jolienta dos Remédios," Barto said, groaning, "please get a move on. The deadline is looming."

"Of course, Barto."

"Told ya, Jola. Ya ready?"

"Yep."

Dave grabbed the lever and wrenched it back as far as it would go. He released it; the weight thudded onto layers of damp blotters sending a shiver down to the concrete floor. She was ready, moved forward, peeled back the blotters, lifted up a portfolio from its registration and examined it. The label displayed the University emblem and the words: SLADE STUDENT EXHIBITION, Printmaking Department, 1983.

They found a pace to suit, and each time, she placed a maroon portfolio on top of an engraved copper plate, took care with the registration, replaced the blotters, and then Dave stepped forward to deliver a manly heave.

"Jola . . ." Dave stopped to rest against the wall. "Fig just had sex in the silkscreen cupboard. That's what everyone's saying."

"Oh, come off it."

"Yeah. True. She had her first orgasm. Ho."

"Naw. The brash punk Fig? First orgasm?"

"*Yeah*. It's a great idea, isn't it?"

"Sorry?"

"Who knows if one of us will become famous in the future? One day, we could sell these portfolios for loads of money."

Dave folded his arms, slouched onto one leg and gazed at her. "Anyway, what did ya think of Barto's etchings?"

"Oh. Surprised, I guess. The etching technician was going on about him being a Master of Aquatint and I was like, Oh, let me see 'em, and when I did, well, I was pleasantly surprised. That told me, didn't it? There was depth, variety of tone and grain, and the photographic imagery mixed in with the artistry was unusual. Anyway, I love the use of maps. I love maps. And what did you think, Dave?"

"Honestly, you do have a nerve. What about the etching based on that Portuguese King?"

"You've lost me."

"Weren't you listening to a word he said?"

"I can't help it. I drift."

"It was based on a true story. One of Portugal's great and tragic love stories. Peter the Cruel was Crown Prince and heir to the Portuguese throne. He fell in love with his wife's lady-in-waiting, who happened to be a Spanish noblewoman. When his wife died in childbirth, he and the Spanish noblewoman went on to have three children together. While he was away, the King seized the woman, basically, because she was Spanish, and had her put to death. Peter returned and was ripe for revenge . . . as you would be. He murdered his father, the others too, became King, and declared his dead mistress to be his rightful wife and Queen. In fact, he had her body dug up, propped on the throne, and forced his courtiers to kiss her bony hand. Cool, huh?"

"Ha ha. Now that you mention it."

They completed the last portfolio. Each one had a label embossed into it.

Now, if I eat in the refectory—salad and chips with lashings of vinegar—the chances are I'll find the studio empty when I get back.

"As I'm clearly talking to myself, Jola, I'll be off. The girlfriend's back from the States. Pepperoni pizza tonight. Chocolate chip ice cream."

"See you, Dave. Send my regards, won't you?"

Six-thirty.

Empty studio.

Perfect.

Jolienta inked up her plate, wiped the surface with scrim, wiped the edges of the plate with a rag. Torn patches of newspaper gave an added finish.

She positioned the plate on the bed and placed damp printing paper over it, laid down tissue, blotters and felt blankets. She turned the handle and wound the bed through once, twice for good luck, and this was always the best bit—peeled back the blankets, blotters and tissue, took a piece of card and eased away a corner of the printing paper to reveal the results of her labour.

Did I get the pressure right? Is every scrap of ink off?

On the other side of the printing press, a piece of tartan flashed by. "What you up to?" Fig said, her Mohican ridge of black hair erupting out of a bleached scalp, a ring poking out of her left nostril.

"It's the Crown Pub in Peckham."

Why did I say that? She'll hate me for being so . . . uninteresting.

Fig leaned forward, grabbed a fistful of hair and yanked. Jolienta kept her head steady and continued to scrutinize the print, which was now detached from the plate, mid-air, and in danger of drooping into a set of folds like a wet handkerchief.

I was ready for that one.

Fig let go and waited for a reaction.

My scalp hurts. My arm aches. The print looks perfect.

Fig slinked away.

Every detail is there. The quality and depth of black is excellent. The pub leans to the right at the corner of Queen

Street; it's ground floor window obscures drinkers behind a brush of aquatint. The surface ink is warm in tone. The burred line is thick. Seven forty-five. Time to go home.

*   *   *

James, Rita, Brillo and Marcus smiled and gave a look of sympathy.

"Alright, Jo-*lien*-ta?" Rita said brightly.

Rita began to stamp on the landing. The courtyard was under a crisp blanket of snow.

"It's cold out her, Jo-*lien*-ta."

There was the wide toothy grin, a bit hesitant today, but full of good intentions. Jolienta gazed at the four people shivering in the cold.

"Come on, Jolly, let us in. Let us in. Jo-lly, Jo-lly."

James laughed. "Come on. Put the kettle on. Hurry up."

Brillo and Marcus laughed.

It must be about last night, she thought. I embarrassed myself. Got drunk. I was sick in James' car. Or did I open the window in time?

"Is this about last night?"

"You remember, Jolly?" James said. "We were worried about you. You drew a picture of an axe on the kitchen cupboard. Come on, let us in. What you up to? We want to see."

"I'm immortalizing The Bouncing Ball Reggae Club."

"Cool." Marcus took a drag of his roll-up.

Brillo moved forward.

"I'll put the coffee pot on then. I know how to use it now."

"Y-e-s! That sounds more like the Jolly I know."

James chuckled. Rita slipped into the living room. The men shuffled in behind.

"So what are you up to?" James said, walking over to the table.

"I'm cutting out this large image. Here's the strobe lighting.

Here are dancing figures. Here's a man with his ponytail bobbing in the air. There's Dan looking mean and cool in his wide-boy hat. You know, he said to me, *Just say the word, Miss. I will see you safe.* Strange he'd be interested in a gangly white northerner. Anyone want a toasted crumpet to go with their coffee?"

"No, Jolly, we've just had a major fry-up."

"Hey, everyone, that's my ponytail," Marcus said.

"Don't let it go to your head. Am I in it? Where am I?" Brillo said. "Who's Dan?"

"Jolly's got better things to do than include you."

"Bwillo, she hathn't done anyfwink in this corner yet so there's woom for you," Rita said. "It's weird, isthn't it? How doeth it work?"

"Darling, it's a linocut. You roll ink over the top and take an impression by running it through a printing press. How is she going to find a press big enough?"

"If anyone mentions potato prints to me, they can't have any crumpet." Jolienta put a tray down at the far end of the table.

"That was quick, Jo-*lien*-ta. No thugar for me. I'm thweet enough, tee-hee."

James, Rita, Brillo and Marcus crowded around the table.

"Hey, you lot, this is really nice of you. I'm pretty embarrassed about last night. Got a massive hangover."

*   *   *

Every year, the printmaking department allowed a percentage of overseas students to buy their way onto the Slade course, and students were only too ready to pay for the privilege, such was the Slade's reputation. Usually, they were mature applicants from faraway countries, much like Omar from Iran, or individuals like the Swede with money to burn. Others had grafted for years, built up a lifestyle and family unit and hoped for a meaningful change in direction. A minority had gotten on board thanks to fellowships, hoped to broaden their horizons and take that home with them. Miguel fell into the last category. Jolienta was sure of it.

He's a small man, a dwarf really. Think Toulouse Lautrec. And the rest of us, including myself, why we're nothing but a bunch of introverts, narcissists and ungrateful slackers like the hateful Fig. In fact, the one thing that unifies us is that none of us can be bothered to speak to him, not even to say *Hi. How are you?*

Without meaning to, Jolienta began to follow his progress. Sometimes, his face was red with effort as he strove to reach the top of a work counter, or wind on the wheel of an etching press.

His workspace was on the lithography balcony, where a couple of English students worked. No doubt they hoped to melt into the background too. Maybe *they* didn't know what the hell they were doing at the Slade, but they didn't have the additional worry about how to order a meal in English, or how to find their way around London, and they didn't have to worry about having two stumps for arms with baby-hands attached to them.

The dwarf looked nice, had warm eyes and frizzy sideburns and she was going to speak to him. "How are you, Miguel?"

No reply.

She nodded to encourage a response and tried again.

"Good? Not Good?"

Miguel froze and blinked back in disbelief.

"Today, you eat breakfast? Yes?" Jolienta nodded again.

No reply.

"No? You no eat breakfast?"

A different approach was needed.

"Weather nice in England?"

She was determined to extract a response. "You like the cold, don't you? Yes?" Her head bobbed up and down.

"No, no. No like cold. No like. Very sad." He shivered and cast an eye around the studio.

"I don't like," Jolienta said, pushing her face into his line of vision. "Have you visited many places in London?"

"Ha, yes. Viseet. Viseet h'many places."

She pointed at him and then at herself. "You and me. We go to exhibition together. Yes?"

Miguel's eyes widened with horror. "Qué?"

"Matisse and Picasso at the Royal Academy. You'll love it."

Miguel pulled his pockets inside out to indicate an absence of money. Done far too quickly in her opinion, anything rather than interact with foreigners or people in general.

"Miguel, money is no problem. Look at my membership card. See. Take one guest in *free*."

She tried to give him the card to read. This time, Miguel edged towards the swing doors and disappeared into a toilet. When he came out, she was there, waiting with the card in her hand. She watched him squirm and waved the card in front of his face.

Whether he realized it or not, he was gradually becoming braver. "Eez free? Royal H'academy? Ha'why? Haw? Ha'when?"

The next day, he tapped her on the elbow and presented her with one of his etchings, which had a pronounced crease down the middle.

Damn. That means, I'll have to give him one of mine and I don't have any that are damaged.

"Miguel. Please. Take a look at these. Which would you like?"

He looked at the selection on the worktable, chose a drypoint of a shop façade, rolled it up and squashed it into his back pocket.

Sigh. He has no qualms about ruining one of my finest pieces, shame he doesn't have the same gung-ho approach towards a visit to the RA.

He was trembling.

Perhaps I should introduce him to Cathy to ease his anxieties?

Cathy was a popular student at the Slade. Cathy roamed between the sculpture department and theatre design, and was her friend, thanks to a connection up north. She adored her friend's prettiness and eccentricities: the large bow in her red hair, the giant plastic flower tucked behind her ear, and the dresses Cathy wore were often yellow, floral, retro, pinched in at the waist, and then they flared out over dainty pointed shoes. Cathy liked to wear lashings of Helena Rubenstein on and about her lips. She projected the joyous figure of a mad ballerina, which lightened up everyone's mood.

Jolienta organized a meeting at once and watched with amusement as Cathy's giant flower mesmerized Miguel in and around the Portland Stones. He was entranced, and it was agreed, he would allow himself to be taken to the Royal Academy by the two women.

The thing is, Jolienta thought on the way to Warren Street tube, it doesn't do any harm to be friendly, does it? If everyone helped one another, the world would be a better place.

They stepped out of the wind and faced a lane of steps and a lane of escalator.

"OK. I race you. You two—take escalator. I . . . the stairs . . . I win . . . of course. One, two, threeeeeee."

Miguel and Cathy bumped and wove past commuters. She took the stairs two at a time. Her legs were going to give in. She couldn't breathe. She *must* win. She arrived at the summit, chest heaving, grasping for air. Cathy and Miguel stumbled out. Miguel laughed so much his eyes were damp. His baby hands were shaking. Cathy tried to conceal a crooked tooth, and in doing so, smudged lipstick over her nose.

They found an exit for Green Park, were back in frosty air, and ascended the red carpet of the Royal Academy. Jolienta handed her membership card to the usher and signed Miguel into the Friends book. They hurried to the last exhibit, where Miguel waited for her return. Out Jolienta slipped, collected Cathy and signed the book for a second time, the three uniting inside for the price of one.

Boy Leading a Horse by Picasso was a large canvas painted in bluish-greys and pinkish-browns, and was located midway along the exhibits. The boy and horse were friends. The boy wore an intense expression. The horse smiled at the boy. The boy, a superb specimen of human anatomy, had an earnest chin, almost dislocated from the neck, which gave the impression of rigorous movement but when her eyes travelled downward, his legs were stuck in mud.

"He's supposed to be leading the horse," Jolienta said to Cathy, while scanning the crowd for Miguel. "But no rope. No lead. Must have got painted out. If the horse keeps to his canter, he'll outpace the boy in seconds."

Cathy giggled. Miguel jumped up from the front of the crowd and waved.

On the wall next to the Picasso, was the curator's idea of a worthy contender. Which do I prefer? she asked herself. Which would I steal if I had the chance? Picasso robbed a piece of African sculpture from the Louvre and then he chickened out and dumped it in the river.

The Matisse is more or less the same size and shape as the Picasso. The artist used similar pinkish browns, but the blues and greens are more of a Mediterranean hue applied by Pointillist dot and Fauvist abandon. In various places on the canvas, his colours create an underwater sheen on . . . a crouched woman . . . clouds in the sky, but the naked women, who dominate the composition, don't have thoughts or fears of their own. Unlike the boy and horse. The design is absolute.

*   *   *

Florescent tubes cast an oppressive yellow over the etching studio and the smell of hard ground sweetened the air. Miguel and Cathy had gone home. Very sensible. She was in the studio for no other reason than she didn't want to be alone with Kris in the flat.

The etching technician was hunched over the alcove, rocking a mezzotint tool back and forth. Each time, it rocked one way or the other it made a sharp incision into metal. A vicious activity. Much like the person doing it. A curious sight though. She had never seen anyone prepare a mezzotint before.

"You have no respect! No respect!" the technician shouted, crisscrossing the plate, adding more cuts and slashes.

Jolienta froze.

She stared at the technician's back and waited to see what would happen next. She studied the technician's angular shoulders turned into the alcove, head bowed over plate. An absorbed stance. Right arm moving back and forth, baggy jeans. A straight up and down figure. The sight made her want to puke.

What have I done? Jolienta thought, racing through the events of the last few days. Is it about Barto?

The technician continued to rock.

"Barto is a Master of Aquatint. You will show him some respect in future. Do you hear?" the technician said.

"Oh?"

The technician scowled.

Gianmarco looked up, his face illuminated by his copper plate. "Barto's invited us round to his Hampstead condo next week. Coming along, Jolienta?"

"She probably won't go. She'd rather hang out with freaks," the technician said, and returned to the rhythm of the mezzotint rocker.

The hairs on the back of her neck stood up. If the technician was referring to Miguel, there was going to be trouble.

She had contained herself long enough. "Freaks? Well, you would know about freaks, wouldn't you? Being one YOURSELF, that is."

Jolienta scraped down the edges of her zinc plate, to show she wasn't afraid. I don't care what happens, she grumbled into the

THE GIRL IN PECKHAM & KOWLOON

pit of her stomach. Enough is enough. That technician slithers around casting doom and gloom. OK, let's see what happens; I've challenged some unspoken law in the etching studio.

*   *   *

The walk from Hampstead tube station to Barto's was a pleasant walk, where branches met at the top to form an archway. Winter sunlight made yellows and golds in the resistant leaves and the pavements were wide and covered in pink gravel, which crunched underfoot. Barto's invitation was an opportunity for the students to get to know each other, but Jolienta was useless at social events. She wouldn't fit in. That was for sure. In fact, the harder she tried, the more spite would come her way. The winter term had been the worst, what with Fig trying to yank her hair out and some other student following her around the studios intent on upsetting her equilibrium. Then there was the etching technician: cold, perverse, impenetrable. She may as well accept the way things were.

She was outside an ivory mansion and a garden of clipped hedges, conifers, holly trees and ivy. A robin landed on a potted olive tree close to the portico entrance, hopped up to the front door and waited. Jolienta knew the bird would fly away as soon as she reached the steps, and made no alteration to her speed. The robin stayed where he was, red breast pulsating proudly. He looked up, mighty tiger of his frosty jungle and sang:

"Twiddle-oo, twiddle-eedee, twiddle-oo, twiddle."

She smiled at the bird and pressed the bell marked Dos Santos. To her surprise, the bird didn't break into a flutter and fly away. It stared at her, looked her right in the eye, winked, and soared into the sky.

The front door sprang open. A voice hollered down, "Top floor. Who ever you are!"

Everyone was eating and drinking. Her social graces collapsed and muteness took over. Luckily, Barto leapt into welcome mode in full-length kaftan. She'd never seen him in relaxed mode before and suppressed a giggle. His physique was hung stout without leather belt and shiny buckle. His medallion was there, lost inside a hairy chest.

I hope he's wearing underpants, Jolienta thought.

"You found ze way den?" Barto said, his nostril curling up. "Have this wine and some tachos and balichão. Gianmarco, change ze music, will you?" he called out.

"Jolienta, balichão eez a traditional Macanese sauce introduced by zee Portuguese. To be Macanese, they say, you have to have a bottle of balichão in ze fridge. Eet's a spicy paste made from dried shrimp, tamarind, coconut milk and chilli. Delicious."

Macanese? He said 'Macanese'.

The word echoed within.

Have I heard it before?

Macanese? Portuguese?

Are they connected?

Barto's wife appeared. "How nice to see you, Jovita! You look well. I like your sunflower jumper. Where did you get it? It looks expensive.

"Made in Hong Kong, you say?

"How did the Peckham exhibition go? Did you sell much?

"You were reviewed in the local papers? Well done! We had a great time visiting you on the Sumner Road Estate and in the Peckham Action Shop. Well done!"

Yes, that was quite something, Jolienta thought, both of them travelling across London to see the exhibition, Peckham, People & Places. Now that I think about it, they've been very kind to me, while I'm always spouting off about some manifesto or other, or petitioning for Barto to be sacked.

Jolienta gazed around the room and tried to relax. The Swede and Geeta were engrossed. Not afraid of life like she was. No sign of Fig. Dave was stuffing his face. A big lad, who likes his food. "What's that you got there then, Dave?"

"It's juicy. Very salty. Basically, it's mincemeat and soya sauce. Barto says it embodies comfort food for the Portuguese-Chinese."

Portuguese-Chinese? The words echoed within.

Jolienta paused at the minchi, balichão, capela and feijoada. The feijoada was a meat loaf made with minced olives and had a cheesy crust. There were pretty custard tarts with brown skins and sweet drinks, English cheeses, breads and cakes, French chocolates, salads, giant prawns in ginger hiding in green leaves, and spicy red sausages.

She didn't know where to begin. She reached for a spoon, was about to dig in, changed her mind and heaped feijoada onto her plate. The etching technician was moving towards her. Jolienta forked cheesy crust into her mouth and willed herself in the opposite direction. The technician was too quick and was in the way. Her face heated up. A lump of crust jarred in her throat.

"You made it, I see?" the etching technician said.

Jolienta steadied her plate. "Oh, hi. How are you?"

"As if you're interested."

"I don't know what you mean."

"Don't give me that."

"Huh?" Jolienta looked for a way out. Dave was chatting up the Swede. Gianmarco and the litho technician were sharing a joke. Omar was surrounded by doting women. "To be honest, I don't understand what you're getting at."

"You make me sick," the etching technician said and walked away.

*　　*　　*

It's a surprise, a compliment to be invited to dinner by Gianmarco. Him of all people. He's the diplomat out of everyone in the printmaking department, the one who says the right thing at the right time. Likes to mix with important people. Can't think why he invited me to *dinner*. Mind you, I'm not sure I should have accepted, I mean, Barto's was a place of luxury in Hampstead, and Gianmarco's is an icy icy rented house in the middle of north London.

Jolienta unbuttoned her coat and gave it to Gianmarco's wife.

"Gian, look. What a lovely jumper. It sparkles in the dark."

"It certainly does, Patsy."

The doorbell rang. Cold air rushed into the lobby. Omar appeared. Without speaking, Jolienta and Omar understood it wasn't a romantic set-up and nodded at each other.

"Come on in, guys. Make yourselves comfortable."

Gian sat his guests down at the dining table and poured out red wine. The log fire, in front of the table, made no impression on draughts sneaking in from creaking windows and draughty skirting boards, and didn't have any impact on the bleak January night. Gian and Patsy were wearing identical jumpers to guard against the cold. She watched in fascination as they fed a mound of dough into a machine and ribbons of pale yellow filtered out and landed onto a tray.

Jolienta pulled at a green shawl and wound it around her neck. Sharpness filtered through the cotton and tugged at her throat. She tucked her hands under her legs hoping to halt her shivering limbs and glanced wistfully at her coat left by the front door.

They could have warned us.

Gian and Patsy were at the sink and cooker. Now and then, the flickering fire picked out a tap or an open cupboard. Omar, still in overcoat, manly and barrel-chested, sipped his wine thoughtfully. According to her watch, it was eight-thirty. Thirty minutes had gone by. It felt more like an hour—an hour of torture.

"Butternut squash with crab, ricotta and herbs in a light sauce," Gian said. "Here." He held out a bowl of Parmesan cheese.

"Sorry about the delay. We're still not used to the Brit kitchen."

Omar took hold of the bowl with a courteous nod of the head and sprinkled cheese over his pasta. His moustache was in glorious shape, glistening in the dark.

"First course, Omar, Jolienta," Patsy said, in case there was any misunderstanding.

"How wonderful."

"Delightful," Omar said.

"Jolienta, how are you finding the Slade these days? Are you thinking of applying for one of the technician jobs when they come up?"

"Er, not likely."

Gian looked pleased. "I know what you mean. The atmosphere at times."

She wanted to say, 'The etching technician's a nightmare', but why spoil the evening with petty gripes?

The first course was extremely tasty.

"What about you, Omar? What are your plans?" Gian said.

"I go back to Iran and teach."

"Are you going into the Slade tomorrow? I am."

"Yes, Gian. Saturdays is good because is very quiet."

"Patsy, how are you finding London?"

The woman stiffened up. "Oh Jolienta, it's cold and gloomy. Cold, cold, cold! But Gian and I have an agreement. I spent the last three years doing exactly as I wanted in New York and now it's his turn to do what he wants."

She noticed a weariness descend on the couple. The cold wine hurt the back of her throat. It was hard trying to make spontaneous chitchat with strangers, hard not to shiver as frosty draughts nipped at your bones. Oh, what to say when you're freezing cold.

Nine-thirty. Gian and Patsy cleared the table.

Jolienta looked at the impotent fire dancing in the hearth and looked at Omar. Lucky Omar in that thick coat.

Patsy laid clean plates and fresh cutlery on the table. Gian returned clad in a woolly hat, which squashed his curls down giving him the appearance of a teenager. He carried over a casserole dish and spooned some of the contents onto a plate. "Chilli lentil and chorizo with wild rice, Jolienta."

"Second course," Patsy echoed. "And afterwards, we got homemade lemon sorbet to refresh the palette."

The plate was cold. The food was cold. The heat had gone out of it. The lump in the middle of her throat started to grow and her whole being wanted to converge on the gnawing ache.

The wall clock said ten o' clock.

"It has been wonderrrrrful," Omar said. "Wonderrrrrful." He patted his moustache with a paper napkin and stood up.

"We must do this again sometime, no?" Gian and Patsy said.

"Yes."

"It was wonderrrrful."

"Thank you, Gian, Patsy."

"Oh, the sorbet," Patsy said.

*　　*　　*

"Tom's out," Jolienta said to the flat, "who knows where. And Kris is away."

She wolfed down breakfast, buttoned up her coat and crunched across the snow in the courtyard.

Today, snow *and* sunshine cast purity over Peckham. The studio will be empty except for Gian and Omar. Nobody will get in my way. No queuing up to use the press. No dissent when the prints need to be hung up or rearranged under weights.

The high street was deserted. The Number Twelve arrived sending a comber of slush spilling onto the pavement. She clambered up to the top deck.

"'Morning, everyone!"

London fresh and new. Everything new.

Elephant and Castle under snow.

Gower Street untouched by footprints.

She crossed the lawn to the corner entrance, stamped her feet on the ground and clambered up the spiral staircase.

Not long now.

She pushed open the studio doors. They swung, creaked and rapped against the walls. She walked past the Euan Uglow studios, quiet and empty. She pushed at the doors of the etching studio and walked into a heavy atmosphere of Xylene and turpentine. She undid her coat.

Almost, almost!

Jolienta picked up an etching plate, hurried to the sink, rubbed it with French Chalk, and sprinkled water over it.

"What do you think you're doing?" a voice said, shattering the silence.

A face contorted with rage confronted her and Jolienta had to wonder, Is this some kind of joke?

"Sorry? What d'you think I'm doing? I'm about to start work, that's what."

"No, you're not."

"What d'you mean—I'm not?"

"You don't have permission."

"Come off it. Gian and Omar are in today. They told me."

"They have permission. You don't."

"I won't disturb you. I don't need your help."

"I don't care. I'm in charge and I order you to leave the premises."

"You're sending me back into the snow when I've traversed the whole of London to get here?"

"Yes."

Gian walked in and shook his coat down.

"Get out, or I'll call security," the etching technician said.

Gian studied the floor and retreated into the corridor.

Her heart pounded. What is Gian going to say to me?

"Jolienta, I'm sorry about that," Gian said. "Don't you know? She's in love with you. Why don't you put the woman out of her misery?"

*   *   *

The bedroom clock said: tick, tock, tick, tock. The room grew dark and the clock said, "Tick, tock, tick, tock". The bedroom door opened. It was Tom.

"For God's sake, don't tell Kris."

His foot was in the room. He lowered his voice and stepped in.

"Jol . . . I've been going out with Veronica for quite a few months. Do you remember her? Would you believe it?" He covered his mouth with his hand.

"Really? You are a dark horse, T-o-m!"

"I didn't ask Kris for her address after that dinner of his. You know what he's like; he'd have teased us mercilessly. It would have been impossible to develop a relationship with her. What I did was, I tracked her down to The Royal School of Music. She said she went there every Thursday. I waited by the gate. To my relief, she recognized me. I invited her to a restaurant I know in Herne Hill, where they do a very good Duck à l'Orange. Afterwards, she asked me to spend the night. I was surprised. Pleasantly surprised."

That Veronica. I knew she fancied him. "I'm impressed, Tom. Impressed."

"It was lovely," Tom continued, in reference to the intimate act of lovemaking. "Unexpected. 'Very nice indeed," and he gave her a knowing look, which sent his mind bouncing back to Veronica's warm embrace.

Jolienta blocked his thoughts out as quickly as possible, removed her socks and scratched the inside of a big toe.

"I'm not going to tell Kris about us until we're an established couple," Tom continued, "because you can guarantee it, he'll play havoc with us."

"Don't worry, Tom. I'll keep it secret. My pleasure. By the way, I heard from Margo the other day. She phoned me at the Slade. Out of the blue it was."

"She and I have nothing in common. To be frank, she makes me feel ill. How is Stanislaus these days?"

Jolienta didn't want to say that Number Thirty-five had told her Stan was *a one for the ladies, always got a pretty girl on his arm.* She didn't believe it for a minute, but in truth, his visits were becoming less frequent, and she had to admit the last time they'd met up at the Slade, he'd eyed up Geeta, and to her intense annoyance, Geeta had wriggled back, pretended to be coy, when in fact, she was a promiscuous bitch with a distinctive body odour.

"By the way, Kris will be back any day."

"To be honest, Tom, I lose track. You know what he's like. He can't be bothered with me. I've tried and tried."

Tom shrugged his shoulders.

The next day, Veronica could be heard singing in Tom's room while he accompanied her on the piano.

There was no end to the amount of privileges Jolienta enjoyed at Number Thirty-three Sumner Road Estate—rent at four pounds a week—shared bills—luxury furniture, an indoor toilet and bathroom—resident pianist and composer—Ghostwriter for the Royal Family, and now she had a classical singer belting out arias next door. It just kept getting better and better.

Sunday. Tom wants to confide in me again, which is reassuring and alarming all at the same time, but it does confirm that we have a genuine connection.

"Poor Veronica," he whispered, "she hasn't got the voice to succeed you know, but she can't see that yet. I plod on with her exercises."

He looked unhappy.

"The exercises will have to be repeated daily until she acknowledges her limitations."

"Oh, I see."

Honestly, Veronica is stunning, tells a good joke, sings well and teaches English and French. Her dress sense is unique, especially the vivacious red chiffon cat suit with the huge frilly collar. Tom's a lucky man. If only he realized it.

The next evening, Tom and Veronica's duet ended with a few cross words. She went to investigate and found Tom laying the table for dinner. Veronica was downing a large glass of wine as if there was no tomorrow. Lashings of mascara made the woman's eyes huge and Irish laughter filled the room.

"Jol," Veronica said, unsteady in her seat, "I've parked ma teaching job in. I'm going ta give ma all to classical singin'!"

"Oh, you are such a darling," Tom said, lighting candles.

Pity was in his eyes, and to her embarrassment, Jolienta felt a surge of envy, much like the first day in Peckham when he dazzled her with his culinary skills. Today, the table was festooned with hotplates of skewered delights, a champagne bucket, and folded linen napkins and silver cutlery. A silver candelabra of yellow candles made the walls dance and glow. The cheese plant was hiding in the semi-darkness.

Bugger Tom and the way he makes me feel. This woman brings balance to the flat. Life's a lot easier these days. Not that I'm in much. Long hours at the Slade, and there's many a time I've struggled to stay awake on the bus, although the muddy mishap on the Old Kent Road is on my list of Do Not Do Again. Anyway, I'll leave them to it. Whatever it is they are up to.

She went back to her room. Tried to sit up on the mattress and fell asleep. Edward Hopper and his wife began to squabble. He threw a few pieces of wood into a stove. Jo ran at him with a kitchen pan, jumped up and hit him on the head. "The cat gets better food than me," Edward said. Very far away, Jolienta heard a soprano voice shrill and vibrant—"Go-od-bye, Jo-*lly*. Jolly-Ju-liv-*en*-ta. *Ta*-taaa", and the front door clicked shut. Now she was curled up into a ball, warm and cosy.

The sound of doors being slammed could only mean one thing.

"WHAT!" Kris pounded into the hallway, slammed another door and charged into the hall.

"Jol! Can you believe it?"

His voice was slurred.

He was waving at her in the hallway.

What unexpected behavior, she thought, and I was having such a nice snooze.

"Tom's been conducting a relationship with Veronica! I walked into her in the courtyard. She told me everything."

He strode around the flat, confused. He'd been deprived of an opportunity to tamper with Tom's vulnerabilities and he was livid.

"You knew all the time. Why didn't you tell me?"

"Well, he told me to keep it secret, so I did. Basically, that's it. No big deal."

She yawned and heard a drawer screech open. A chocolate wrapper was squashed and tossed across the table. Ry Cooder went on full volume. He fixed himself a drink. He slammed the living room door in her face.

*　　*　　*

"Jol?" Tom tapped and waited outside. "Could I ask you for your advice again?" he whispered.

"Sure."

What advice can I possibly give Tom? Oh, I do hate these moments.

He looked harassed. "It's about Veronica. I just don't know what to do about our relationship."

Honestly. They've only just got together.

"What's happened, Tom?"

Tom pulled in his lower lip.

"Well, she keeps crying. I don't know what to do. I'm very fond of her, but quite frankly, the situation is getting on my nerves."

His face hardened. "We bumped into Nicky the violinist. Do you remember her? Veronica became considerably upset, because, I was, er, shocked to walk into Nicky like that after such a long time. Now she keeps crying and asking for commitment. To be honest, I'm not sure I can tolerate much more."

"Oh? What d'you want out of the relationship, Tom?"

"I'm happy with the way things have been, but if she keeps on crying and pushing for more, then I'd rather end it."

He stood there, defeated, which was not like him at all.

"Tom . . . you know, I understand her behavior. Speaking as a woman . . . er, being a female myself that is, it's easy to fall into a trap of feeling insecure. I've done it myself. I've just sounded like I'm whining all the time. And then you can't get out of it. Like a record stuck on a loop. Look, if you care about Veronica and want to do the right thing, this is what I suggest. Reassure her. Tell her how much she means to you. Explain that you're not interested in commitment for now . . . with anyone in fact . . . and that isn't going to change in the immediate future. Thirdly, tell her the crying is making you uncomfortable. Lastly, stick by her until she regains her composure. You can reassess the situation then."

"Thank you, Jolienta. I'll give it a go. I also want to apologise for the many times I've corrected your speech."

*　　*　　*

April showers. The Peckham exhibition was on show for a second time in the high street. Exhibits had been re-installed due to popular demand. New press releases had been sent out. She was in the Peckham Action Shop, invigilating, inviting neighbours and locals by personal invitation. Sometimes, she stopped pedestrians and persuaded them in. Jolienta liked to ask all visitors to comment in the guest book, and at the end of the day, she liked to read the comments. One woman must have been optically-challenged, because she'd written, *What a load of abstract blobs*, but the photographers from Number Thirty-five had penned, *Jolienta, you're a genius and we love you*. Emma Johnson of The South London Press wrote, 'The paintings bring Edward Hopper to mind and at times the characters are reminiscent of Edward Burra. Not only is this exhibition worthy of our attention as a collection of art, but the artist has collaborated with the local community, a community which is threatened by a six-lane motorway intent on tearing out the heart of Peckham High Street, and thus Jolienta dos Remédios shows her credentials as a recorder of social injustice. It must be serendipitous that Ms Dos Remédios teamed up with photographer, Brillo McKenzie, whose photographs—portrayals of a Turkish Cypriot couple, and even more startling, a panorama of Rastafarians smoking marijuana in the Britannia Pub—capture Peckham in all its beauty and diversity.'

So many compliments mixed in with crass ones, it didn't matter that Tom and Kris hadn't crossed over the road to see what she was up to. And were they missing something—The Britannia Pub. That had been an event and a half. Only she, in all her enthusiasm, could have dreamt of asking a photographer to set up a tripod in the middle of that pub. You could have heard a pin drop when Brillo pointed the lens at the customers. Every Rastafarian in the bar twisted to the left, a wave of dreadlocks mid-air. At times like that, it was good to be young, girlish, giggle, and hope for the best. Dan raised a glass.

Peckham, People & Places.

No sign of Tom or Kris.

She closed up shop for the day.

*   *   *

Tom was in the kitchen making a supper of grilled peppers with toasted pinenuts, kebabs of pheasant and a red currant jelly with a hint of elderflower. A brass bucket on the kitchen draining board cradled a bottle of booze, a type she'd never heard of. Tom's voice was very close to her ears, spinning around.

"Jol . . . Veronica and I have decided to move in together."

"Oh, Tom, that's great. Really great."

She almost wrapped him up in her arms, but she would never have actually dared to touch him.

"As you know, this is my flat, Jolienta, and I've decided Veronica should move in."

"Hey. That's great. You'll be nice and cosy then. Easy access to the piano, eh? More singing lessons for you to accompany. Ha ha."

"Actually, we've decided it would be best to have a room each. Veronica and I wouldn't want to live on top of each other, would we? This will, of course, mean that either you or Kris move out."

"Oh."

"In actual fact, I've mentioned this to Kris already. I'm sorry, Jol, he became agitated. The problem is, he's going to create mayhem. Therefore, I thought I'd better warn you. You see, he said *you* should be the one to go, and he was quite aggressive about it. However, I must say, Veronica and I would rather *you* stayed and *he* left."

She hadn't anticipated this.

She drifted into the safety of her room.

Who's worse? Tom or Kris?

A panic started up. Her chest felt tight.

Call yourself a Labourite, Tom? Think you can lord it over people and dispose of them when it's convenient?

And Kris?

You Judas. I let you buy my Hubble Factory. It was beautiful, that drawing.

Jolienta sobbed.

I don't know what it is about people in London. It was never like this up north. Or maybe it was?

She got up and went to the kitchen. "Don't worry Tom, I'll go." She hadn't meant to say it. Anyway, she must embrace change.

Tom looked shocked. "Jol, we'd rather *you* stayed and Kris left."

"I've made my decision."

She put her coat on and went out on the balcony. Rain shot down in sheets of glass. Out in the courtyard, rain scattered at odd angles on her shoulders and frame. She was saturated. Out on the high street, rainwater gathered around her ankles and flowed angrily into gutters. A lake was forming under the railway bridge. The traffic had disappeared in an area normally packed with shoppers. Too dangerous for driving. Jolienta laughed. She was shrouded in water with no person in sight, except for a solitary figure with an umbrella in the distance. She jumped into the gutter. Icy water rushed up her legs and sent a shock to her loins.

She waded on towards Peckham Rye, where the floodwaters encircled her. The heavens had truly opened. She found a bench under a thorny arch and sat down and wept.

The Polish Anthem

TULSE HILL WAS QUIETER AND LESS GRIMY than Peckham and there wasn't much to see of Edward Hopper in the buildings or situations. In fact, Belgravia Avenue was the opposite to the Sumner Road Estate. The road was grand with oak trees cracking up the pavements. The houses had gravel drive-ins, slicing up gardens of sago palms, climbing roses, lavenders, lupins and Continental Poppies.

Home was Number One hundred and eighteen. It had a front garden that differed from the rest. It had a lawn of weeds spreading from the gate and low brick walls up to a door that opened into two parts, the way patio doors do. The high street was non-descript. The station was immediately there, just turn left, and better than trekking up the Rye or taking a bus to Elephant & Castle.

There hadn't been time to think. She had left Peckham and Hopper behind. She had left Number Thirty-five behind. Stanislaus would take the new address in his stride. Something about the landlord had bothered her, niggled at her.

Something's not quite right about him, but when you're in London, you don't really know many people and you're desperate—you take a chance, don't you? Besides, Rita came with me to view the flat, and she didn't have a bad word to say about Mr O' Brian, or the flat. So it must be OK. Geeta's going to move in soon; I won't be alone. There's a phone box outside. No worries about who pays for what call. It'll be OK.

Home was in a discreet part of London. The avenue rose into a gentle hill and no children hurried along it to school. There were no bustling mums with prams. No strident office workers marching along with brief cases.

"Stan," Jolienta was in the phone box putting money into the coin slot, "you're in. I don't believe it. The Tulse Hill flat's gigantic. It's got floor-to-floor carpeting. Purple. Lovely on bare feet. Monumental-sized furniture you can lose yourself in and drapes that reach the floor. The rent's a bargain at twenty pounds per week each." She fed thirty pence into the slot.

"Darling, you are a marvel. I don't know how you do it and I was born in London," Stanislaus replied.

"Maybe the landlord, Mr O'Brian who's Creole, doesn't understand London prices, Stan? He and his wife live on the ground floor. His wife's a nurse; too shy to speak. You know, she seemed kinda shocked when she met us—Geeta and I."

"She was dazzled by your beauty, darling."

"There's no private door to the flat, but who cares? The landlord's married. The flat doesn't have a phone. That's why I'm in the phone box outside. It's right outside! Anyway, when are you coming over? I haven't seen you for weeks."

"I'll be around tomorrow evening, darling. Miss you."

"Good. See you then. I'm late for the Slade. You'll find Tulse Hill Station is two minutes away from Belgravia Avenue. Bye for now, my love."

Jolienta hurried over to the other side of the avenue and turned left into Tulse Hill Station. On the train, she opened up a book called 'She knew the Polish Anthem'. The main character, she had discovered, travelled from place to place looking for somewhere to live and was always in search of a home. The character had no knowledge of her family or forebears and desperately wanted to belong—belong anywhere, belong to someone. The parallel between the character and herself had not escaped her notice. And whatever circumstance arose in the novel, there was one thing the character could rely on—the sound of the Polish Anthem. This reverberated in the character's dreams and memories.

Jolienta followed the woman's journey, savoured each word and was reaching the end of the book. In the last few pages—to her great relief—as the train rattled into London Bridge—the woman got a job baking bread, married the baker and lived happily ever after. It happened very quickly. Jolienta re-read the last few paragraphs and looked at the book cover. It showed a stocky creature in front of a blushing sunset, with an oval face, short fair hair and penetrating green eyes. The ghostly woman wore a wide-rimmed black hat and had a black cloak draped around her shoulders. The train screeched to a halt.

Jolienta set to work in the studio. An easel was loaded with a drawing board and a heavy imperial sheet of paper. She scratched into the paper with crayons, chiselled out a landscape and a face, stopped to sharpen tips, smudged and blended oil pastel with a stubborn thumb until the friction became hot and pulled up fibres, did what no artist should do with oily and non-oily products, and dug deeper into the resilient paper, a purchase from Faulkner's. The black hat filled up the width of the paper. Below it, a luminous face confronted the unknown.

One day, Barto stopped to examine her progress. Jolienta scribbled. Jolienta scraped. Other staff stopped to observe. She took heart in their silent approval and was aware that the students kept a respectful distance to avoid spoiling her concentration. She acknowledged the end of each day with disappointment—the Slade would be locked at eight o' clock and she must go home.

A week later, she was working on The Woman in the Black Hat

and considering the background, which was not quite right. She wanted a hint of the sea inside the sky. The silkscreen tutor made a few comments. She stood there, open-mouthed and dribbled.

The next day, Barto, clearly agitated, said, "Wad eez it you are doing? You are hypnotized by this woman! Eed is narcissistic. I prefer ze Bouncing Ball Reggae Club on Japanese Mingei!"

Jolienta glared at him and reconnected with The Woman in the Black Hat; the blushing horizon became a panorama of lavender, cool-pale-algae-turquoise, yellow ochre and lemon, with shreds of sharp orange, which flicked with electricity.

Another week disappeared, and another tutor, a guy who had a beard, which resembled a toilet brush head, resumed the attack. "I think you should move on, Jolienta. This ain't getting you anywhere. I hate the idea of you wasting months on an image that ain't going anywhere.

"Jolienta!" he said, adding volume to his voice. "You're depressed. Why don't we go get a cappuccino?"

She liked this man; he played the saxophone, had a New York accent, however nobody, nobody was going to shift her from The Woman in the Black Hat.

The drawing told her it was ready to proceed.

She cut the woman's face out of four squares of linoleum. At the top of the main square, she carved out those five special words: 'She knew the Polish Anthem'. She selected Japanese papers—deep red going on purple, deep blue going on turgid yellow, and poured a mound of gold dust onto the counter, lined up pots of translucent medium and tubs of printing inks. Jolienta rolled on inks, registered each piece of printing paper and burnished the backs with a barren. Finally, she hung the results up to dry. The Woman in the Black Hat waved back. Her sky was a blinding gold. Her hat was very black. The words shone out. She knew the Polish Anthem.

Polish Stan said she had developed a Polish fetish. He said she was obsessed with all things Polish—Polish sausage, Polish films like Man of Iron, and was addicted to Lech Walesa, and in three hours time, she would peel off his clothes and clutch his invincible Polish body.

*   *   *

Those moccasins, they made her want to run like the wind, chase wolves, travel endlessly until the end of time.

"Hello Mr O'Brian. How are you? Did you want something?"

Mr O'Brian was in flat cap and tweed jacket and following her tread as she descended from the upper landing. His nurse-wife was nowhere to be seen; the woman would normally peek out from behind him in her NHS uniform, two anxious eyes darting from side to side waiting for something to happen.

"I'm just going to make a quick phone call, Mr O'Brian. Bye."

Mr O'Brian sniffed.

The avenue was empty. The station and high street were close by. No one seemed to walk down Belgravia Avenue; they drove into their drive-ins and then vanished from view. An oak tree embraced the telephone box with branches and disorderly roots. She put an umbrella in the corner of the kiosk and dialled.

"Sweetheart, sorry to call again. Are you staying over? It's more relaxing if you stay over."

"Darling . . ." Stanislaus replied.

A young man in a leather jacket walked by.

". . . darling, can you hang on for a second? I need to take care of something."

"Okey-dokey, Stan."

A breeze entered the phone box, she was about to say, "Sorry Mister, won't be long"; the words were in her mouth, then he was next to her, pressing his face against her. The man in the leather jacket shoved into her, squashed her into a corner of the kiosk, and slapped his hand between her legs grasping whatever he could find. She was jammed solid, her pelvic bone throbbing. He bared his teeth and muttered. She pushed. She got out. The receiver swung to and fro and she could hear Stanislaus say, "Jolienta? Jolienta? Jolienta?" She got to the other side of the avenue and looked back.

The man emerged from the phone box and smiled. She tried to shout, "Help". An inaudible yelp came out. "Sorry love," he said and held the umbrella out.

Does he think I'm stupid? Does he think I'm stupid?

He whipped the side of kiosk. He thrashed it with so much hate that the umbrella snapped and collapsed into a broken heap. He let out a cackle and threw it down. Jolienta staggered to the station and dialed nine nine nine. From the safety of the main road, she checked the width and depth of the avenue. He was nowhere to be seen.

"I was worried. I caught a taxi. Are you all right, darling?"

"Stan! You're here. Incredible. I live over there."

They walked up the garden path towards the patio doors and went up the flat. He sat on the edge of the bed. He was still wearing his raincoat. "Are you going to tell me what happened?"

"I had to call the police."

"What happened?"

"Someone at the door," the landlord shouted.

A policewoman was outside holding a notebook in her hand. The officer came up the stairs. Stanislaus excused himself.

"That's sensitive of him," the policewoman said. "So . . . this man . . . he sounds sadistic."

The officer wrote out a report and left.

"Darling, tell me what happened."

Stanislaus, he was so handsome. His body was perfect and his chin irresistible. All of a sudden, she felt shy. She flung her arms around him and held on tight.

*   *   *

The Saturday was bright and brisk as she travelled from Tulse Hill to Peckham High Street. Jolienta turned into Pelham Road, fur coat wafting in the breeze. She was wearing more make-up than usual. A plastic carrier bag swung at her side in time with each stride. She was on her way to clean out her old bedroom on the Sumner Road Estate and wanted to collect a few books. It was also a good excuse to say goodbye to The Alliance and other places she'd battled with in paint and charcoal.

She strode past Thos. P. Headland Engineers Merchants, one of the buildings she'd painted for the Peckham exhibition—a familiar landmark, what with lurking shadows turning parking meters into vibrant guitar-shapes, red brick walls bouncing back the chilly sun, and blue office windows full of grime and emptiness masking industrial activity; Peckham was a part of her. She had embraced every shop, market stall, street and alley in the pursuit of beauty and truth, yet she was the one who'd left Peckham—not Tom or Kris with their affluence and indifference.

She passed a disused tennis court, moved closer to Number Thirty-three Sumner Road Estate. Green wire fencing and sunlight flicked patterns across her retinae, weaving the pavement, tarmac, litter, weeds, walls, windows, roofs, trees and birds, into the sticky membrane of her brain.

"Tom insisted I take the cheese plant to Tulse Hill with me," she rambled, "the spindly thing that struggled for light. *Well, you are the only one who looks after it*, he said, which wasn't true at all. I never looked after it. And I remember, when I held it in my arms, it was heavier than I expected. I staggered to the door, pot in arm, fan-shaped leaves poking my face and a deep crunch in my belly. What a brouhaha. Kris went berserk after I'd gone. Fancy him throwing his typewriter at Tom's door and turning his bedroom into a locked arsenal. I'm glad to be out of it. *That Veronica's a whore*, Kris shouted, according to Tom.

What a hoot. The way he behaved behind my back! *She's going.*

Not me! Minnie Mouse is going!"

A figure, directly ahead of her, was growing larger and larger.

We are going to collide. Why should I move out of the way?

The figure was Kris. Regal, blond, blue-eyed and beautiful, arrogant and threatening. She had spent a year, give or take a month, living with this man.

He caught sight of her and squinted back in disbelief.

"I demand you bring that cheese plant back," he said, the end of his nose jabbing hers.

"How absurd."

And it was—his nose prodding hers.

"It's in my new flat, on the landing, where it's especially bright. It'll probably flourish."

"You dripped oil paint on my shirts and carpet!" he yelled, and with so much venom, she held her face up and waited to be slapped.

He unbuttoned his camel coat and gulped. "How dare you use my room to paint in, Jolienta dos Remédios, when I expressly forbade it!"

She stepped aside and continued to the Sumner Road Estate. She turned into the courtyard. She was going to take one last look at The Alliance from his window whether he liked it or not.

North Peckham Estate

A RIGHT TURN INTO SOUTHAMPTON WAY led to a cul-de-sac and to one of many stairwells into the North Peckham Estate. Rumour had it taxis wouldn't stop in this part of Southwark and nor would anyone else. Except for Bill that is.

"Hi Bill. How d'you do? Fancy seeing you here."

Bill King, owner of The Crown opposite Manze's Eel & Pie Shop, was bent over his car engine and identifiable by his check trousers. He pushed his spectacles into place with the back of his hand and let the bonnet drop. "Hello, Miss er Um. I broke down. Haven't seen you in a while. Hope you haven't forgotten us."

"Oh Bill, I do miss Peckham and chatting to the shopkeepers, and I miss all of the places I used to visit and paint. I must give you an etching of The Crown. It sold well during the exhibition. There are five of the edition left."

"How about lunch Sunday week? My treat. You can bring it with you. What did ya call it? An itching? Bring that picture of my pub with you."

He peered into her face, and in doing so, exposed the tunnels of his mind. 'Unhappy', his face said. 'Am I worth knowing?' his insides whimpered. 'I can see she doesn't want to accept my invitation. Old skin, sacks under the eyes. What does my future hold? I will wake up one morning, my soul trapped inside my dead body and I'll never have known Love. Never have tasted it.'

Oh, really, Jolienta sighed, he shouldn't have asked. It's not fair. I've only met him twice; once to talk about the six-lane motorway, the other time to investigate the inside of his pub.

Bill shoulders drooped. His face sagged.

"Bill, I'd be delighted to have lunch with you."

His shoulders bounced back up again. "That's for definite, Olienta?"

"Yes. Look, my diary says that's the twentieth. I've got your number. Must hurry now, Bill; I might be moving back to Peckham!"

Jolienta cantered up the stairwell into the North Peckham Estate and entered a complex of identical walkways and stairwells. Not a person in sight.

Which way now?

She scanned the anonymous maze.

Dog shit. Dog shit. Look out!

Goodness me, every door and walkway is the same.

Oh, here it is—Number Seventy-four.

Carl opened the door a few inches. "Hi, Jolienta. Come in."

Carl was a quiet man. Not much to say for himself. Exactly what she needed. Out of everyone in their clique, he was the unassuming one. If she moved in, she wouldn't have to worry about a thing.

Carl took her on a tour of the flat. It wasn't what she'd expected. It was larger and had a third floor to it with a darkroom at the top and a large balcony overlooking concrete cubes. The kitchen was large, tidy and strangely unwelcoming. Not a wrapper, wrinkled packet or plate in sight. It contained an old washing machine and a tumble dryer. Back in Sumner Road, there hadn't been any washing machine, an odd fact considering Tom's predilection for home comforts.

"So your friend's moved out then, Carl? Is that for sure?"

"Yeah. Keith got married and they've moved into a flat of their own on the other side of the estate. I hope she doesn't regret it. He's ugly. She's beautiful. She's Turkish with long fair hair. I made lunch for us," he said, pinning her down with two big puppy eyes.

"Oh, that's nice. I didn't expect that. You are considerate."

"One of my signature dishes. I have two. My mother showed me how. Chicken Marengo's my favorite. The other one is Beef Stroganoff."

He pulled a Pyrex dish out of the oven. She could smell gravy.

"Are you going to tell me what's been going on, Jolienta? The other flats . . . What went wrong?"

"Sure. If you really want to hear. Groan, Carl. Oooo, this tastes good. Thank you. OK. Where was I? Dear me . . . the Tulse Hill flat was palatial, the rent was a bargain, there was no private door to the flat, no phone, and the landlord lived downstairs. I thought everything would be fine, because he was married, his wife was with him, there was a telephone box in the avenue and Tulse Hill Station was only two ticks away."

"Tell me about Geeta, Jolienta. I hear she's stunning."

"Hang on Carl, I'm trying to tell you—seeing as you asked. Give me a chance. One evening, Mr O'Brian, the landlord, came in without knocking. A man wearing a Docker's jacket walked in behind him. There we were, two uninvited men in our living room, Geeta-in-sari cross-legged on the settee, me by the window and cheese plant reading about American printmaking, when blow me, Mr O'Brian fell to my feet. I'm telling you the truth. I'm not exaggerating. He fell to my feet, hands clasped together ready for prayer and begged us to go on a double date with him and his mate. Geeta and I gawped at each other. I declined of course. We ushered the men out. Unfortunately, we couldn't lock the door, because there was never any lock there to begin with. We plugged a chair under the door handle. Another evening, Carl, we were leaving for the pub, on our way down the stairs, when the landlord and his wife—a nurse—came out. She was always in

110

uniform and never actually spoke. Well, Mr O'Brian started shaking his fist at us. I mean, he started to shout, *Get out of my house, you prostitutes.* I shouted back—*We are not Prostitutes; we're Postgraduates!* And with that, he ordered us to leave. I started flat-hunting, got my bags ready. Geeta decided to stay put. She got it into her head she'd be all right, because she's a 'person of colour'. That's what she said. When I told the etching technician, *she* said Blacks hate Asians. As if the technician would know; she's as white as French Chalk. I've never heard of such a thing."

"And then what happened?"

"I forgot to say . . . before that happened . . . I was in a telephone box outside the gate to the house when a young man jumped in and attacked me. I was terrified, and you know what, he was handsome. For God's sake, I ask myself: WHY?"

Carl gulped back his tea and put the cup down. "What exactly did he do to you?"

"Oh, come on. I'm not going into detail."

Puppy eyes enveloped her. "What happened after that?"

"Oh! Sigh. My tea's getting cold." Jolienta drained the cup dry.

"OK. It was Goodbye, Mr O'Brian. Goodbye, Mr Telephone Box Assailant. I moved to Camberwell Green near to a railway bridge. I'd passed that way many times before on the bus. I loved the curve of the archway and the idea of a train rumbling past my bedroom window. I wondered what it would be like to live there. The landlord was a white guy, about thirty-six years of age. The rent was OK at twenty-five pounds a week. I met his girlfriend, bizarrely another nurse and as mute as the last in Tulse Hill, would you believe. The room was small and had a lock on the door. That swung it; I'd be safe. But when I moved in, I discovered a musical card inside the bedside cabinet. 'Congratulations on Your Divorce'. That's strange I thought, he's letting me know he's available. I threw it away, no problem, whereas before I'd probably have asked for his permission. Ha. I left it on the top of the bin for him to see, get any funny business out of the way right from the start.

"I settled in, hung blue velvet curtains up, drew charcoal drawings of hats, and put the cheese plant in the living room on the upstairs floor, where the light was bright. My room was cold but nice. Stan said it was marvellous. Well, a few months went by, I was in the bathroom getting ready, washing myself at the sink—I'm not one for having a bath first thing in the morning and there was no shower—I was looking in the mirror, completely naked, soaping up my nether regions, when I happened to glance outside and downwards. The bathroom window overlooked the back corner of the property. It gave a limited view, but, blow me, the landlord was staring right up at me from his bedroom window. In that instance, I realized he'd been watching me every morning, seen everything . . . me urinating . . . everything."

"And what happened after that?"

"Well, that's why I'm here, Carl, to look at your spare room, and what a difference it would make, having a landlord who's a friend."

"Yeah. I need someone to move in. What happened to Geeta, Jolienta? Where is she now?"

"Well, as I explained, Geeta thought she was immune to eviction. The silly woman went back one night to find her belongings out on the lawn. Mr O'Brian had opened the window and chucked the lot out. I lost my deposit, because of her stupidity, hundreds of pounds from my grant; all because she thought she was well in with Mr O'Brian. And when I think about it, Carl, she had several lovers on the go, plus the regular one. That must have been what did it; that's why he thought we were prostitutes."

"Oh." Carl sat up straight and crossed his legs.

"And if her family find out, they'll have her killed . . . She went and married one of them to stop him from being deported."

"The landlord threw everything onto the lawn? I have a lot to lose, Jolienta. Gangs patrol this estate. They have organized 'look-outs' waiting for you to go out. They just hang around waiting to break in. People get mugged every day around here. I think that's why Rita and the others don't visit.

"I worry about my cameras, my lenses, my tripods and the enlarger too. It's a good one. I've got developing tanks, trays and chemicals—all inflammables. To be honest, I feel as though I must stay in most of the time to protect the equipment. Getting contents insurance is impossible. I've tried. Taxis won't come here. Did you know that? You'd be doing me a favour if you moved in, Jolienta. Safety in numbers and all that."

*   *   *

The cheese plant was left to fend for itself in the Camberwell house. Carl helped ferry boxes and paintings up from the cul-de-sac. The new bedroom was unpleasant and lacked character. The metal windows wouldn't take the blue velvet curtains. The bed was a single and dipped in the middle. The futon mattress was dumped in a corner.

*   *   *

That Tulse Hill landlord is welcome to my deposit and that Camberwell-bag-of-potatoes can go and rot. Carl, he's such a sweetie. What a change of fortune. And just as well, there's only so much a person can take. He makes nice dinners too—a bit repetitive perhaps—and endless cups of tea, and he lets me use the darkroom whenever I like. He never uses it himself. Strange, what with him being a professional photographer and all that.

Jolienta switched on the infrared light and pressed the door to.

You'd have thought the others would have been to visit by now, seeing as there are two of us here from the same gang living at the same address. I hate the fact that they haven't been round.

This flat. It's huge.

The furnishings are grim.

Carl's in every night.

I must admit; I wish he wasn't so repressed. Those eyes. You just want to stroke him and give him a doggie biscuit.

She pulled out a sheet of paper from a tray and dipped it into cold water. The image was over exposed.

Anyone might accuse me of being a fraud for changing my approach to painting, that is, not working directly from life anymore. Oh, I can just hear them at the Slade, especially the Euan Uglow mob. "What a kop out. She's using photographs", but I wouldn't be copying the photo; I would keep on painting and repainting it until the image was mine.

She removed the strips of negatives from the contact sheet gripper, inserted another set of negatives, switched on the enlarger, counted out the seconds and slid the paper into developing fluid. Images of Choumert Road Market appeared.

"Well, it's safer to use a photo. Today's affront," she said in the rosy darkness, "could easily become tomorrow's assault. OK, I'm older and wiser now, however, bad things still happen. Like the time in broad daylight when two guys dropped their trousers in front of me. I was trying to paint chimney pots on the Camberwell New Road. I mean, OK, as a response, I took up karate for a while, bought the white robe, and Geeta—a brown belt—she got angry with me, said my blocking was hurting her and then she refused to partner me. That incident with those guys. It bothered me. The way they stuck their naked backsides at me in broad daylight like that, scoffing into their navels, and I had to pretend I couldn't see them and keep on painting. The truth is . . . I can't paint outdoors anymore. I hate the fact they've won. But there it is. I use photos now.

*　　*　　*

Carl's dad whistled as Jolienta carried in a tray of tea and buns. His mum, a tiny woman, hung her head and tried to shake the shame out if it. Carl ran his eyes over her too. He just couldn't believe he was living with a woman and was under the impression he'd achieved his ambition—found a wife.

"My Mum and Dad have bought you a carpet, Jolienta, for your room. They drove it all the way here from Wales."

His parents nodded in the direction of a carpet roll on the first floor landing. They looked desperate, desperate for closure on their son. She could feel their anxiety.

No turning back now, Jolienta thought. What's done is done. I live here now. She poured tea into four teacups. Carpets? Eee, they're only good for accumulating mites, dirt and wriggly centipedes.

She offered out the buttered buns, glanced at the carpet and saw that it consisted of a nasty red and black swirl.

Carl and his parents were absorbed in her every movement. Embarrassing. They were measuring her grace, the brilliance of her smile, and no matter how many times she repeated herself to them—that she was allergic to synthetic carpet and couldn't afford to pay for it either—the parents insisted she accept the carpet as a gift. The father, a tall man, not like his son, got up, flexed his muscles and bear-hugged the roll to the second landing.

The TV was on. His mum and dad were filling cupboards with tins and packets of pasta. She could hear them say they had a long drive ahead, and when they'd gone, Jolienta decided to get the carpet problem out of the way, hauled it into her room, unrolled it and left the edges of it overlapping the skirting board. That way, it could easily be rolled up again and given to some other poor bastard. Canvases, prints and drawings were stacked under the window.

The next morning, the alarm clock danced on the carpet. The smell and colour of the carpet made her feel sick. From the bare metal-framed window, the sky was blank.

No sign of Carl.

Coffee! Jam on toast!

Today, Coldharbour Lane Tyre Shop awaits me.

A discovery during a rambling walk, the premises of the Coldharbour Lane shop had been three or four individual shops in bygone years. Its giant windows had been blackened out for reasons unknown. The main wall had been painted a violent crimson. Notices had been drilled in between the windows and coronet cornices. The boards said, *Engines, Gear Boxes, Back Axles, Prop Shafts, Dynamos, Starters, All Makes of Engines*. Bullet holes dotted the frontage where a juggernaut-sized tyre stood on its side. The tyre had dwarfed a mother and child cuddling in an armchair. The image kept going around and round in her head, like evolution itself.

*   *   *

Barto dos Santos closed the aquatint box, banged on both sides of the seven-foot box three times so that it shook, and rotated the handle so that the contents were riled and spinning out of control. He monitored his wristwatch for two minutes, opened the lid, put the zinc plate inside, taking care not to disturb the falling resin inside. He closed the lid again, not wanting to disturb and swung the hook into place. If she wanted to make sure no one interfered with the plate, he said, she had "better stand guard for fifteen minutes until zee last speck of dust has fallen".

Jolienta stood guard for twenty minutes and extracted the plate with care, a true balancing act. The plate was covered in a fine layer of resin ready for the grill, where a Bunsen burner would melt the powder to a transparent crust.

"Barto, when d'you know the sugarlift solution is ready?" It had been bugging her for ages. How many hours was she supposed to spend shaking a jam-jar up and down?

She hated not getting answers to her questions.

No one says how much sugar, or how much water to use, and exactly when the solution is ready. And if someone does answer, they can't give me a straight answer; one I can understand.

"You keep adding ze sugar until ze solution cannot dissolve any more grains," Barto said.

Great.

The etching technician announced it was time to close the studios. "Evaculate," the etching technician said.

Jolienta hurried home, ran beneath the street lamps of Southampton Row, sprinted up the stairwell and zigzagged along the dog-poo walkways. The route from the cul-de-sac to Carl's front door was a daily mystery. Every door and walkway was identical. Despite the confusion, by magic, she would find herself in front of the right door.

No sign of Carl. Is he asleep?

Carl. What a character. Lying in bed all day with the heating blowing dry air over his face and pillow, and by the time I get back, the fumes are enough to kill him.

The heating vent in my own room is always closed off. If you wake up to greet the day, there's no point allowing artificial hot air to send you back to sleep again, until one day you never wake up. It dries you out. It makes you cough. You know you're being poisoned.

Jolienta wandered into the living room. He wasn't in his bedroom after all; he was on the settee in pyjamas. The TV was on, a sturdy four-legged thing resting on green-matted carpet.

"I bought the replacement shampoo, Carl."

"Yes, I saw it. My mum and dad dropped by on their way to Plymouth today."

"Nice. Was it good to see them?"

"Yeah. It was nice to see Mum. Always is. My dad . . . we don't get on. We don't connect. Never have. He's bought you a second-hand bicycle by the way. You'll be able to cycle in and out on the ramps. It'll be safer."

"Goodness. That was thoughtful. Will you thank him for me? D'you know? It will be safer getting in and out that way."

"It's in my room. It needs a bit of attention. It's rusty in parts."

"Thanks for letting me know.

"Carl, you know whole days are racing by. You're either in a daze or lying in bed half-comatose due to the heating vent in your room, or you're falling asleep in front of the TV. Frankly, it worries me. I am worried. You need to get out and about more, Carl. You need to close up that vent in that room of yours."

"It won't close."

"Well, move the bed away and open the window."

Anger darted across his eyes. "Jolienta, I've got something to say."

"Yes?"

"You're never in."

Oh-oh. What's next?

"The washing machine doesn't work and you were the last one to use it."

"I'm onto it. It'll be fixed at the weekend."

"My parents are annoyed, because you didn't pay for the carpet."

"Ah. I was wondering when that one would crop up."

"And I've made Chicken Marengo."

"How lovely!"

The phone rang. It was Polish Stan.

"Hang on, Stan, I'm just moving the phone into the bathroom." She pulled down her jeans and sat on the toilet. "Sweetheart, I must have tried to catch hold of you at least four times last week. You're never in."

"I'm busy. You know what it's like. But there is only one Jolienta dos Remédios, and I love her!"

Her bladder opened. It demanded release. She had the distinct impression that Polish Stan could hear the torrent batter the bowl and funnel down the U-bend. The need was too great.

"What I need to ask you, Stan, is . . ."

"Is everything alright, Jolienta? What's that noise?"

"I'm running a tap. What I need to ask you . . . what I need to ask you . . . is—the last time I stayed with you I found photos of a naked woman in your house."

"Ohhhh? Bob haircut?"

"Ye-s."

"That would be Carol, darling."

"Who's Carol?"

"Carol is Carol."

"What d'you mean, "Carol is Carol"? Who is she? Your lover?"

"Darling, I love you both in equal amounts. I do."

"Owwww! Why didn't you tell me? I thought we were in love."

"I couldn't tell you. We *are* in love. I knew you wouldn't accept my open policy and you're a hard person to let go of. You're special."

"Stanislaus, I don't want to see you ever again for as long as I live."

"I'm sorry that's how you feel. Goodbye, darling. One day, you'll be famous and I'll say to my friends, I *knew* that woman."

Jolienta filled the toilet bowl with a winding trail of brown waste just thinking about the woman with the bob haircut and large breasts pointing in opposite directions.

God, I thought we were in love.

There's no getting away from the evidence.

Open policy, he said.

Am I capable of an open-policy relationship? I don't think so.

The last thing I want is a gloating Carl. Jolienta bathed her swollen face and hovered on the landing. Crimewatch was on. She could hear it. She slipped into the room and settled in front of the TV.

"I think you should move out," Carl said.

"Yes, of course. May I keep the bicycle? It will be very handy."

Ha, ha, I was ready that time! I'm tired of ol' Puppy Eyes anyway. Him and his unreasonable attitudes. Tired of justifying how much toilet paper I use, tired of the contrast in personality between us. He's so predictable. I actually knew this was going to happen.

The next morning, a housing officer on the estate, a puzzled man, gave Jolienta a form to fill in, which more or less offered her instant access to a studio flat on the North Peckham Estate. He tossed the keys across the counter. "Good luck, Miss."

Well, that was easy then.

Bill King

THE NEW FLAT WAS THREE MINUTES AWAY and one of two flats at the top of an enclosed stairwell. Everything inside the flat was new—grey floor tiles, white walls and ceilings and very large windows on one side, which gave a view of the estate's hollow core. The housing officer had described it as a studio flat, but in reality, it was full of possibilities. Jolienta speeded up the process of packing, carried boxes and canvases, and tiptoed through the faeces—dog shit zigzagged and trodden into the walkways by the wheels of prams and feet of children.

A heavy fire door separated the walkway from an enclosed stairwell. Her new home was two minutes away from Carl's removing any expense, but it was a cumbersome task. Each trip involved the fire door jerking back into position, catching the back of her foot, and ended in a loud wallop. She was getting a headache. The door slammed on the bicycle twice, which didn't do the back wheel any good.

The shunting was over. Artwork was stacked next to the bicycle. She sank to the floor. She was surrounded by things, her things, humble things, things that didn't matter, and she was rid of the red and black carpet. The futon mattress in its new settee base smacked of luxury, and brought a smile.

"The engineer's coming tomorrow. My own phone. Can't wait. Coming up in the world."

The clock indicated that it was eleven-thirty. She was fully dressed slouched against the futon settee, sitting on the floor, daylight pouring in through the windows, and in exactly the same position as the day before. She hadn't moved a muscle. That's how tired she was.

The engineer was at the door. Jolienta opened up and saw two girls and a young man out on the landing minding their own business.

"Black or cream?" the engineer said.

She looked at the telephones. "I've never seen a cream one before. I'll have it. It's a novelty."

He unpacked the phone and connected it without any fuss.

When the engineer departed, she saw the three people on the landing smoking themselves silly, and hurried back in to admire the phone. The living room-cum-bedroom-cum-kitchen was looking cool—beige futon settee, cream telephone. Jolienta picked up the receiver and listened to the tone.

*   *   *

The fixtures and fittings of The Houndsditch of Peckham were from another era—chunky chiming clocks of brass ornamentation and not for sale. They were there as a form of customer service. The Dior perfume counter had a vast selection of products in frilly bottles and boxes. There was always plenty to see in Peckham, and she was back in among it, although nothing would ever recapture that first summer of discovery in the high street and the year of painting that followed. Hopper was a distant memory now and she'd changed, moved on.

Saturday. Market day. The smell was reassuring, earthy and musty with a sweet undertone of rot. Most of the stalls were packing up; Jolienta backtracked to Prestos and bought groceries and two papyrus plants.

This time, the fire door was not as difficult to handle and it swung to with ease. She took the short stairwell in a few bounds and passed the three friends on the landing. Bottles of wine were on the floor. Two more friends had joined them, tucked away to the side on the next flight of the stairwell, which ended in a brick wall.

I suppose they like it here. It's private. Better safe than sorry though. I'll double-lock the door.

The phone rang.

"Hello? Not many people have this number . . ."

"I'm calling to remind you about tomorrow."

"I didn't forget. Bye."

This phone. I'm thrilled. I love to hear the click when I put the receiver down.

Onions in garlic sizzled on the camping stove. In went mince and chilli powder, chopped tomato, red kidney beans and finally, a bouquet garni and a stock cube.

Candles, close to the papyrus, decorated the ceiling and walls with thin strips of shadow. The estate's nightlights illuminated the core of the estate and shone on the papyrus plants adding more shapes and tones of grey. Feathery shadows tickled the cupboards and the sink.

The chilli was delicious. The herbs, spices and garlic would help the remainder of the dish survive the night without a fridge.

Jolienta gazed at the room in disbelief; the space was full of possibilities, and the bathroom was something else, right off the Richter scale.

She switched on the bathroom light to make sure it was true. Gleaming white tiles and a bathtub unfettered by human bacteria assaulted the eye. The cabinet mirror revealed a young woman with long dark hair. It had grown long all of a sudden. Her body had become thin too, a result of jogging in and out of the estate and into the cul-de-sac, and more recently, cycling up and down the ramps and even around Trafalgar Square. There was a worry at the back of her mind, a feeling that she was losing her grip. Thick hair fell onto her shoulders. The end-of-course exhibition would flush out the slackers, she thought. For a start, she was the only one in the printmaking department with a toolbox. Not long to go and she would walk away from the printmaking studios. She wouldn't miss anyone. She'd stay in touch with Dave and Cathy. That'd do. Miguel was back in Mexico.

Jolienta tossed from side to side under bedding of tangerine cotton—the kind Jules would approve of, he being a lover of peach whites and apple whites and ecru settees. He was another guy. Just another guy. He had a darkroom too. He was the one who'd taken her photo for The South London Press during the early days of Tom and Kris.

She was unfolding under the duvet, spreading out. The bedding was pristine, still creased from the packet. She stretched fingers and toes to each corner of the mattress—firm stomach, firm breasts, firm legs, firm arms. Her skin felt soft. She ran fingers up and down her stomach. It felt nice. The room became sunshine, green trees and a meadow of wild flowers.

The next morning, she washed her face and hands, rinsed and wiped the sink, folded the bedding and put the bundle on a sideboard and clicked the futon base back into position. It looked wonderful. Someone banged against the front door. The peephole revealed the same five people on the landing. Some were standing. Some were sitting. They were smoking. Bottles were on their sides ready to topple down the steps.

Don't they ever go home? Don't they ever sleep? Why there's Jules picking his way through them. He's very early!

"Hi, Jules. You're early. Come in."

"That was quick," he said laughing and holding out an ice-cold bottle. "Were you watching from the peephole? How about this . . . Buck's Fizz to go with our brunch. I brought a carton of orange juice too."

"Good stuff. What do you reckon they're up to Jules?"

"Let me in properly first. Ah, the living room has large windows. Plenty of light. Very nice. How are you? Is everything all right?"

They kissed.

"You've lost weight."

They kissed again. He rammed his tongue inside her mouth.

"Where are you going to move to next, Jolienta?"

They sat down at the foldaway table.

"I've only just moved in, you silly bastard."

"Yes, I know, but you can't stay here. There's a gang living on your doorstep. They're doing cocaine. They're doing syringes. They're doing everything."

"Oh. The Peckham Action Group said there was a spare room going in Crystal Palace. If things go skew-whiff, I'll go there."

Jules nodded. "What's on the menu?"

"Chilli, side salad and your contribution."

"Smells good. You've been busy. The table looks nice." He glanced at the green tablecloth and turned in his seat to look at the camping stove. "Hmm, I never say no to a plate of chilli. Kidney beans remind me of south America. Give me that tea towel." He got up, threw the towel over the champagne bottle and uncorked it.

"Thanks. Here we are. Tuck in Jules."

"How's the cycling going? Have you been negotiating the streets of London as per usual looking for the next painting?"

"Yes. Didn't last long. Not by bike anyway. An ice-cream van knocked me over as I was coming out of the cul-de-sac that leads into Southampton Row. The back wheel's buckled. Mind you, when the compensation comes through, I'll be buying a ticket to China. I've wanted to go there for as long as I can remember."

"You were run over by an ice-cream van? Were you hurt?"

"I'll tell you about it in a moment."

"Why does everything happen to you, Jolienta?"

"China is going to happen to me, if you don't mind. Being run over was a slice of luck. How else would I get the money to go there? I have this theory that if I get there, I'll feel more whole, more real. I'll make enduring art. I'll make paintings that will stand the test of time. On that note, let me tell you about the ice-cream van that ran over me, and my encounter with Bill King, owner of The Crown. It went something like this—

"Bill, how nice to see you. I moved into the North Peckham Estate after all y'know."

"Hummmprh. It's you. You didn't show up for Sunday lunch."

"I know. It was quite a few Sundays ago, wasn't it? You probably won't believe me, Bill, but I had an accident on the way, and what with everything going on, I clean forgot to get back to you. I've only just remembered now, to be honest."

Jules, he didn't believe a word, so I said—

"I ended up in hospital, Bill. I can prove it. Show you an accident report. I was cycling along Southampton Way and an ice-cream van ran over me. I was taken to King's College Hospital and had stitches to my leg."

Jules, I was shuddering as I spoke. Surely he could see that? Anyway, I continued on hoping he'd hear me—

"The driver didn't see me and I had right of way. He knocked me, and the bike, to the ground. I scrambled up. He continued to advance. I banged my fist on the bonnet as hard as I could or he would well and truly have squashed me into the tarmac.

A man and a woman sat me on a low wall. The woman said I was bleeding. Then an ambulance arrived and took me to King's College Hospital. It seems part of the bike had pierced my leg. The flesh wound was at the top of my thigh, about one and half inches long and revealed the strange texture of exposed flesh. The doctor

126

produced a needle and thread, puckered up the edges
of my torn skin and began to sew. It wasn't a good job.
He apologized, said he was a trainee, took the thread
out and began again—pulling up tents of skin."

Guess what he said back?

"Oh, I must be off. I've campaigning to do. The motorway
is going to plough through my business."

and off he shunted with a pronounced limp, because he was
recovering from a stroke what with the strain of it all."

"I don't mean to laugh," Jules said. "It's the way you tell 'em.
Well, let me know if you need a lift to Crystal Palace or if you go to
China. Stay in touch, won't you? Thanks for the brunch."

"The bottle's empty."

Jules laughed. They kissed and hugged. She felt his hands
explore her body and pulled away.

That night, Jolienta heard the sound of partying on the
landing, checked the lock and checked the phone's dial tone. The
futon was full out, bedding in place. From under the duvet, she
studied the papyrus leaves jostling in the moonlight and
nightlights, and grew sticky and hot. The teenagers were being
rowdy. They were brushing against the door. Someone fell against
the door. How thoughtless. Their voices carried into the living
room. Their music penetrated. The pillow over her head didn't
make any difference. She got up and made a cup of tea.

The dial tone. It's OK. Let me put socks on. I'll tiptoe along.

The peephole showed the same women with the same men, on
the landing, swigging from bottles and smoking. The women had
fabulous hairstyles and wore elaborate jewellery. The outlines
bulged towards her eye and were distorted by the kaleidoscope
view.

It's four in the morning. If they knew I was behind this door . . .
this thin door . . . Hang on. Am I not a social recorder? I will draw

them. Get the drawing materials. And a weapon too.

Jolienta drew. Jolienta trembled. A hammer lay at her feet.

The next morning, the coast was clear. She sprinted down the stairs, out of the maze and into Southampton Row. The hammer tapped away at her hipbone as she ran.

Someone is going to get a surprise one of these days. Someone is going to push me too far.

She jogged across the pedestrian crossing.

It's saying something when you don't relax until you're standing at a bus stop to take you away from your own home. Did I feel this bad when I lived on the Sumner Road Estate? No, the neighbours were friendly and I never felt threatened. It was only Tom and Kris who were the problem.

It's the design of the North Peckham Estate. That's what it is. It allows a subculture to develop. That's why there are break-ins and muggings.

I wonder which is worse: being undermined by Tom and Kris, or having a gang live on your doorstep?

How I miss Number Thirty-five. They never came to see me at Carl's. I haven't bothered to ask them to come to the new flat. Why bother? Accept the way things are. God, they criticized me for not reimbursing Carl for that hellish carpet. I can feel my face tightening up.

It never fails to surprise me that people who've known me for years, two years, they must surely have a measure of me by now—yet they are so quick to believe Carl, a man too scared to face the world, a man who says I owe him money for a carpet. Well, while Number Thirty-five are busy assuming I've swindled him, I've been busy missing them so much it hurts. I even called on Veronica at the old flat, hoping all the while to bump into Rita and James—to see their lovely faces again. They're never in. Veronica had transformed herself into a Stepford Wife with a silk scarf knotted around her neck. She was proud to show me the revamping of my innocent wardrobe. She'd covered it in flowery vinyl, and turned my room into a pink blancmange.

Her relationship with Tom was blossoming, Veronica said, and she'd given up on the idea of becoming a professional singer. I should imagine that was a relief for Tom. Kris apparently left the flat in a cloud of smoke, address unknown.

The atmosphere was terrible, Veronica said, *warfare*, and the council had received a stream of complaints on BBC letterheaded stationery. Mind you, it was a good idea I called that day. I found myself gazing around that living room wondering whether I missed it or not, and wondering if the settee made Veronica itch too. Oppressive was the word that popped into my head.

I ended up telling her that it was a relief not to have to mind my P's and Q's, and to be able to drink instant coffee without criticism, and I told her it was really weird not having the men put me down. She was a bit shocked to hear that. I must admit I was quite amused to see the shock on her face.

I wonder does she know she's lost her sparkle?

Veronica, she said she wished I'd never left the flat. That was nice to hear, although it would have been nicer to hear that from Number Thirty-five.

*   *   *

Jolienta ran up the steps from the cul-de-sac and into the estate, hopscotched along the slippery walkways and pulled the fire door open. A weave of knees and legs had to be stepped over. Luckily, her key was ready for the latch. A teenager, barely a man, was in the way.

He raised his hand. He was an astronaut on the moon. He cupped his hand over her breast and squeezed the marshmallow.

"Get off!"

His hand floated to his side.

The door to the neighbouring flat clicked open.

"Let the lady go."

The group melted away.

"You're brave," a man said. He shook his head. "I can't take it. I'm leaving as soon as I can. Going back to my parents in Chingford. I was in a phone box yesterday down in the cul-de-sac, and the same gang attacked me. I'm not jokin' you. They threw a brick at me. My name's Steve by the way. Are you OK, lady?"

"Steve, you're the one who's brave. How can I thank you? You saved me. I'm shaking like a leaf. Look. Did the brick hurt you?"

"Bruised. You can't tell. The black skin."

Jolienta held her hand out.

"Come on, lady. Now, now," he said holding her hand. "Don't cry. Maybe you should go back home too?"

"I would if I could. London is the only place to be if you want to be an artist in the UK, and as for my family up north, well, I couldn't go back." It would be far worse going back. Back to a threadbare bedroom, foot-washing in the kitchen sink, the innate lack of communication, my mother forcing me to accept the man in the string vest, the one she moved in, the one who smokes, farts, drinks stewed tea, and doesn't know the meaning of 'father'. *Have you got a lock on your bedroom door?* she said to me. *He's angry. I'm not sure what he'll do.* That isn't exactly a springboard, is it? Besides, I'd go insane there and all my efforts over the last two years would go right down the drain.

"I'm from Nigeria, Jolbienti. We moved to the UK five years ago. I'm telling you, I'm going back to my parents. Next Thursday. Who cares about the rent I paid in advance."

"Are you studying, Steve?"

"Yes. Law at King's College. And you?"

"I'm at the Slade School of Art, part of the University of London. Hey, Steve, if you need to use my phone, or anything else, please, please, just ask. But say your name loud and clear. Say, 'Jolienta, it's Steve' through the letterbox before you ring or knock, or I'll be terrified. Are you definite about leaving then?"

"Definitely. I'm definitely leaving. My parents are coming to pick me up."

"Well, I'll always remember you and your bravery. If I don't see you, good luck with everything."

That night Steve was embellished in her mind.

The next day, she drew a picture of him standing on the landing in a blue shirt and gave it to him.

Thursday arrived. Alone again. Jules packed the car. The lid to the boot wouldn't close. It took two journeys. Papyri swayed in the breeze.

The new room in Crystal Palace was the smallest one yet. It was clean and square in shape, and smaller than Tom's room at Thirty-three Sumner Road Estate. Most mornings, a biker revved up his motorbike under the window, which was like being wired up for electric shock treatment. The landlady's baby cried in the adjacent bedroom, and the husband was too attentive to the point of being a nuisance. Much to her amusement, the landlady found it impossible to manoeuver her into babysitting. One morning, a cheque arrived from a solicitor settling the ice-cream van incident. The cheque was for three thousand pounds.

"Jolienta, it's very nice having you live here," Janice, the landlady, said during an uninvited visit to her room. "We all like you. Especially the baby, except . . . Excuse me if I'm blunt. I don't know what to make of you. You don't eat with us and you don't want to come out of your room. Do you mind me saying this?"

"I'm preparing to travel across China, Janice. I have a lot to do. Look. The maps and guidebooks on the table. Here. This cassette tape. *Teach yourself Mandarin Chinese*. I play it over and over again in an attempt to get the accent right. I'm trying to get my head inside China so I can make the most of it when I get there. I can afford to go now. My personal injury cheque arrived. I'm booking the ticket next week with a tour operator in Islington."

"Oh. I see what you mean about maps and guidebooks. Well, why don't you join us for dinner tonight? We'd love to hear all about your plans."

"Sorry, every minute counts. I have too much to do. Hope you don't mind. I need to learn the language. I need to swot up on the history. I can't afford the time to eat lunch with your husband. He asked me to show him how to switch the washing machine on the other day, but I've never used one so I wasn't of much use."

"Honestly," Jane said laughing, "you're as bad as each other."

"Jane, I can't concentrate if he knocks on my door. He knocks quite often while you're at work."

*   *   *

In the fourteen hundreds the Chinese explored the seas, an interesting fact obscured by later Portuguese and Spanish seafarers. By the fifteen hundreds, smugglers and pirates were rampant. The sixteen hundreds brought strife, civil war and more invaders. The seventeen hundreds? The eighteen hundreds were about exports of tea, silk, cotton, lacquer and porcelain, at which stage Western powers took advantage of China's out-of-date governance. Addiction was rampant in China. The Opium Wars ensued. Great Britain waged a war against China in order to maintain its trade in opium. The British won and continued to ply drugs. Hong Kong and Kowloon became British territories.

World War 1. Thousands of Chinese signed up. China declared war on Germany while in the throes of a civil war with the Kuomintang and the Communists. During the first Sino-Japanese war, the Japanese killed an estimated three hundred thousand Chinese people in the Rape of Nanking. A second Sino-Japanese war followed with an estimated twenty million Chinese dead and fifteen million wounded. In nineteen-forty, the Japanese Imperial Army bombed China. Hitler attacked the Soviet Union, and before you knew it, World War II was underway. There was the battle of

Pearl Harbour. An atomic bomb was dropped on Hiroshima and Nagasaki. The People's Liberation Army and Mao Zedong ruled and seventy million more deaths in 'peacetime' followed. According to the list she was scribbling down, the numbers added up to one hundred and thirty million dead Chinese people.

Opium wars: 18 to 20 thousand Chinese dead

World War I: 140 thousand Chinese helpers recruited, don't know how many dead

Civil war from 1928 to 1936: 2 million Chinese military dead

Sino-Japanese War I: 35 thousand Chinese dead and wounded

Rape of Nanking: 300 thousand Chinese dead

Sino-Japanese War II: 20 million Chinese dead and 15 million wounded

Japanese Comfort Stations: 20 to 40 thousand women sex slaves, three quarters died, 36% were Chinese

World War II: 35 million Chinese dead

Civil War from 1945—1949: 1 to 3 million Chinese dead

'Peacetime under Mao Zedong': 70 million Chinese dead

Mao was a charismatic figure, who led epic marches. He captured the world's imagination. Chinese intellectuals were sent to work in the fields. No couple could have more than one child or suffer the consequences. Sometimes, girls were disposed of at birth. Boys were of value and were not left to die.

Mao instructed his people to reduce the population of sparrows. That is, he ordered everyone to keep making a noise until sparrows fell to the ground dead. Crop-eating pests took over and a great famine followed. He and his followers fought and fought. The bodies piled up.

Jolienta rolled out a map of China. It showed the mountain ranges and river valleys. She measured the distance between Hong Kong, Amoy and Macau. She followed the length of the Yangste River with its splayed out tributaries running into the South China Sea.

Imagine travelling all the way to China and being too shy to speak, or being treated with scorn, because you, foreign devil, couldn't say a word like 'Hello' properly? Research revealed that Mandarin had four tones to one word. A person might easily say "horse", or "but", or "hemp", or "mother", depending on the way they pronounced the word "ma".

Cantonese had even more tones to one word. The only time she had heard that language spoken was during a rare outing to Chinatown, when a woman came to visit the family and treated them to a restaurant meal. Later, in death, the same woman had bequeathed the camphorwood trunk of treasures. She had died alone in her American apartment.

There were many Chinese authors to take on board, learn from, and authors of mixed blood too. There were younger generations of writers as well, such as Maxine Hong Kingston and Amy Tan. They all wanted to make sense of their past.

Portuguese devil

TOO LATE. THE DOORS CLAMPED SHUT. The train trundled down the tunnel without her. 'Newbury Park via Hainault' dissolved into pixels and faded into nothingness. The digital timer on the electronic board said fourteen point thirty and forty-nine seconds.

"Jol!" a voice shouted. The sound resonated.

Who's that? Her eyes searched the crowd.

The voice repeated its cry. "Jol!"

This time, it was louder and it was a man's voice. The crowd hid him from view.

A man in a desert-camouflage hat, brim flopping over eyes and wearing a long camel coat, stepped forward. He stood legs apart and stared at her. She saw a square chin with a cigar sticking out of it, and for a second, her heart missed a beat.

"Jol!" the man repeated with a sense of urgency, "it's *me*. Kris. How are you?"

What? Kris? Is that really him? After all these years?

The platform emptied. They circled each other.

"How's Chopin then?" Jolienta said, a faint smirk on her lips.

"You mean Tom? Terrible. Everything fell apart after you left. I had to put a lock on my bedroom door to stop them from emptying the room. Can you imagine? They were a bloody nightmare. They tried to have me *evicted*."

Jolienta imagined Kris's typewriter flying through the air and crashing against Tom's door. The dynamics would have been intense, hilarious, although it was hard not to feel some sympathy for Kris against the precise Tom and the hapless Veronica.

"Their cosy candlelit dinners," Kris ranted, "shish kebabs, baked pumpkin, steamed turbot! Wankers!"

His head reared above her. She gazed up his nostrils and for a moment she was back in Pelham Road outside Thos. P. Headland with its parking meters, waiting to be slapped across the face. She hadn't missed him. Not once. That was her revenge. She'd missed Tom though, and the absurd sense of establishment he brought with him—leafleting Peckham on behalf of The Labour Party, supper-ing on honey-glazed salmon and quaffing Bollinger champagne. "Kris, I bumped into Tom in the Queen's Road years ago. His parents had died and left him and his sister, Margo, three hundred and fifty thousand each."

"That's the privileged for you, Jol," he said with a clenched jaw.

"Don't forget, Kris, he was adopted at birth. Good luck to him, I say. Mind you, I did laugh after we spoke in the post office that day, because what he said was, *Decent amount they left us. I'm really a home-counties boy at heart, Jolienta. I'm going to buy a converted barn. Veronica and I—we're married now. Have a son.* You see, after all that leafleting on behalf of the Labour Party, he just couldn't wait to get out of Peckham. Where exactly are the 'Home Counties' anyway?"

"Bloody hypocrite," Kris said. "Veronica," he gasped, "she's nothing more than a whore. I told Tom, *She's a whore.* And now they have a child! God—Tom has fathered a whore's child. He made a big mistake—that Tom—messing with me. You'll see."

He's ranting. Nothing new there then.

"In the end, I bought a flat in Battersea, Jol."

He scoured her face, gulped, and crushed the cigar between his lips. "What about you, Jol? How many years has it been?"

"Dunno. Eight? Ten? More? Less? I'm living in an Acme House

now, in Leyton. Still haven't gotten over the day the letter arrived. Acme Houses are like gold dust, you know."

"Acme?"

"They're an arts organization. They provide short-life housing for professional artists at miniscule rents. I rent the entire house for ten pounds a week and get to use it for the purpose of making art, that is, until Delmont Road, gets pulled down for the M11 link."

"Interesting. I didn't know such schemes existed. So how is the art coming along?" Kris said with a smile.

"I finished at the Slade . . . of course. My uncle told everyone at the end-private view that it was "inappropriate" to ask about prices. Consequently, I didn't sell a thing. Figure that one out. I lecture in art colleges up and down the country. I've just had a piece of work purchased by The Victoria & Albert Museum—I set myself a target to be collected before I reached my thirtieth birthday. I was only a couple of years out."

"Congratulations. What was the painting of? Was it of Peckham?"

"No. I couldn't maintain the connection. I moved away from Hopper; my work's more of a spiritual nature now. The V&A bought a painting called The Tree of Life."

"Brian didn't appreciate your Hubble Factory. I did. I tried to buy it back from him, but he refused. He's a different man now. He and his wife both have affairs. I don't know. What's the point?"

Kris stopped to gaze at the black and white checkered floor. Trains came and went. Crowds meandered in and out.

"I'm off to Los Angeles, Kris, to meet my Great Aunty Cheeki. At long last, eh?" Jolienta glanced at him and waited for a sarcastic response.

"Don't forget to take your own *ginormous sombrero!*" Kris replied.

He'd remembered everything. But still.

"You never did cross over the high street to see my Peckham

exhibition, did you, Kris?"

He blew smoke over his shoulder.

The silence was unbearable.

"By the way, the six-lane motorway set to plough through Peckham High Street was shelved due to a lack of funds. After all that, eh? Can you believe it? And Bill King went and died of a heart attack. Sad."

"Jol!" His voice boomed around the curved walls. "Alison, my ex . . . Do you remember?"

"Yes."

How could I forget? I found them both at it on the settee. It wasn't the first time I'd walked in on a couple and to be fair, I've been caught out myself, kitted out in suspenders in front of the gas fire.

She tried to picture Alison. She had met her the one time. Alison had been a red-faced woman rearranging her skirt. Alison hadn't been what she expected at all. The woman had a big nose and a great big arse.

Well, I suppose she was striking. Oh, OK, she was beautiful, and it was a pretty pleated skirt she wore that day. She reminded me of Helen Sukova, the tennis player. Then the incessant phone calls began again. So Alison hung on in and got her man, eh?

"We're getting married this summer, Jolienta. Wanna come to the wedding? What about you? Married?"

He didn't wait for an answer. An act of kindness perhaps.

"Oh, I forgot to tell you, when I get back from L.A., I'm going to China. It's taken me a long time to get organized."

Kris looked impressed.

"I must go now, Jol. I'm on my way to see my analyst. I go once a week. Been doing it for years." He fiddled with his hat. "I'll be in touch . . . Alison and I would like our portrait done. I just thought of that one."

He walked towards the exit and vanished.

The tube doors opened. She got on.

What on earth is going on? After all these years?

Go to his wedding?

I should have stayed in Peckham. *They* should have gone. I should have *stayed*.

The tube drew into Leyton.

*　　*　　*

Turning the corner into Delmont Road, it was reassuring to see a woman in a beret wheeling her invalid boyfriend over their doorstep. A husband and wife with three bonny children waved. The train moved along the overland track.

She reached the front door, grateful for the Acme House.

The front room, of ripped floor vinyl and lumpy woodchip wallpaper, was the main studio and had a view of trees and wire fencing. The kitchen housed a converted clothes-mangle equipped to edition prints and looked out onto the back garden. Upstairs, hand-stencilled curtains decorated the walls when the sun rose. Cigarette burns from the previous occupant lay under well-placed rugs and second-hand furniture.

Mother's due. I never thought I'd see the day. Her in London visiting me. It's Uncle Fufu; his surprise has achieved the impossible. Neither she nor I can resist an offer of a free ticket to L.A. to visit the legendary Great Aunty Cheeki. I can't wait. Then I'll be travelling across China. What a year. Who knows how things will pan out?

Cheeki is from an older generation. She might be willing to talk about the past. Explain why Mother ended up in England. Explain to me why everyone decided to settle in different parts of the world. There might even be relatives living in China. I can visit them.

Jolienta emptied groceries onto a side counter, washed red and green peppers and dried them with a tea towel.

*   *   *

"Poooooop, poooooop" and "poooooop!" Uncle Fufu's flatulence echoed around the grotto toilet, blew into the bathroom and flapped around their ears and nostrils. She and her mother looked at each other. The table took the full force of their amusement and rattled on the floor like a roadside drill.

Oh, ha, ha, thanks to you, Uncle, ha, ha, I'm going to America to meet Cheeki, and shortly, ha, ha, I will sample your cooking—Diabo—a traditional Portuguese dish, which will no doubt send us off on a flight of methane gas.

"Oh, Fufu. What a big fart!" Dora said. "Whuhaha whuhaha."

"Hold your nose, Sis."

"Whuhaha. Fufu, you are naughty. Don't forget to wash your shitty hands. Whuhaha."

Opposite them, the red and green peppers stood, a sparkling henge of shape and colour.

"Stupid Jolly. Look Fufu. Look at what Jolly's done! She's arranged peppers over there. Whuhaha, whuhaha. How stupid!"

Her mother sat back clutching her midriff. False eyelashes closed tightly over smooth brown skin. Mother had slept in those eyelashes for the last thirty-two years; she had never seen her mother without them.

"Stupid Jolly," Dora said, foraging in her handbag. "Why don't you work in a bank instead of all this art nonsense?"

She sent a pleading look to her uncle. Fufu, he had a ferocious face at the best of times—slitty eyes, the teeth of a piranha, the breath of a distillery, but really he was her ally.

Fufu smiled, unpacked his shopping bag and said in that drawl of his, "Well Jol. Reach for the stars. That's what I say."

He gazed around the kitchen. "Jol, this is your new home? 'Acme'? What are they?"

He began to dice onion, garlic and ginger and cut up pounds of beef stew, roast pork, roast duck and chicken.

"They're an arts organization. They rent me the house for ten pounds a week. It's classed as short-life housing. Eventually, it will get knocked down to make way for the M11 link."

"I see."

Fufu rinsed Basmati rice, peeled potatoes and carrots, lined up salt, sugar, mustard, white vinegar, Worcestershire Sauce, sweet pickle and green chillies. Into the pot went tomatoes, the onion and garlic, spices, herbs, red wine, the meats, a jar of mustard and a bottle of sherry.

"Diabo, Uncle? Smells like the devil too."

Fufu clutched a glass of Merlot and sat down to refortify his strength. Dora found a tube of glue and a hand-mirror and began to repair the growing gap between eyelid and plastic eyelash. Talking Heads thudded from a cassette player.

"Do I smell? I smell home cooking.
It's only the river, it's only the river."

"Stupid Jolly. Stupid music. Fufu, look," Dora said, "don't you think Jolly has the nose of a collie dog? Whuhaha, Whuhaha. Look. And poor Enaida," Dora said, changing the subject, "after all Enaida did for Naldo. He let her die alone in an old people's home. How could he do such a thing? When you think she carried him with a gunshot wound to safety and saved his life."

"Did either of you do anything for Enaida yourselves?" Not that Jolienta knew who Enaida was; she had given up asking such questions long ago.

"Did you know Naldo received an award for bravery?" Dora muttered, contradicting herself.

"What was it for?"

Dora blinked the question away. "Don't know. Can't remember."

Fufu brought the saucepan over and ladled Diabo onto three plates. The pungent mound spread over the plates.

Her mother ate and ate and her stomach grew bigger and bigger. Mother dug deeper into the pan, sweat dripping off her brow. They finished with chocolate pudding and chocolate sauce. Daylight was fading. Fufu said it was time to go and grandly wished them a safe journey to America.

"Sis, give Cheeki my regards."

"Goodbye, Uncle Fufu. Thank you."

"Poop, poop, Fufu. Poop, poop!"

When Fufu had turned the corner at the top of the road, they decided to check their tickets, passports and luggage. Dora washed off her make-up, careful to leave the lashes in place, pushed rollers into short black hair and smothered her face with moisturizer. She was too excited to sleep she said. Jolienta told her to keep her sticky face away. Dora said her daughter's breath smelt like the sewers. Jolienta opened her mouth and breathed heavily on her mother.

*   *   *

Five-thirty a.m.

Dora opened up her make-up bag and began the process.

Eggs on toast. Fresh coffee.

The driver honked. There was a panic. They went out and put the luggage in the boot. Jolienta instructed the driver to go to Holborn for the first of the Piccadilly trains. The driver drove into Stratford Broadway and asked, "Which way now?" She took command, verbally slapping the imposter with directions.

Dora snorted, "Clever Jolly. Clever Jolly. Whuhaha!"

*   *   *

The airhostesses waved as the passengers disembarked. Dora groaned, "I'm dizzy Jolly", grabbed a plastic bag and threw up. Jolienta held onto the luggage, dry throat from too much coffee, the passport check was over, they were jetlagged. Seconds passed and Dora erupted, "Aaahhhh, Aunty Cheeki! Aunty Cheeki!"

Jolienta scoured the airport lounge. The Great Aunty Cheeki! I'm going to meet the Great Aunty Cheeki at last. At long last.

Dora leant in and pecked a small fat oriental lady on the face.

Cheeki dos Remédios was a bulldog of a woman, a pensioner of eighty-nine years of age, breasts held in place by the waistband of her summer dress and white hair scraped back into a tight bun. The old lady had a sweet face, looked Chinese, looked very old.

The old lady accepted Dora's greeting with relish and grabbed an arm. "Dorotéia, is this Jolly? Myyyy, she look big and hefty. Why didn't you give her a brace for her teeth?"

Dora coughed into her hand. Cheeki chuckled, shook her fist and led her guests into the California sun and onto the soft leather seats of a yellow Cadillac.

The taxi glided along the San Diego Freeway, passed liquor stores, passed fast-food parlours, dour supermarkets, lines of telegraph poles and row upon row of palm tree. Jolienta blinked at the sky and traffic. Every detail needed to be committed to memory.

The driver slowed down.

"Here we are Jolly. In Gardena. This is my house."

Everything dazzled—the heat, the sky, the houses, the gardens, the Pacific breeze. The pavement was burning through her sandals.

Dora and Cheeki were arguing about who was going to pay the driver, but she had better things to do. Number Three Hundred and Seventy-two Chanera Avenue was a sort of chalet made out of wooden slats and faded to a sage green—the type of home she'd always wanted to live in and in the right kind of climate too. Chinese wind chimes sprinkled notes across the porch. A rocking chair leant against the wall.

Jolienta hurried to the taxi and dragged the luggage out, eager to see inside.

"Henri, my beauty!" Cheeki cried, one foot in the lobby.

Henri fluttered overhead and landed on the old lady's head. Cheeki cooed, tried to stroke it. It clambered across her scalp.

"Oh, Cheeki, you always loved budgies," Dora cried.

The rooms inside were typical of a great aunt. If anything can be called typical. White lace curtains, plenty of ornaments, photographs in sepia, black and white and then full colour, all shrouded in the aromatic semi-darkness of garbage fumes, cookies and Chinese spices. Pink crochet dollies dressed up the toilet rolls. Their room was nice. The air conditioning came on.

*   *   *

I waited to see what would happen next.

Cheeki covered a saucepan over and brushed up against Mother. "Myyy, you look much prettier than you used to do Doroteia. Myyyyy! You've improved with age! Hee, hee, hee. How d'ya do it?"

Mother blushed in yellow summer dress with frilly epaulets, straightened up, a good foot taller and puffed her chest out.

Cheeki pretended to cower and brought her fists up—one two—ready to box. "Tell me Doroteia, how come you went to live with Naldo back in Hong Kong days? You knew which side your bread was buttered, didn't you?" Cheeki searched Mother's face; her eyes were pools of watery blue.

"Oh Aunty, I don't know what you're talking about," Mother replied, and in such a way, I knew something was going on.

"Oh, Cheeki, oranges and lemons," Mother called out from the garden. "You're so lucky. Olive trees too."

What *is* she playing at? One minute here, one minute out there? She's lying too. I can tell.

"Chee-ki . . ." Mother was in the kitchen again, hovering, "Fufu and I were wondering . . . er . . . what happened in Kowloon when we lived in Alvege? What I mean is," Mother hesitated, tried to hide her discomfort, "wasn't there an inheritance for everyone and we missed out on our share, because we were orphaned at a young age? Everyone forgot about us."

"Dorotéia, inheritance?" Cheeki barked. "All the sisters received diamond earrings and diamond necklace. All boys drink and gamble! Your father, Luiz, did what all the men did. He gambled his share away!

"Jolly, we sisters were suffragettes, but the men . . . Sorry Dora." Cheeki dropped to a kinder tone. "When the Japanese invaded, the Chinese looted Alvege. They stole everything they could to survive the War. Then all hell break out.

"Bah," Cheeki punched the air. "We have left all of that behind. I told you Dorotéia. We all warned you, if you went to UK with *that man*, and we knew nothing about him, we wouldn't be able to help you if anything went wrong. But, you wouldn't listen!" Her body shook. Her jowls shook.

So Mother had hopes of an inheritance? Who is 'that man' Cheeki is referring to? My father? What is Alvege? Why is Cheeki so angry? Is it because Mother ended up in the UK, alone and impoverished?

Time for dinner.

"Dorotéia—pig's trotter in star anise and garlic. Your favorite."

Cheeki and Mother ate in silence. I picked at the food—a large orange potato surrounded by bloated flesh. The gravy was oily, and it didn't smell right.

*   *   *

"So Jolly, what do you want to talk about today?" Cheeki was wagging her stick in front of her.

"Tell me about our family during Hong Kong days?"

"Oh?" Cheeki swung about; her face trembled with the pull of gravity. "Jolly, our name—Dos Remédios—comes from a devotion to Our Lady of Remedies in Portugal, our homeland, but we always regarded Macau as the place of our roots. Didn't you know that Jolly?"

"No. I didn't. Say it again, Aunty. I'll write it down."

"Dora," the old lady exclaimed spinning on the balls of her feet, "why didn't you talk to your daughter about the past?"

Mother looked as though she was far away. "I work all day and when I get home I'm tired."

Well, that's true. She's spent years writing out parking tickets, dodging irate motorists, and over time her body has tilted forward due to the sheer exertion involved. It was all to feed us kids. Her feet must have stung with each step, each pound onto pavement. It was the same thing every evening. She'd get in, be worn out, prepare dinner while still in uniform, fall asleep in front of the TV; if you moved, dropped a book, changed the TV channels, or sneezed, she'd wake up and slap you right across the face.

My offers to cook were in vain. Either she thought I was too stupid, or she wanted to keep me the impotent child . . . this is the most likely . . . or it was because the tangle of utensils and rubbish piled in the middle of that rotting kitchen, was ready to come crashing down?

"Jolly we lived in a house called 'Alvege' in Kowloon," Cheeki said, picking up from where she'd left off. "Our parents—your great grandparents—Eugenio and Cecilia dos Remédios, took the first letter of each daughter's Christian name to make up the house name 'Alvege'. Alda, Lina, Valda, Ermima—that's me! Griselda, and Enaida—Enaida was the eldest."

Cheeki used her fingers to spell out the word. "A - L - V - E - G - E. See? Jolly . . . in Portuguese, Alvege means evergreen. We were six sisters and five brothers you know."

"D'you have any photographs?"

"Look Jolly. Here. Everyone at Alvege. Names on back."

A lump in the middle of my throat started up. No one had ever responded to any of my enquiries before. The photo showed a group of children, smartly dressed, eleven in all, huddled together in order of height or age, standing on a set of steps. On either side were stone pillars and potted palms—an impressive façade for any home. At the back were the proud parents—a dark brown mother with a soft face, hair swept back, a mix of Portuguese and Indian blood perhaps. The father had a stern expression, looked more Chinese, had a lighter skin-tone. Someone had written names on the back to correspond with each figure. Cheeki was a cute doll-type with hair billowing over a white lace collar, and she was standing in front of a young man. I turned the photo around. The young man had been labelled 'Luiz'. My grandfather.

He looks about nineteen here. He doesn't look like a drunk or gambler. I have his eyes. The family looks successful, complete, not like the mess we are—strangers, who have lived in the same house.

"Jolly, any question?" Cheeki said.

It has always puzzled me that Mother speaks English, Cantonese and Portuguese, and why did everyone leave for the USA? Why did Cheeki choose Los Angeles? Why did some go to Canada? Why did Mother decide to go to the UK with a man she hardly knew? The words came out. "Cheeki, what happened to Luiz, my grandfather?"

"He died of TB a young man Jolly."

*   *   *

Cheeki rotated a teacup in her hands, round and round, tilted it towards the window, peered inside, and read the sprawl of tealeaves. Mother was asleep, head on the table, a globule of saliva about to break.

"Cheeki, tell me about your childhood before Mother wakes up."

The old lady rinsed a dishcloth, wrung it out, wiped the fridge—on the top, at the front—opened it, organized cartons and popped open a jar of pickles.

"Jolly, I used to cycle around our ballroom when I was a little girl."

"What? There was a ballroom in Alvege?"

"When I was older, I looked after all the nieces and nephews. We'd play horsey and gunnysack race on the lawns. Daddy watched over us. He used to wear a dicky bow, you know."

Cheeki concentrated on the onion in her mouth.

"What about the adults, Cheeki? What did they get up to?"

"The ladies played mahjong. Luiz would take the boys hunting in the New Territory. Fufu and the others would run into the woods throwing up firecrackers, and POW, your grandfather would shoot down white doves with an English twenty-gauge shotgun. At school Jolly, the boys dipped grasshoppers into inkwells and flicked them at each other's shirts."

Cheeki sent an imaginary insect across the kitchen.

"Your mother was quite a gal you know."

"Aunty, was . . . the family cruel?"

"What d'ya mean Jolly?"

"Did my mother and uncles experience violence as children?"

"Jolly, no children was ever treated badly; Alvege was happy place."

"But Cheeki, Mother put holes in my sister's leg with a Stiletto shoe. I remember the blood pouring out. I was hiding under the table. If you were a minute late, y'know, she'd thrash you. One night she came at me with a leather belt. I was fed up with being terrorized—I was sixteen—sweet and innocent. I kicked her down the stairs. She never hit me again after that."

"Jolly I am shocked."

"And Uncle Fufu is always as pissed as a newt.

"And Uncle Rico tried to show me pornographic magazines in his mouldy bedsit."

Cheeki gasped. "Jolly all I can say is, they were orphaned at a young age and got divided among the family."

Cheeki stopped to think, but it was a long time ago and beyond reach. "I can't remember who got who. Then the Japanese invaded Jolly, and everything changed."

Henri scrambled up a curtain. Cheeki went to clean his tray. Mother was waking up. Thanks to Cheeki's presence, Mother had begun to glow in recent days.

*   *   *

Cheeki slopped haam yook chung onto a plate. "Eat up Dorotéia."

Mother took the plate. "Stupid Jolly doesn't know what's good for her."

"Come on Jolly, you try too." Cheeki heaped bamboo leaf parcels onto a third plate.

They began to eat with gusto. I played with the food and tried to think of a way out.

"Tell me a story, Cheeki."

"OK Jolly, I can.

"Pirate story?"

"Ha, ha."

"Pirate captain Cheng Yi married beautiful prostitute called Ching Shih in year eighteen oh one. Now, Cheng didn't think she was the girl of his dreams, but he thought it was good investment and wife-to-be agreed to marry on one condition—she get share of power and wealth. So for six years, Cheng and Cheng I Sao grow pirate business in South China Sea. When he die all of sudden, instead of grieving widow, Cheng I Sao took over business."

Cheeki's eyes twinkled. "You know Jolly, I still hungry. Piece of Battenberg Cake?"

"No. No. Carry on!"

"Whuhaha, whuhaha! Cheeki!"

Listen to Mother laugh.

"Cheng I Sao's new husband became captain while Wife attend to business, military strategy and ruffian fleet. She brought more and more outlaws under banner of Red Flag Fleet. Wife became responsible for eight thousand pirates in region—exceeding navy! Then Wife expand into blackmail and extortion. Helped by vast, spy network, she controlled local farmers . . . her law became revolutionary, if order disobeyed . . . scoundrel beheaded!"

Cheeki karate-chopped the air to indicate no mercy. "Most famous law was about female prisoner. Ugly women taken back to shore, free of charge."

"Whuhaha, whuhaha, Cheeki!"

"Wife fought off attack from Chinese, Portuguese and British bounty hunter. Then Government offered amnesty. Wife jump at chance. This mean no pirate punished and even less executed. Most kept booty and get military jobs."

"What happened to Cheng I Sao?"

"She retired with loot and second husband, opened up gambling den in Macau. Died a sixty-nine year old grandmother."

"Whuhaha, whuhaha!" Mother dabbed her eyes with a tissue.

I grinned. I must get the old lady to tell me more, more about everything—about Hong Kong and Macau and about why she chose Los Angeles out of all the places in the whole wide world.

Ancestral roots

"So Jolly, what do you want to talk about today?"

"Tell me about the relatives we're about to meet."

'They're from your mother's side. Your grandmother."

"The De Silvas?"

"Yes Jolly."

"What are they like?"

"You will meet them soon enough."

"What is Jolly talking about?" Mother said.

"The De Silvas.

"Jolly, your grandmother die of a brain tumour. We didn't know about those things in the old days. The family thought she was mad. She would groan and cry out. The elders locked her away in a room at the top, where she could groan and cry to her heart's content. Only the amah went in. Sometimes, every blue moon, they let your mother in too. Your mom would sit on the floor and rest her head in her mom's lap. Come on, time to go, you two. Hurry up."

According to Cheeki, Chinatown was the Hollywood equivalent of Shanghai and only one bus ride away.

The air-conditioned bus stopped at Downtown. We followed Cheeki through a gate of bronze dragons and entered a vast plaza—a ghostly, sanitized square of searing heat and brash sunshine. No clutter of smells or eastern paraphernalia here then.

151

Cheeki stopped outside a small red pavilion. An elderly couple and a man were inside relaxing in the shade. The younger man shook hands and said Hi. The couple didn't smile or offer any kind of greeting to me, but their presence and impeccable grooming more than compensated. The woman's hair was a pure white, a stark contrast against leathery skin and black dress. A diamond broach sparkled on the lapel of her jacket. The husband, thin in pinstriped suit and stiff white shirt, had little control over his body. He reminded me of an elegant puppet I used to own, although how I came to be in possession of such a gift is a mystery.

The woman made a regal gesture—all dialogue must cease. A flicker of amusement appeared on Cheeki's face.

"Jolly," Mother whispered as we all walked towards a restaurant, "it's sad; Agousta says you remind her of Guiomar, my mother. Aaaaaaaah."

I ignored her. The fact is she had never mentioned any grandmother or grandfather to me. Ever.

"The younger man is Tio," Cheeki interjected, grinding a cigarette under foot, "Toto's grandnephew."

"Ohhh! Toto?" Dora echoed. "Toto? He taught me shorthand in Beco da Boa Vista. I became a stenographer in a Hong Kong courthouse thanks to him. Is he still alive?"

"Jolly, Agousta doesn't want to talk to you about the past," Cheeki said gently. "She's old. Don't worry, Tio might."

The elderly couple, Agousta and Freddie, took charge of ordering lunch in Cantonese. The waiters jumped into action and laid the table with hot towels in plastic envelopes.

"Hey Dora," Tio said, "been to the supermarket lately to buy some yau cha kwai, paak tonk ko or hah kao, hey?"

"Oh Tee-o, I miss these things. I miss siu mai and smelly chau towfoo. Whuhaha, whuhaha."

"It's great to meet you, Tio."

"Jolly? How's London? It's been years since I visited the UK."

"It's the only place to be if you want to be an artist, Tio."

"Artist? Hey, Cheeki says you're interested in your heung ha."

"My roots? Yes. Tell me, Tio, why did your parents move to California out of all of the places in the whole wide world? I've always wanted to know."

"Didn't they call it the Gold Mountain? I think reports came back from brave Filomacs and after the War . . . well. Why, Uncle says moving to the States was the best thing he ever did. The Brits, he says, they ruled the roost and we Macanese were subservient. I can hear him now."

"Oh no Jolly, the British were wonderful," said Cheeki. "We followed a lot of their ways. Really we are anglophiles Jolly."

"Uncle would say . . ." Tio was wearing a generous smile, "we Macanese were sandwiched between the privileged Caucasians and the oppressed Chinese majority. Hey, y'know what really got his goat? In Hong Kong days, my uncle wanted to open up an ordinary bank account and they treated him like a *cheena pobre*. But when he arrived in 'Cisco in fifty-six . . . would you believe . . . he got a job as a bank clerk and was signing checks for millions of dollars on his first day."

"I love to hear these stories. I love to hear them, Tio."

The waiters cleared away dim sum trays and began to lay out barbecued meat, ginger chicken with cashew nuts, crispy fried shrimp balls in stainless steel trays, black mushroom with shellfish and abalone dried scallop.

I listened to the chopsticks clicking, the mouths sucking and the occasional—"Weather hod"—"Whad's the weather like in Liverpool, Dorotéia?"—"Isn't it terrible, Cora married a Chinese." and, "Whuhaha, whuhaha!"

"Well Jolly, what would you like us to talk about now?" Cheeki said, wiping her mouth. "Jolly wants to know about the past everyone."

"Alvege, please. Thank you for asking, Aunty."

"Oh, Jolly. Alvege? Hear that everybody?

"OK. It was a large house on a hill and the road was called Peace Avenue. The area was called Ho Mun Tin and was occupied mainly by us Portuguese families. Sometimes one rickshaw on road. That is what it was like. There was a staircase carved into a fifty-foot rock at the back and a tall guava tree was in the garden. A giant wooden horse in garden too. Don't know where it came from. The Kowloon-Canton Railway ran parallel to us, which was handy."

"How did Naldo get shot?"

"You know about that one Jolly?" Cheeki said somewhat impressed. "One day, Naldo hear people shouting and run down armed with baseball bat—everyone looked out for each other in those days—as he got closer, he saw a mugging taking place. Naldo charged and looter fired at him. The bullet entered his left side, close to spinal cord and went out through right armpit. Lucky hospital wasn't busy; he made complete recovery.

"When the Japs invaded, the British surrendered on Christmas Day, you know. We were sent to refugee centres in Macau. At first it was terrible, people got separated, but really, we were safe under the Portuguese flag."

A waiter wheeled a desert trolley towards the table. "Wah, they copied the custard tart from our pasteis de nata!" Cheeki yelled.

"Refugee centres," Tio continued, "don't think of the prisoner of war camps you see on TV or in the movies. The Macanese got clubs, schools, the Bela Vista, and a military depot to stay in. No POW camps for us. I wasn't born at the time. Dad was seventeen and was brushing his teeth when the Japanese planes flew over to bomb Kai Tak airport. He could see the deadly red circle on the planes as they flew by. And his dad went to work as if nothing was happening. Everyone did. One of my uncles became a Volunteer. He was killed a week later. The family all went to hospital to see the body. That is when it hit them—*WAR*."

Cheeki frowned, "That is what it was like. We were safe, but terrible things happened. Valda died in Stanley Prison. Heart attack maybe. She was all alone. We don't know what happened."

I examined their faces. Agosta and Freddie seemed oblivious to our conversation.

Perhaps one day I will end up like Valda, dead and all alone?

I am grateful to hear all of this. I have wanted to know if Mother and her brothers had been prisoners of war. If they had been POWs that might account for her violence and inability to communicate and it would explain Fufu and Rico's eccentricities.

I looked around the table. Everyone had stopped talking. The last thing I wanted was for everyone to stop connecting.

"Did you move back to Alvege after the War, Aunty Cheeks?"

"No Jolly, Alvege became school."

"Did the family run the school?"

"No Jolly. Canadian nuns."

I couldn't figure it out. Did they have to sell Alvege? Or was it no longer theirs to sell?

Cheeki lit a cigarette and sighed. "I am the only living member of the Dos Remédios clan of Alvege Jolly, and really, us around this table, we are the last of the Macanese people. Jolly, you look like an English rose, but really you are the last of the Macanese people."

*   *   *

"Jolly, you are intrepid," Cheeki chuckled. "I leave your Las Vegas ticket at the Greyhound Station. We see you there."

"That'll be great, Aunty. Thank you."

"But, Cheeki," Mother complained, "I want to go to Albuquerque with Jolly to see the cowboys and Indians. Jolly, take me with you. Let me come with you. I demand to come with you. I am the mother. I am the parent."

155

"No way. You're going gambling in Vegas with Cheeki. You can't be in two places at the same time. Besides my reasons for going there are professional. I have an appointment."

"Oh, stupid Jolly. Stupid Jolly."

Mother stamped her feet on the floor.

I hurried onto the porch with my rucksack and waved. "See you in Vegas later, ladies."

One of the best things about L.A., I decided as I left Chanera Avenue on foot for the Amtrax train—besides the constant sunshine of course—is the abundance of palm trees anointing roads and boulevards. And one of the worst things about L.A., my logic continued, is being automatically reduced to bag-lady status if seen walking along these humungous roads.

Los Angeles Union Station, more of a grand Catholic church in appearance, stood before me, dressed up in palm trees against a vivid blue sky. A very nice businessman helped me find the platform for Route 66.

The train, a metallic mountain, took my breath away. I climbed to the upper deck, a novelty in itself for a Brit. The train started up and before it had a chance to gather momentum, it stopped to add on mail cars and picked up speed for Flagstaff, Gallup and Winslow. It was due to arrive in Albuquerque in sixteen hours.

The ticket collector explained to passengers that blankets were on sale in the café, and that the shop closed at eleven-thirty p.m. "Eleven-thirty-one is a terrible time to discover you're cold," he said. "The rail tracks between Los Angeles and Albuquerque are notoriously rough, so watch out when you're going between carriages."

At times, the train did lurch, sending passengers careening. Halfway, the train drew to a halt again, ending a succession of saguaros and Joshua trees. The ticket collector explained over the tannoy that the delay was due to a fire in the Mojave Desert, which was becoming "more and more commonplace due to the proliferation of Cheat Grass and Red Brome".

The hours dragged on. Eight went by. Eight hours of sunshine, burgers, doughnuts and cardboard coffee, and enough time for me to question my reasons for visiting the Tamarind in Albuquerque. Occasionally, the ticket man appeared to check for new passengers, but for most of the journey, the carriage was largely unpopulated.

I tried to ignore the empty seats about me. It grew dark. The desert view changed to hazy reflections of empty seats and a sad white face. The train passed the Rio Grande and the Acoma Indian Pueblos. Twenty-eight hours later, it reached its destination and I staggered onto the Albuquerque platform.

The station looked pleasant enough with a homely sign and a few hanging plants. I was worried though. Instantly worried. What a stupid plan. Why have I come here? I know nothing about Albuquerque. I didn't do any research. My whole plan is based on the Slade lithography tutor's comment that the Tamarind would give me a warm welcome and that I "should mention his name".

I hate networking. But it has to be done.

I walked into the centre of Albuquerque Old Town and booked a room in a budget motel named, of all things, Budget Motel. I sat on the bed with my rucksack. The enormity of my folly hit me; I could have been in Vegas, watching Cheeki gamble. Imagine: Cheeki at a roulette table, whacking people out of the way with her stick and saying rude things.

I lurched out of the motel and ducked into the nearest shop. I bought a brass buckle of a steam train, a weighty thing. I clutched it, felt the weight of it.

Later, when it was not quite evening, I phoned the Tamarind to check on our arrangements. Beth Martinez, the manager, answered and confirmed that our appointment was at eleven.

I ate a double burger with fries followed by a vanilla milkshake and decided to enjoy the setting sun and go in search of the

Tamarind. It was my habit to check my destinations in advance and Redondo Drive off Central Avenue was easy to find along the grid of roads.

The flat-roofed building of the Tamarind glittered in the dipping rays of the sun.

I began to beef myself up in preparation . . . Why, I've sold artwork to museums, Beth . . . taught special needs groups . . . published articles about the arts . . . I was invited to have a one-woman touring exhibition in the UK and collected reviews along the way. Been interviewed on TV by Jason Beauford, the art critic. I've taught in a variety of art colleges around the UK . . .

Satisfied with my preparation, I went back to Budget Motel and sat in front of the TV. That didn't work. I took a shower. Hot water poured down erasing my anxieties. How lovely it would be, I thought, to stand naked under a waterfall and walk barefoot in a tropical jungle.

I slipped between the cool sheets and switched off the table light. Round and round to the sound of the sea, I pushed a small fat stone over a large wet stone in a figure of eight motion. I poured sand and water onto them. The dream faded away.

The next morning, I ate a McDonald's muffin with a poached egg, bacon and hash browns on the side with maple syrup and a giant beaker of coffee with two sachets of cream.

Redondo Drive.

Beth Martinez was a plain woman with short brown hair and she was wearing a white shirt and black trousers. Beth invited me into her office. We sat down.

"Exactly, what is the purpose of your visit?"

I laughed. "I'm under the impression that I conveyed my intentions already in my letter to you. Didn't you receive it?"

I reminded Beth about what the lithography tutor at the Slade School of Art had said— that I "should mention his name" and I'd "be sure of a good welcome".

"Yes, but what exactly do you want, Ms Dos Remédios?"

I recounted my achievements as a painter and printmaker, my use of experimental techniques, my commissioned articles about printmaking societies in the UK, and so on, and that I'd like to write about The Tamarind and stone lithography. "I mentioned my ideas in my letters to you. Didn't you get them?" I repeated.

I explained it all again, and added, that the Slade tutor had said I "would receive a good welcome" if I mentioned his name.

Beth Martinez glared at me.

"Beth, it's an absolute pleasure to travel all the way from London to Albuquerque to meet you," I added in confusion.

A technician was allotted the task of showing me around the studios. I observed Tamarind stones being moved from sink to table by hydraulic lift truck and watched as air-powered and electronic levigators ground down the surfaces of the stones.

The technician explained that the Tamarind had exhausted a quarry in Bavaria, known for yielding stone of uniform molecular structure. Hence, they had been forced to find a new supply of used stones. Materials were a constant problem, the technician said. "The label on a can of ink does not reveal that a factory has been sold, bought and sold again by corporations. One good pound of light-fast ink does not guarantee a second good pound."

After the tour, I waited for Beth to re-appear. When the waiting became too hard to bear, I left. The only other person I spoke to in Albuquerque was on the departure platform of the station—a huge man with a tiny feather in his trilby, who said he got up early every day at six o'clock and went to bed early every night at seven o'clock, and he didn't look bad for seventy-eight years of age, did he? I stared at the blue-tinged mountains behind him and nodded in agreement.

The train arrived in L.A. without mishap.

Hurry up, Jolly, I told myself. Get to Vegas. Get to Cheeki. Downtown—the Greyhound Station. That's where my ticket is.

159

Oh, see the pickpockets in action at the bus stops. He's seen me. Quick. Hurry.

A vengeful-looking man did a U-turn and headed towards me. I ran to the station, which occupied a corner on one of the junctions. My heart thudded. I threw myself through the double doors. Inside, it was calm, less crowded.

The Greyhound staff, two women and a man, in grey uniform, didn't know anything about a ticket left behind by a Cheeki dos Remédios. I asked again. I stood there. I tried to figure it out. I was stunned. Cheeki had forgotten to leave the ticket. I queued for a bus. Night was moving in. I had no contact details for Cheeki or my mother, no door key, and no surplus money.

I gazed out of the bus window.

Gardena! I'm here.

Here's the alleyway, the one where Cheeki beat off a mugger with her walking stick.

Chanera Avenue.

I carried on walking and stopped outside Mrs Wallace's house. Mrs Wallace had a spare key. I knew that much.

A shadow appeared in the hallway and Mrs Wallace emerged.

"I'm sorry to disturb you, Mrs Wallace. I realise we've only met briefly. The one time. Do you remember me?"

Mrs Wallace screwed her eyes up.

"I'm Cheeki's great niece. We met the other day. She gave you a spare key."

"I remember. What can I do for you?"

"I was supposed to meet Cheeki in Vegas, but the plan's gone wrong. I need a key to get in. Obviously, Cheeki won't mind. I've been staying there for the past three weeks. I'm family."

Mrs Wallace didn't look happy and closed the door.

Oh dear, what am I going to do? It could be days before they get back.

Seconds later, Mrs Wallace returned, thrust a key at me and

closed the door again. I was relieved to see Cheeki's porch and glad to get back into the chalet. Mrs Wallace's behavior wasn't worth a second thought.

I sloped into each room and gazed at Cheeki's things and the way they'd been left. Henri chirruped and hopped to the corner of his cage. The evening passed slowly. I ate cinnamon bagels washed down with cups of milky tea.

The next day, the wind chimes on the porch announced that Mrs Wallace was outside on the porch. The woman had an especially ugly expression on her face.

"Hello Mrs Wallace, would you like to come in?"

"Why aren't you in Vegas with Cheeki? Why are you in Cheeki's house when she's not here?"

"If you must know, I went to Albuquerque on my own and Cheeki was supposed to leave my Las Vegas ticket at the Greyhound Station in L.A. When I got there, there wasn't any ticket waiting for me. I'm very upset about it, actually."

"Why didn't you get off the Amtrax at the Las Vegas stop?" Mrs Wallace snapped, and then, much to my great annoyance, the woman ran from room to room to check that everything was as it should be.

"Because," I replied to the running figure, "because I didn't damn well know it stopped there. Please leave. I. I am the great niece of Cheeki dos Remédios. Get out." My statement was absurd, but Mrs Wallace ejected herself from the chalet.

I slammed the door. "Good riddance!" The wind chimes settled into a peaceful rhythm.

*   *   *

Two days later, Cheeki and Mother hurried towards the porch with strained expressions on their faces. Both plied me for an explanation about my absence in Vegas.

"Oh, Jolly I sorry. I forget," Cheeki said. "I getting old."

Later, Mother whispered that all Cheeki did in Vegas was eat muffins and play slot machines. "Please tell me about Albuquerque," she cried, vexed that her daughter had had adventures and she had had none.

*   *   *

Cousin Sophia drove away from the Pacific Ocean, continued up Harbor Freeway, turned right into San Bernardino and left into North New Avenue. Mother groaned as the vehicle took another corner. The car continued to rise, glided along South Ramona Street and passed a landmark called the San Gabriel Mission, "Where," Sophia informed them, "many Indians died of European diseases".

Cousin Sophia finally drew to a halt outside a white bungalow fronted by two patches of brown grass. Like most L.A. homes the blinds were down to keep the sun out. She showed us where we were going to sleep and warned us not to flush the bathroom toilet unless it was completely essential. This was in compliance with a drought policy for the region, which all residents took extremely seriously. We went to inspect the toilet, and sure enough, it was brimming with brown and yellow human waste.

"Who wants coffee?" Sophia called out.

I was shocked. Mugs of coffee were being heated up in a contraption called a microwave.

"We heat everything up this way, Jol."

"My God, Sophia, I've never heard of a microwave, never mind used one."

She laughed. "Let's sit down. Do you have any ideas on what you'd like to do?"

"Can I look at old photos of Hong Kong and Macau?"

"Oh, now you are asking. I'll have to check out the attic."

Mother sat down. "Jolly, it's lovely, isn't it? Black shelving, black lacquer cabinets, black three-piece suite."

"Yes. It is nice. Not like our house."

"Ssshhh!"

"I've found the albums." Sophia said spreading them across the coffee table.

"This one is of your wedding day in Hong Kong, Dora."

Before Sophia could finish, Mother snatched the photograph and slipped it under the hem of her dress.

"Let's have a look at that," I said.

"No. None of your business."

"It's my history too. Why shouldn't I see it? Married in Hong Kong, were you?" I asked.

Sophia was as stiff as a board. 'Dora never told her children? Myyyy.' She remained silent.

I got up and wrenched the photograph from my mother's white-knuckle grip. "No, Sophia, she has never told us anything," I replied. And there Dora was—a demure bride—front teeth like a rabbit—arm-in-arm with her groom—a tall British Naval officer—and they were standing next to a Hong Kong signpost.

People of the Southern Ocean

WE GOT OUT OF THE TAXI and surveyed the ultramarine sky streaked cinnamon-pink. We followed the signposts, arrived at Check In and waited. An official examined our tickets. He explained that we were booked on different flights, two days apart.

"Please," Mother said, "we are mother and daughter."

"It was Uncle who booked the seats, not us," I spluttered. "That's Fufu for you; pissed again."

"Jolly! Whuhaha, whuhaha. She is naughty," Mother said to the official.

The official glanced at the two women. One was small, dark-skinned and wearing false eyelashes. The other was young, lily-white, tall and hefty with buckteeth. Both of a nervous disposition.

After some dialogue on the phone, the official came back with two boarding passes.

We turned to each other.

"Oh, Jolly. I almost had heart failure!"

What a nice man, I thought. One of the crew gave up his seat.

I looked at him and sniffed his cologne.

"Ladies, I'm here to help. We try our best not to separate family. Have a good flight." The official gave a well-practiced smile, which showed off an attractive nine o'clock shadow, and pointed to the departure lounge.

His good looks galloped through my mind as I observed the changing hues of the sky though the lounge window. Oh, it has been amazing, I thought. It has been truly amazing. Cheeki's stories about the past—her feisty nature—the photographs and information about the family—Redondo Beach—Chinese restaurants—meeting new relatives—the shopping malls with no daylight or fresh air—Hollywood and palm trees galore. Watt's Tower, and San Gabriel with its graveyards. It's sad too. Will I ever see Cheeki ever again, I wonder?

We clambered aboard.

The plane took off.

The sky turned indigo.

"Oh Jolly, I do hate travelling," Mother said and grabbed a paper bag in readiness.

The next morning, the plane touched down at Heathrow and a light drizzle covered the terminal. Mother roused herself with difficulty.

Once passports and Nothing to Declare were done, we caught the Piccadilly Line to Green Park, changed to the Victoria Line for Euston Station, and found ourselves ascending into the middle of the station. A few cleaners were operating ride-on-floor scrubbers, and stalls were switching on lights and machinery.

"Jolly, let's have a final toast to Cheeki," Mother suggested, and she went off and bought hotdogs with mustard and frothy cappuccinos too.

"Delicious."

"Yum yum piggy's bum."

Her false eyelashes were beginning to disengage. One was dangling in front of the left eye.

"It's time for me to go. I'd better go."

The train departed.

Mother waved and shrank into the distance.

*   *   *

As with all profound journeys followed by a return to reality,

Jolienta felt rejuvenated and lost, both at the same time, and stomped around the house, clicked on a mosaic table lamp, which had a pink-pleated shade, shoved letters and bills into a pile, emptied the fridge of old food and cleaned out the toilet.

The living room was for leisure only, yet the walls displayed a line of unfinished paintings. Softwood was stacked in a corner of the room. A handsaw and a drill lay on the floor.

Jolienta wrenched herself away from the sight of so many incomplete paintings. The Coldharbour Lane Tyre Shop painting—the mother and child had kept on reappearing. The juggernaut tyre had been painted out.

"Hopper's well and truly gone. That's why I can't finish the paintings. I suppose my new direction is the right one to take.

"I have to accept change.

"Working from the soul instead of directly from life—that's bound to bring some bumps along the way, except aren't I moving away from what really matters—the bond between people and places?

"The Woman in the Black Hat got a mention in The Guardian. It sold well . . . I need to earn money. Everyone's entitled to earn a living. Even me."

Jolienta picked up the newspaper and read the text again:

> Supermarket art - reach for your trolley. Buy an
> Edvard Münch-Das Geshrei pastiche by artist,
> Jolienta dos Remédios.

"Polish art critic? Hmmpfh! Oh well, they say all publicity is good publicity. On top of that," she said to the room, "that photo of Sophia's is in my head chomping away like a maggot. Who was the man in the naval uniform? Was he my father? Is he alive? My sisters and I, we have different fathers?

"I'll never get over the shock—that she married twice . . . we have two fathers. What was the British Navy doing in Hong Kong? It must have been to do with the War. To not know anything is a curse. I am my mother's youngest, the whitest, the *Stupid, stupid Jolly. Nose like a collie dog.*

"Am I really of the same flesh and blood? I could be someone else's daughter, couldn't I? She almost had me adopted. If she'd let me go, I could have been living in Canada or some other country. I could have been normal. I might have been happy."

Jolienta began to unpack souvenirs and arrange them on top of a dresser next to the bed. There were plastic soup ladles with bamboo motifs, several framed photographs, some Mexican ceramics, including a Tree of Life candelabra decorated with tiny figures and green leaves, and there were several gifts from Cheeki.

"I didn't get anything for Fufu. I forgot. He's hard to buy for. He doesn't go in for presents unless it's whisky. Still, I messed up, big time.

"Here's the champagne glasses Cheeki gave me." Jolienta removed the tissue paper with care. "Five inches in height. No chips or cracks."

According to Cheeki the glasses were over one hundred years old. The glass itself was dense and uneven. The bowl section and stem were octagon-shaped. Most surprising of all, the stems were hollow, crying out for red liquid. A bottle of Merlot was ready to do the job. Jolienta admired the shape and texture of the glass and the hollow stem. "That woman," she said.

Cheeki was in front of her, punching the air and was surrounded by forty relatives in a Chinese restaurant. "Rah, rah, rah, the Dos Remédios clan!" the old lady cried. Cheeki swished her mink coat. Everyone laughed. The image dissolved.

On went Cheeki's dressing gown—another gift. The blue fluffy polyester reminded her of the old lady's watery eyes.

The next day, Jolienta peered out of the upstairs lounge window. It overlooked trees, the wire fence and rail track and a cemetery of untidy graves. Graves. Dead people.

"I'll never get to meet my forbears."

She picked apart a packet of Blutack, shaped portions of it into small lumps and began to plot out sea routes on a world map.

"The Portuguese were the first to go to sea in search of land and spices; spices more valuable than gold. No, they weren't the first. They did a sort of duet with the Spanish. No, that isn't right either.

"The Portuguese and Spanish competed with each other until they agreed on a line of demarcation from Greenland to the mouth of the Amazon River. Once the treaty was in place, they raced in opposite directions grabbing as much land as possible, taking African prisoners as slaves—setting in motion a new and terrible form of oppression.

"To think my ancestors dealt in slavery! The history books say that the conquistadors were cruel. Were the Portuguese as cruel? I hope we were better than that. Is everyone cruel if they have access to power?"

Jolienta pressed two lumps onto the map, two lumps for two ports on the west coast of the Congo Basin, the route taken by Prince Henry the Navigator. Fernão Gomes sailed further. Vasco da Gama made it past the Cape of Good Hope and reached Calicut in fourteen ninety-eight. The Portuguese captured Malacca and usurped Muslim domination of the spice trade: pepper, cloves, ginger, cinnamon and nutmeg.

She gazed at the blue lumps, entranced by seas and mountain ranges. Over thirty lumps made up a trail of forts and factories from the north coast of Africa to Sofalia and as far as Nagasaki. As for Macau, Great Aunty Cheeki had said the Portuguese had been rewarded with Macau for ridding the waters of pirates in fifteen fifty-seven. Other research implied that the settlement came about following the bribing of a Mandarin official.

Jolienta tried to imagine the reaction of Chinese people to the first influx of foreign devils. "They must have been fascinated, horrified, entertained—what with our big noses, beards, hairy sweaty bodies and coarse manners. No wonder the Chinese ruled out inter-racial marriage. Except, except—a boat-dwelling people named Tanka were happy to marry the Portuguese sailors. And the Portuguese men went on to marry Filipino, Indian, Sinhalese, Malay and Japanese women.

"Were my forebears more Malay, more Tanka, or something else? Chinese mythology had Tanka as snakes able to last for three days under the sea.

"I hope I'm Tanka.

"The Chinese despised Tanka and forbade them from living on the land. Some Tanka were pirates. Some lived as prostitutes who punched their clients, but kept a clean tidy boat. They called themselves People of the Southern Ocean or Sui Seung Yan, and considered their Chinese name meaning 'bowlegged', 'people on water', 'egg' or 'vermin', an insult.

*   *   *

The alarm clock danced away. Jolienta opened one eye and saw it was the wrong time. Henri would have done a better job, skydiving from the curtains.

She sat up. She wasn't in L.A. anymore. A month had gone by and Pacific breezes had continued to waft under her nose.

The postman was at the door. Letters and leaflets were on the floor. She tugged at the gummed seal of a blue airmail envelope.

'My dear dear Jolly'—Cheeki's handwriting was clear and loopy and showed a slight shake of the hand—'It made me happy to get your phone call. You will be glad to know a new pill is working wonders at ninety years of age. I have no fear of death in fact will welcome it. Weather here turned cold. Thinking of going to Vancouver in March, the month I can eat mangoes from Manila.

'Henri died,' Cheeki continued, 'and I have moved into a rest home run by Franciscan nuns. Come and stay Jolly. Nuns not charge you. No relatives in China. No one lives there anymore. During the War, Fufu won a bet at the Happy Valley Race Track, went round the world and left everyone with nothing to eat.'

Jolienta waited until midnight and dialled Cheeki's number. The ring tones echoed and faltered as if the call might not connect.

"Oh Jolly. How nice to hear from you," the old lady said gaily. "Yes, I will ask the fucking nuns. Jolly you are intrepid—China and then L.A. again—I see you on your own this time."

*   *   *

They were interesting. Slides of Chinese men with plaited hair, dressed in silk, slumped over opium pipes. Jolienta popped the last slide out of its viewer and returned it to its plastic envelope.

"Unfortunately, you can't take them with you," the librarian said, and filed the envelope inside a metal cabinet. "However, you can order copies. The Opium Wars were around eighteen forty-one. The British won. Took Hong Kong as their prize. Macanese men, brought up by Cantonese amahs and educated by English-speaking Jesuit priests, arrived to take up the demand for white-collar workers in Hong Kong. The Macanese became indispensible; their education and language skills were compatible with the British. Does that help?"

"It does. Very much. I'm beginning to understand why my mother speaks English very well, Chinese well, and speaks a smattering of Portuguese. It's always puzzled me. There's so much I don't understand. Why did the Macanese leave China? I suppose most of what they had was destroyed."

"You've booked your ticket, haven't you? It's the Beijing to Hong Kong tour, isn't it? I envy you the truth be told. I can't go this year," the librarian said.

"It's taken me a long time to get organized. I didn't want to go unprepared. I couldn't think of anything worse than insulting the Chinese or making a fool of myself," Jolienta replied.

"Are you finding the language lessons useful?"

"Yes, Mr Chang is from the mainland. Teaches etiquette too. I supplement his lessons with taped ones at home. Listen to this: *Ni hao, laoshi. Tianqi hen hao.*"

Maisonette

THE TRAIN PASSED OVER THE TRACK in the direction of Hainault, it was midday and the road was deserted except for Camilla, who was on the doorstep waiting to be let in.

Jolienta let go of the curtain. What does she want? I could pretend not to be in.

"Hi, Camilla, how are you?"

"Hi. I'll come on in, Jola."

"Of course. I'm about to have lunch. Want some?"

Camilla cast a bold eye around the kitchen, paused at the printing press, dissected its wooden frame and clever joints, and sat down. "No, thanks, I've eaten. I have to be careful. My colon."

A plate of chilli was on the table waiting to be eaten.

"You mean you actually cook for yourself?" Camilla said.

"Yes."

What a stupid thing to say. Of course, I cook for myself. What am I supposed to do? Eat out of a packet? It's only a plate of chilli. Here we go. Why is she here? It's the first time she's been to my Acme house and she wants to comment on my cooking? I mean; there's a press behind me. I constructed the frame myself. Isn't that more interesting? Look at her—her brain is going ten to the dozen.

"So what brings you here, Camilla?"

"'Thought I'd see how you're getting on in your new home."

"That's nice. Excuse me if I tuck in, won't you? Cup of tea?"

"Why not? By the way, Phil's back with Gill."

"How predictable and regrettable."

"He's sorry. I told him, Jola, next time I'm calling the police."

" . . . so you won't need to hide the knives away again, you mean?"

"He's not that bad."

"Not that bad? He gave Gill a black eye, threw her over a brick wall. You ran into the kitchen to hide the knives. Do you have amnesia or something?"

"He's changed. He's left his wife for Gill. He's going to settle down. He wants to make amends with you. He wants his portrait done. He'll pay you—commission you. He's sorry he upset you."

"No. Why would I want to get mixed up with a cokehead? I don't give a shit that everyone idolizes him 'cos he's some hotshot avant-garde director. You banned him from the house and two weeks later you let him back in and he beats Gill up."

"He wants to commission you, Jola."

"Don't you dare give him my number. I mean it."

Down went the chilli—more satisfying than any drug or fracas.

Camilla rotated the cup. "You make a good one."

"Thanks."

She always takes me by surprise. Camilla. She used to be so sweet. Really really lovely. Now she's a monster.

"Ready for the move, Jola?"

"I got onto a housing list."

"Which one?"

"I was tipped off about a list in Hoe Street. The receptionist asked me how I met the criteria. I told them about the Acme house, that it was getting bulldozed for the M11 link and therefore I'd be homeless. They said the list was too long and there was no point in me adding my name, so I said, "Well, I'll add it anyway. I don't mind waiting". This went on for some time.

I wouldn't budge. Eventually, the receptionist let me onto the list. Ten days later, I received an offer to be re-housed. How bizarre is that? I thought housing lists took years. Anyway, it looks like I'll be staying in east London after all."

"We're all leaving. We're moving to Brighton . . . the largest community of artists in Europe moving in bulk. You'll be the only one left here, Jola. Ha, ha. Left behind."

"Oh, really. Is that so? Brighton? Good luck to you, that's what I say."

Camilla looked at the wall; she was searching her mind for something and needed a blank surface to help her locate it. "So how's the work coming along, Jola?"

"I finished a Tree of Life painting. Sold it for five hundred quid. Needed the money. It was worth treble, you know. Mind you, what are the chances of meeting someone with five hundred pounds in their pocket? Unbelievable. At Spitalfields Market too."

"If you make sculpture like I do, you don't get to sell to the ordinary person. You have to be collected or commissioned. That's how sculptors survive."

"You could sell your drawings, Cam." Except, you can't draw, can you? You silly woman.

"Maybe. Hadn't thought about it."

"By the way, I'm ready for China."

"You're actually going?" Camilla replied with pretend surprise.

Jolienta laughed, skimmed her finger over her plate and licked the finger. "What about you, Camilla? What are you up to these days? Go on, impress me."

"I'm having a solo at the Ikon. I'm a friend of the curator. I'm going to be on TV, on 'This Morning' Richard and Judy. I won the Jerwood Prize. Oh, the Tate asked me to design their annual Christmas Tree . . . I might just hang it upside down; I'm behind schedule with my own stuff. Anyway, while I'm here, Jola, Phil wants to know . . . "

She glared at Camilla. "Could you please stop asking? I don't know why you're persisting."

"Are you teaching at the moment?"

"Part time in Loughborough. I have a great rapport with the students."

"Printmaking isn't really art though is it, Jola? It's only technique."

"I'll let Rembrandt and Goya know what you said."

Camilla sat back in her chair. "We're all going to the ICA tonight. Tickets only."

"Are you inviting me?"

"Nah."

Jolienta tried not to laugh.

"Gill told me to say 'hello' by the way."

"Is she OK?"

"Yes, she's over the abortion . . . on the mend. Started therapy. Just left to go on tour. Flying into Tokyo right this minute. Earning loads of money with the Quartet. Guzzling champagne. Overdoing the speed. She bought a washing machine before she took off. I've been using it every day."

"She's incredibly talented, that one. When I listen to her play the viola, I'm dazzled."

"Yeah. See ya, Jola. Actually, you might never see us, because we're all moving to Brighton en masse. Don't get isolated. Don't cut yourself off, become a stranger. It must be terrible being on your own all the time. No social life."

"I'll manage. What is it you're always saying? *Survival of the fittest?*"

"Ha ha."

"Let yourself out, Cam. Bye."

She made herself another cup of tea, piping hot, not strong, no sugar, not too much milk, not full fat.

Who cares? I'm moving to a new home, Jolienta thought. I'll

make a fresh start. Build a new life. Keep my head down. I *will* make it. I will make it on my own terms though, not by trampling on other people.

Jolienta had a start date for the tenancy of a ground floor maisonette. No point telling Camilla how beautiful the property was; Camilla would make it sound like it a disadvantage to be offered a beautiful home with a large front garden—a garden waiting to be Paradise—a garden waiting for fruit trees, herbs and flowers.

Besides, Camilla originally orchestrated her isolation.

Jolienta grimaced. Took a while for me to work that one out, didn't it? I used to be so sure of myself then I came to London. I have loved people, loved them as friends, loved them as family.

There's no point in bothering with them. Leave it as it is.

I've told you before, Jolienta, believe in your instincts. You allowed her to erode your confidence bit by bit in a way more powerful than Tom or Kris. You allowed that happen.

My new home will be next to a forest glade and boating lake. Epping Forest cattle trot up and down and chomp on peoples' gardens. I've seen them. The road is wide and gives off a sense of affluence, a sense of space. Opposite the maisonette, there's a row of shops: a butcher's, an off-licence and a grocery store manned by a very nice family from Sri Lanka.

*   *   *

Jolienta knelt on the ground and ran her fingers through the crumbling soil, pushed primroses into the earth—red, yellow and blue, and planted irises by the front door with the tubers left exposed to the sun. By the gateway, French and English lavender blossomed next to a miniature potted apple tree. The sky was infinite and Polish Stan had ceased to exist, Kris was a friend, and she had Cheeki in her soul. Cheeki was always there, inside her, ready to fill the gap or erase the pain. And thanks to Cheeki, she felt fairly whole and mostly real, which was a good start.

A new voice—rasping, rough, gruff, assaulted her ears. The man spoke behind her so as to take her by surprise. He stood too close to her so as to ingratiate himself, and he breathed on her neck to garner intimacy. Seconds later, the unhealthiest white bony skull of a man was jammed in front of her.

Jolienta shrank into the ground.

The man ventured into the pathway and scratched his head. He was thinking about what to say next, but his face said it for him. 'Looks like a soft touch. Don't mind givin' this bitch a goin' over', and, 'Hey, I've really landed on me feet here, pal'.

He spoke out loud. "Me name's Albert. Bert to you. I'm movin' into the ground floor flat, darlin'. Bin inside for GBH, but yer got nathin' to warry about. I promise ya."

She looked at the primroses and back at the man. If she legged it now and locked the door behind her to blot him out, he'd know she was terrified.

"Watch d'ya do fer a livin', lady? D'ya 'ave a job?" He extinguished a cigarette with two rusty fingers and stuck it behind his ear.

Jolienta sighed. "I'm a painter. An artist."

"Ah, really? Great stuff. Anytime yer want to barra me rollers and trays, just arsck. I'm thinkin' of startin' up a paintin' business, meself. I'm movin' in on Friday, darlin'. I'll be under yer . . . so to speak. We'll be able to confer."

Friday arrived.

There'll be many times when I can't avoid him. For a start, the vestibule is small. There's no point feeling sorry for myself. Make the best of it.

She turned into the station underpass and into Leytonstone High Road. Cage Rouge was open. She paid for a croissant and a cappuccino. The shape and size the cup was typical of an Italian café. The café was full of nice people.

She checked her watch.

Nine o'clock. I wonder what time he's moving in? What shall I do now?

She browsed the ladies section of Matalan, which was next to the Co-op. Bert's bony white skull loomed in front of her.

He's going to be trouble, that man. When the post arrives, we'll both be in the vestibule. It's inevitable we'll rub shoulders. I could buy a letterbox and install it outside. But when I come home with bags of shopping and I'm trying to open up the front door . . . When I'm opening and locking my own door in that cramped space. When I'm carrying in art materials and paintings.

Jolienta continued to wander around the shops of Leytonstone. There were no letterboxes for sale in Woolworths.

Abbey National? Do I need Abbey National? Closed. Six o'clock? The day is over. What now? Explore Wanstead? Look at hundred-pound dresses in boutique-windows?

She meandered along the edge of Whipps Cross Lake and stopped at a log cabin. It smelt of fried onions and was managed by a pleasant man.

Egg and chips.

On the way back and through a side road, the houses were lined up on one side. Owners had left apples in cardboard boxes on the walls. On the other side was the forest glade. The moon throbbed in the sky. Jolienta turned left at the end of the road and crossed over for the maisonette, walked quietly up the pathway, opened the front door, opened the door to the flat, double-locked it and padded up the stairs.

She tossed and turned in bed and in the early hours heard Bert scramble into the vestibule. As he exited, he slammed his door and the door to the house. Two hours later, he came back, slammed both doors again, oblivious to the way the building shook. Great. I've got a burglar living under me and he doesn't know how to be quiet.

Morning filtered in.

"I live in Leytonstone now. Who would have thought I'd go from south to north-east and end up in east London again?"

A snore filtered through the bedroom floor.

"With a bit of luck he'll sleep all day and only come alive at night."

She put the kettle on and cracked open a couple of eggs. Jolienta could see Bert's garden at the back. It was overturned soil with a few clumps of nettles and the beginnings of hardy poppies. The size of it was vast and the walls made it private.

Bert's radio filtered through the kitchen floor.

"I'll go and finish the garden; what better way to spend a Saturday morning. The planting's done. Now to sow grass."

Jolienta began by levelling off the soil with a garden fork, sprinkled down sand, added a dusting of dark soil, and combed in grass seeds. It was obvious by the two eyes drilling into her backside that Bert was at his bay window rubbing sleep out of his eyes, and lighting up a fag. "Nice arse," she heard him say. Or did he think it? Both actions were interchangeable in her world.

One thing she didn't fancy—and she was certain about this—was finding herself alone with him in the vestibule and having to smell his donkey breath.

The postman was at the gate. He winked and threw a bundle of letters into the vestibule and closed the gate behind him.

She picked the bundle up and undid it.

There's a lot of letters here. One for Albert Cornell. Albert Cornwall? Albert Courtney? For Bert Cordell? Humph!

"D'yoo mind not interferin' with my fackin' letters?"

Bert was inches away and about to explode.

"I'm not interfering with your letters, Bert. I'm casting an eye over them. That's all. You must know that surely? These letters, they're mine." She pretended he'd finished speaking and got her key out. "Must get on, Bert. Bye."

179

That evening, she heard Bert pace up and down his corridor. He was talking to himself. Occasionally, he bounded along with the energy of a dog let off the leash. Profanities ricocheted off the walls and ceilings. Piff. Paff. He punched a wall. He ranted. She heard him say, "the facking wife", "the facking man next door", and the "facking bitch upstairs".

*   *   *

Bert had taken to wearing a suit and aftershave and waiting upon her arrival. He was behind his door ready to pounce. At the sound of her, he was in the vestibule, that is, until she got her key in the latch and blotted him out. After a fifth such encounter, she was ready to lie for England.

"Bert, I never, ever, speak to anyone at the front door. That's the way I am. One of my quirky ways. Haven't you noticed I don't talk to anyone at the front door? What an eccentric I am! We all have our peculiarities, Bert. Must go."

He seemed to buy it. However, he was bound to turn the conversation over and over in his mind. He would go over her words like a hot spin until he decided he'd been insulted. Then, he would pop.

She leafed through the post. One of the letters was a blue airmail envelope postmarked Los Angeles.

> *Jolly, still smoking the fags. Nuns said Yes,*
> *you can sleep on the floor. Hurry up back from*
> *China and tell me everything.*

Cheeki's letter was excellent timing. And so was the trip to China. Her tartan case and rucksack were ready. Jane was to water the garden. Jane had strict instructions not to let Bert pass the threshold.

Beijing

THE PASSENGERS UNDID THEIR SEATBELTS, scrambled high and low and snatched at their hand luggage. The eight-hour flight had taken its toll; she was welded to the seat, no feeling in either leg. A gap among the passengers appeared. She lifted herself out and swung into the aisle. Thank God for strong arms.

The pain. The pain!

I'll be OK in a moment, she thought.

How embarrassing. I'm stuck at a right angle. This isn't how I planned to enter China—bent over like an old lady—nose facing the ground. At least, I know in thirty minutes or so I'll be back to normal.

Beijing airport was all grey floor and pairs of feet.

"Ha ha, ta shi meiguo ren," someone said.

I'd like to give that man a piece of my mind, Jolienta thought, but I've got more pressing needs right now, like getting through Customs.

She followed the feet in front. The feet belonged to the UK group. One or two of them noticed her condition and sneered. The tour guide, a young woman called Lynn, didn't look too pleased either, and began to carry out a body count of the group. Once it was clear that three people from the USA were not on the coach, the driver pulled out and edged into the streets of Beijing. Members of the group pointed at people practicing Tai chi on the pavements and in parks.

The driver steered the coach into a forecourt and stopped outside a hotel. Congratulations were in order; the October weather was not hot enough for mosquitoes, Hotel Huguosi was glamorous, and the lobby was magnificent. Jolienta eased herself onto a marble bench and watched with amusement as a line of cases flew through the air and hit the floor in a series of slaps. A few leather trunks burst open. Shirts and socks spilled out. Some cases collided and spun into a twirl. The group—mainly retired schoolteachers, doctors, administrators—responded with loud "Tut"s and "Really"s. Meanwhile, the porters set about hurling cases into the lobby, hatred glimmering in their eyes. Her own luggage lay at her feet, light enough to skim across the ground with two monkey arms.

She had two objectives only: to lie down, to get the pain to stop.

"Excuse me, mademoiselle," a woman in an explorer's hat said, "May I present myself to you. Je suis Madame Thierry. You and I are to share a room for the duration of the tour."

Madame Thierry was a retired woman of culture, archeology in fact, and wore a hat with a cord tied under an ample chin. She was a stout woman and also wore a dowdy raincoat, which couldn't fasten at the chest, and she had a monocle dangling out of her breast pocket. Madame said she had paid for her place on the tour through the sale of a Renoir etching found in a Paris flea market.

"It's a pleasure to meet you, Madame. A Renoir? What a lucky person you are. Extraordinary. Did you know I'm an artist? That is, I understand the etching process. Shall we go to our room straightaway? I see you have the key. I must lie down. My back is painful. As you can see, I'm bent over. My face must be a picture of anguish."

Jolienta extracted herself from the group and went in search of an elevator. Madame bustled beside her.

"I must explain to you, young lady," Madame Thierry began.

Jolienta put all of her concentration into yanking a heavy metal grill to the side, shuffled into the elevator and tried to stand up straight. The elevator creaked to the third floor.

Madame had the key.

The room was large, grey and peeling due to the passage of time. Huge windows consumed one wall.

"I must explain to you," Madame continued, "I'm rather deaf and my eyes are very sensitive, which means I must exclude all light from the interior."

"What d'you mean, Madame? Draw the curtains to?" Jolienta adjusted to fresh spasms of pain.

"Non. No. I must blacken out ze windows with plastic bin liners and wear a blindfold or else I cannot sleep. Curtains are never enough."

Not wanting to disturb the balance between pain and discomfort, Jolienta unfastened her sandals and waited for torture to fizz through her body. When the moment was right, she got up, boiled a kettle, filled a flask with hot water and placed it next to a packet of painkillers.

At the back of her mind, she had the curious feeling that her purse was missing. Probably the pain, she thought. Jetlag on top.

The shape of Madame Thierry balanced on a chair, was followed by the rustle of tape being stretched across plastic as Madame banished all light from the room. A minute later, jasmine tea swept past her nostrils, followed by Madame's snore. And then nothing.

A dream has come, or has it?

My aches and pains have gone.

I am in a forest glade.

Sunlight is filtering through a canopy of leaves and the sound of silence is but a flute playing a timeless melody.

A crane calls out and struts towards her chicks.

Madame's alarm clock tinkled.

Jolienta remained still and listened. There was no movement in the dark from the other bed. She waited to see if pain would return, rolled onto her knees and onto the floor, gripped the edge of the bed to lessen the impact, and waited for pain to contort her limbs. "Bonjour, Madame Thierry. Il est sept heures moins le quart."

"It eez time to rise?"

Madame fought with blindfold, curlers, quilt and pillow as if they were an unwanted lover.

"I found eet 'ard to sleep," Madam said with floundering arms, legs and Cocker Spaniel eyes.

"Do you need to use the bathroom before I take a shower, Madam?"

"Quoi? I can't 'ear you?"

"Do you need to use the bathroom before I shower, Madame?"

"Pardon?"

"Do you need to use the toilet before I go into the bathroom?"

"Zer is no need to raise your voice like that."

Jolienta winced. The pain. She showered, brushed her teeth and examined her complexion under the dusty light. A thump landed on the bathroom door.

Perhaps Madam doesn't like to be kept waiting?

"Here we are, Madam. All yours. See you at breakfast."

"You are not attendez for me?"

"No," Jolienta replied in French out of sense of innate courtesy, "I need to elongate my legs."

On the ground floor, the entrance to the hotel restaurant opened into a huge empty dining room for 'Westerners Only'. A skinny woman in a yellow cheongsam advanced.

"You English person London?

"Yes. Shi ying guo ren."

"Aaargh." The young woman recoiled.

Perhaps my pronunciation is ungainly?

Or is it my foreign devil features?

Or is it because I'm bent at ninety-degrees like an old lady?

"I am with twenty-four soft corpses," Jolienta added in Mandarin Chinese, trying to be as helpful as possible.

The woman checked her list and found the UK group. "Ha, ha. You follow me, lady."

The woman kept her distance and guided Jolienta to a collection of round tables laden with teacups, bowls and plates. Several waiters emerged from the kitchen, allowing a din of cutlery and voices to escape. Madame and an Englishman appeared. Madame poured out tea for herself and the man, and gave her a shrill look of disapproval. The Englishman, who had a pugnacious lumpy red nose, appeared to have been briefed by Madame, and also gave her a dirty look.

Someone said the three Americans had arrived in the early hours and they weren't pleased. Apparently, the UK organization had given them the wrong information and this had led to the expense of a later flight from London. Waiters appeared with steamed buns, deep-fried dough sticks, "zongzi", and white pots of green tea. A young man with a golden face, tall, thin and wearing a dark suit with a white shirt and black tie, set himself apart from the British at breakfast. It was his aloof manner that made it easy for her to identify him as Mr Wu, the official Chinese guide.

He's the Chinese guide, all right. He probably doesn't want to sit down and crease his trousers. He's looking at me the same way as the woman in the yellow cheongsam. He's staring at my nose, the nose of a Collie dog.

"Tianqi bu lung bu re?" Mr Wu said with a bow.

"Tianqi heng hao," Jolienta replied.

"Aaargh." Mr Wu looked away.

Once the novelty of the first group Chinese breakfast receded, Lynn got down to the business of dealing with the group's issues and the day's itinerary. After a visit to the Great Wall of China, apparently they were to finish off the day with a sixteen-course banquet held in their honour, organized by Hotel Huguosi.

"Everyone, meet Mr Wu, your official guide," Lynn said at last.

Mr Wu took a bow and smiled. The group applauded.

"Jolienta, Mr Wu will take you to the police station today to report the missing wallet, and then he'll take you on to the Bank of China. It's a shame you'll miss the wall. You must come straight back to the hotel afterwards and wait for me. You can't go off on your own. I know you want to, but you cannot. Do you hear? You can watch TV in your room if you get bored."

Mr Wu added his own instructions. "You pay for taxi to Gate of Heavenly Peace."

"Can we go by bus, Mr Wu?"

"No."

Jolienta eased herself into the back of the taxi. Mr Wu sat in the front. The roads to Beijing were unexpectedly wide and smooth. The driver passed a long stretch of cyclists and halted. Mr Wu didn't acknowledge Tiananmen Square and gazed sullenly out of the window. She peered out of the window. A blanket of fog was covering the Square. The truth be known, she was afraid. Afraid of the unknown. Uncomfortable too. She had no control over Mr Wu and he didn't want to communicate.

She got out. Mr Wu got out and watched as she counted out the fare from a roll of crumpled renminbi yuan. He looked up at the sky and beckoned her to follow him into a concrete building, a peculiar place, out of keeping with the historic Square. Inside, a policeman behind the counter, dealt with Mr Wu's enquiry straightaway. Mr Wu stifled a yawn and waved her off to the far end of the station.

The hairs on the back of her neck shot up.

Two officers, pistols tucked into black holsters, confronted her. Their uniforms were olive green, their hats edged in red and yellow. Collar patches offset braided epaulettes. Leather belts were pulled in tight to show off muscle and black batons.

"Sit down, lady!" one of the officers yelled.

Jolienta sank into one of the chairs. The officers began a rapid discussion in Chinese. Jolienta's gaze hopped around the room. She was confused by the reception she'd received. Once or twice, she heard a familiar word. Other than that, the dialogue was incomprehensible. In a corner of the room was a small metal bed, the kind of bed found in a prison cell. A blanket was resting on it, folded neatly.

Does Lynn know I'm here? she wondered.

How long will they keep me here?

Does Mr Wu, know I'm being treated this way?

Is he laughing about it right now?

The men are cackling coldly, murderously. They're not the Police, are they?

Are they soldiers?

What's that hammering sound?

It was her knees. Her knees were banging together under the table. She pressed her hands down on them. The knocking wouldn't stop.

The nearest officer addressed her in precise English. "What is your report, lady?"

"My wallet was stolen coming into China, sir. I need to report it."

"Wallet stolen in China?"

"Yes. It was a black wallet. It contained traveller's cheques."

"Wallet stolen in China?" the officer repeated.

"Yes." Jolienta trembled. "I need to report it to get a refund. Get the money back, sir."

"Wallet stolen in China?" the officer repeated.

"No, sir. I make mistake. Wallet not stolen in China." She wanted to sob, 'Please, please, wallet not stolen in China. I am stupid lady'.

The two officers of the Zhongguo Renmin Wuzhuang Jingcha Budui were satisfied they had scared the tourist witless.

"Goodbye lady," the soldier-policemen said.

Not a word passed between Jolienta and Mr Wu on the way back. Hotel Huguosi's maids were making beds and changing towels, and one minute she was lying down trying not to aggravate her back, and the next, she was gazing out of the window shaking with fright.

They had nothing but contempt for me! I was just another westerner, a tourist, a foreign devil. They couldn't see *me*. They don't know *me*.

A rainbow arched the sky. She had to get out. She shuffled across the lawn and saw that the rainbow disappeared into a pond. No pot of gold was to be found. Droplets of rain fell onto the pond's surface. The air was moist. The rain increased in intensity. A willow tree sagged. The pond's face gyrated. Orange carp swam to the surface. A kingfisher darted out, dived into the pond, held a fish in its beak, and flew off on a horizontal trajectory.

*   *   *

As soon as Lynn arrived, the UK group filed into the hotel's public restaurant on the first floor. Jolienta didn't know where to sit; almost everyone was part of a married couple or had a relative or friend with them. Madame Thierry was with the pugnacious Englishman again. Even Lynn had brought someone along for the duration of the tour—a skinny white boyfriend with not much going on between the ears.

"Listen up, everyone," Lynn said, "the hotel restaurant has gone to a lot of trouble to prepare a sixteen-course banquet in our honour. It doesn't really matter what you choose from the menu; you have to eat sixteen dishes whether you like it or not. If you find that you reach the stage where you're beginning to flag—at least take a nibble of each dish. We don't want to offend, do we?"

"Is this how the Chinese normally eat all year round, Lynn?"

"No, Norman. I think the average person mainly eats rice and noodles. Some vegetables or dumplings. Maybe an egg in the morning. Special occasions would be another matter."

"How can they expect us to eat so much, Lynn?"

"I honestly don't know. I think the idea is to stuff us to the brim so we won't be of any trouble to them while we're in the country."

"What happens to the leftovers, Lynn?" a married couple said. "Can staff take it home?"

"Unfortunately, all waste gets thrown away. They can't take it with them. If they got caught, they'll be severely punished. Lose their job."

"The noodles are greasy, aren't they, Lynn. Do you find them greasy?"

"I'm bloated already. Are you bloated?"

"Call me a moron, but aren't our London Chinese restaurants better than this?"

"Has anyone seen my dentures?"

"I didn't sleep a wink last night, did you, Lynn?"

"I dropped my camera down the lift shaft, Lynn."

"Does anyone have any chamomile lotion? I'm itchy."

"God, I'm tired. Those steps. Arthritis."

"Who built the Great Wall, Lynn?"

"Lynn, I've lost my passport."

"Pass the soya sauce someone."

"Snake? Who wants stir-fried snake? Anybody?"

"We had to survive on snake when we were evading the Japs. Tastes of chicken."

"Deary me, the wine is sweet, isn't it?"

"Lynn . . . what does that poster on the wall say?"

"It says, *Smile at the foreigners or else punishment.*"

"Good grief."

"How did you get on at the Great Wall today?"

"Incredible. The view was superb. Weren't you there, Gemima?"

"I'm Jolienta, not Gemima. Gemima's over there. No, I wasn't. I had to go to a police station and then go on to the Bank of China to get my stolen traveller's cheques refunded."

"Don't tell me you went on your own."

"Mr Wu took me."

"How interesting. What's he like?"

"A bit of a dark horse actually. I see he's not dining with us this evening."

"Jolienta, did you manage to get everything sorted out?" Lynn said.

"Er . . . yes, but nothing went quite as expected."

"What do you mean?"

"Mr Wu wasn't friendly."

"What do you mean?" Lynn looked nervous.

"Oh, I got the refund all right. The bank was obstructive to begin with because I didn't have a police report, however, I remembered what I'd been told in the UK. I was told to always be polite but very persistent, and then, if necessary, ask to be put through to a UK branch on the phone, then they'd pay up."

"You didn't have to persist, did you?"

"Er . . . yes. I had to be very persistent. They put me through to Head Office, Abbey National, and then Abbey phoned the Bank of China back. I have to tell you . . ."

"Tell me what?"

"Tell you about the police station."

"Lynn, what are we doing tomorrow?"

"Lynn, can you teach us Chinese?"

"Lynn," a number of people said, "how do you say, 'Hello', in Chinese? We want to say Hello to Mr Wu tomorrow morning."

"Ni hao. That's how you say it."

"Can you say it again?"

"Yes, Benjamin. Ni hao."

"Knee how?"

"No. Ni hao. Goodnight everybody. See you all tomorrow."

"How do you say 'Goodbye', Lynn?"

"Zai jian."

"Sigh ten."

"Goodbye, everybody."

"What a nice young lady. Terrible, the amount of food left over. Terrible. A feast gone to waste."

Lynn bent down and whispered, "Jolienta, I've made an appointment for you to visit the hotel doctor."

"The hotel has it's own doctor? Wow. Will you come with me? Don't fancy going on my own. Who knows what might happen."

"I'm sorry, no. I'll point you in the right direction. Let's go outside and take a look.

"You see that cobbled courtyard over there lit up by Victorian gas lamps?"

"Yes."

"Cross over it at a diagonal and you'll find the main entrance just around that corner. In case the doctor doesn't speak good English, I've written a note for you to give to him."

"That's very kind of you. Who would have thought my back would still be stuck at a right angle? The pain is terrible. It's getting worse too. I'm exhausted. Thank you, Lynn."

"Tomorrow evening. Seven fifteen. Don't forget."

"Thanks for that. 'Night, Lynn."

*   *   *

The group spilled out of the coach. Mr Wu looked very smart. Sally, a tall woman, started to jump up and down to get the circulation going.

"While we are here," Lynn said, "if you see anything you like, buy it, because you might not see it again in China. I've often regretted that I didn't buy goods I liked, and then I never saw them again."

"You mean we're going to wander around on our own, Lynn?"

"Yes, Duncan. We'll meet back here at twelve-thirty."

"She's leaving us."

"Oh God, someone make a note of the name of this place."

"Has anybody got a map?"

Mr Wu whispered in Lynn's ear.

"Stay nearby everyone. There are plenty of shops and stalls in this area. No need to stray. Twelve-thirty. Back here for lunch. Buy lots of nice things."

"Can we stay with you, Lynn?"

"No. I'm spending time with my boyfriend."

"Oh dear, we can't stay with her. Did you hear that everybody?"

Jolienta shuffled into an alleyway. "Hey, everyone, I'm going in here. Hey, where is everybody?"

*   *   *

Not a soul in sight. The Victorian lamps lit the way over the cobbled courtyard. Their glow picked out delicate saplings and neatness. The entrance for the medical centre was signposted in Chinese and English. A receptionist greeted her and took her straight to the third floor. Jolienta tried to stand up straight; the pain had left her sore and tender.

"Hello, Miss Rem-e-dios. British guide say you have bad back?"

"Ni hao, Dàifu xiansheng, British guide gave me this note for you."

The doctor was tall, as tall as Mao himself, and well built. He had a hearty face and looked as though he enjoyed nutritious food and led an active life.

"Ah, speak Chinese. Very good. You get on bed. Come."

Jolienta shuffled forward. "Ow, ow."

"You very tense lady."

Jolienta thought of Bert in the vestibule ready to punch her face in. Then she thought about the man in the airport laughing at her bent posture. A tear slid down her cheek.

"On to bed. I sort you out. Turn onto front, Lady."

"Ow, ow."

"Back very red. Back very sore."

"Yes. Ow, ow."

"I give you massage and medicine with deer's horn."

Dàifu xiansheng placed a warm towel at the base of her back and began to rub the sore muscles with the palms of his hands.

"You wake up now, Miss. I give you medicine. You get up now and try to walk normal."

Jolienta let out a big yawn and slid off the leather couch. Inch by inch, she stood up and waited for pain. The doctor laughed and slapped her on the bottom.

"One per day, Miss," he said, smiling at her bottom with longing and desire.

"Thank you, Dàifu xiansheng. Xie xie. Thank you."

*   *   *

Jolienta nibbled the black ball the doctor had given her. It didn't taste medicinal; it tasted of rubber tyre. It had to be eaten. She grabbed a beaker of tea.

She decided on a white dress, added a coral necklace and was ready. Madame Thierry, who had been napping, pulled up her stockings and darted about the room. Occasionally, they bumped into each other. Finally, they converged inside the elevator, where Madame growled. Jolienta rolled her eyes and snorted. A collection of stern faces was waiting for them in the vestibule. "My fault," said Madame Thierry.

Punctuality was a popular topic among the guides and the group had been warned never to be late. Not only did the Chinese consider it rude, the schedule relied on punctuality.

"Knee how, Mr Wu," the group sang from their seats. "Knee how. Knee how. Knee how."

Lynn looked at Mr Wu, who was laughing. Lynn laughed and grabbed a megaphone. "OK, everyone, just so you know, I'm losing my voice, hence this contraption. What was that, Duncan?"

"Where are we going now?"

"We are going to a popular haunt called Tianqiao Happy Teahouse, located in the Xuanwu District."

Madame Thierry, aware of the venue, had decided to put on a string of pearls. Sally was wearing a black dress and her husband was in a smart grey suit. The elderly brothers were kitted out in linen. Jolienta could smell perfume and aftershave.

The coach tackled a hump bridge and several narrow streets. It squeezed into another narrow cobbled street and stopped; the group gasped with delight. Tianqiao Happy Teahouse was picture-postcard-pretty. Inside, colourful lanterns hung like bunting and cast a fruity glow over dining tables.

Jolienta sat next to Sally and her husband. She could rely on them not to be full of instant disapproval like Madame Thierry, who was sitting on the other side of her.

Shortly after the first course was served, velvet curtains parted and an actor, in a long black wig with a thin moustache and painted features, emerged. He moved sideways across the stage in a squat motion brandishing a sword. Drums, clapper and symbols belted out his song. Projected scrolls on the walls explained the story—the *huashan* aristocratic young woman was in love with the *xiaosheng* peasant. Once their love was exposed, the peasant was to be imprisoned and the woman would be left to lament the execution of her beloved.

Jolienta giggled. Jolienta tittered. Fortunately, Sally and her husband were engrossed in a soft domestic argument. Tears of mirth began to pour down like the rain on the willow trees by the pond. Madame Thierry looked at Jolienta with astonishment and produced a handkerchief, but the more horrified Madame was, the more Jolienta giggled, releasing strings of mucous from each nostril. The peasant was about to be beheaded yet her eyes and mouth continued to insult the opera.

"It's the medicine, Madame. The black lump. The deer's horn. It must be . . . no control . . . ha ha, ho ho, boo hoo, hee hee."

The next morning, the group complained to Lynn about the accruing damage to their suitcases and trunks. They also complained about being constipated. Food was plentiful, and all sorts of meat, from dog to cat to rat to snake, but there weren't many fresh vegetables to be had. It was agreed, the food lacked roughage for the delicate Western digestive system.

Lynn said she would try to speak to the porters, but the problem was each new destination brought a new set of staff.

Next destination: Chengde.

The venomous porters threw the cases into the coach-hold. The group climbed on board, indignant. Mr Wu and Lynn huddled over the megaphone.

"Ni hao, ma?"

The group responded, waved and cheered, "Kneeee hooooooo-oowwwwwww!"

Jolienta watched Hotel Huguosi fade away.

Across China

BEIJING, THE CAPITAL OF CHINA, lies between two rivers and is surrounded by mountainous land. The Yanshan Mountains sit in the west, north and east. In the southeast, the Yongding River flows into a plain. Chengde is one hundred and twelve miles from Beijing and reached via the Jingcheng Expressway.

Forty-three miles from the capital, the route became steep and winding. The Badaling Great Wall was "firm and strong to keep the marauding nomadic tribes out. Twenty feet wide for galloping horses, five abreast. There are holes in the wall to be used by archers," Mr Wu said. "Now," he continued, "we are driving through the primeval forest of the Huairou District, which offers an abundance of rare trees.

"After seventy-five miles, the Simatai Great Wall has thirty-five beacon towers and is deliberated for steepness, queerness and intactness. There is the Mandarin Duck Lake fed by two springs—one is warm, the other is cold. In winter, the lake never ices up."

Chengde came into view. Jolienta pressed her face against the window. The driver looped a statue and fountain and halted outside Tian Fu Nest Hotel. Cases were jettisoned onto the pavement. Many of the group scrambled to lodge a protest, but the porters didn't take any notice. Sally, six foot four, a good ten inches taller than her husband, jumped up and down to get the circulation going and broke into an army exercise. "One two. One two." The brothers, Panama hats shading their eyes, tottered down the steps of the coach. They inhaled the clean air, glad to be alive. A retired headmistress with tight peroxide hair tried to hide a mosquito bite, which was ballooning from her nose. Madame repositioned her monocle and regarded the hotel. Jolienta shuffled along as best she could, her back at an improved angle of twenty-three degrees. Finally, Mr Wu alighted with a small black wheelie case and began to supervise the twenty-four soft corpses and one half-breed.

Madame and Jolienta were amazed; the hotel interior was Tibetan-style. Their room glowed with copper and gold ornamentation. No luxury had been spared the foreign devil.

Jolienta looked in the mirror. "I'm not hungry, are you, Madame Thierry?" Every day, breakfast and every other meal they'd eaten on the tour had been wasteful in terms of sheer excess, while the average local had to make do with noodles and a cup of cha.

Madame Thierry glowered at her. She groaned. She had offended Madame again. "Would you like me to help you blacken the windows, Madame?"

"How dare you."

"You keep misinterpreting everything I say. It's not fair."

"But you speak zo quietly and it eez still midday," Madame said, throwing her arms in the air.

"I can't help it if I talk quietly, Madame, just like you can't help being deaf."

Madame Thierry sat on the bed, crushed.

Hmmm, I'm not hungry, which is a shame, Jolienta thought, because they serve spicy Sichuan food here doused in huajiao pepper, which turns your mouth numb. "Madame Thierry, you must try the Sichuan food. You must try the steampot. It's a big pot simmering in the middle of a table"—and it will burn your mouth off.

Madame Thierry began to sob. "Many years ago, I received a telegram. My husband was killed in action on zees very day."

"Madame, maybe the steampot is not a bon idée. We're going to visit a couple of temples this afternoon and, would you believe, *monks* are going to make us lunch."

Madame Thierry smiled. "Une bonne idée. Your pronunciation eez terr-*ible*."

*   *   *

Putuo Zongcheng Temple gave a limitless panorama of forest, pagodas and mountains. At Wenshu Temple, the group ate the meal prepared by the monks. In the evening, Madame Thierry blackened out the room's windows and rested. It had been a perfect day, in which Jolienta had found herself sitting next to the three Americans for the first time.

The next morning after breakfast, the group took up their seats on the coach and brayed, "Kneeeeeeeeeee hooooooooowwwwwww!" and reverted to stony-faced expressions as the porters began their attack on the luggage.

Next stop: the airport. Which airport? It was easy to lose track. The driver drove to an airport. There were no brightly-lit shops selling Western items or Chinese souvenirs, nor were there any coffee bars. Only greyness.

The group found themselves standing on tarmac in front of a tiny plane with a rusty ladder.

"Eh up. Do you think it's safe?" said Norman.

"Everyone up. Don't wait all day," Lynn said.

The ladder clanked under the strain.

"Oh, Lynn, I'm not happy about this."

"Mr Wu says the plane is in good repair. Hurry up."

Disgruntlement was overtaken in the fight for a window seat. Jolienta was intrigued to see that the interior signage was in Russian. The intercom began to emit greetings and instructions in a variety of languages. The plane lifted off, shuddered into the sky, flew parallel to the Great Wall, soared over the Yunzhong Mountains, gave a view of the Luliang Mountain range, and then a valley gave way to a ribbon of Yellow River. Jolienta reached out for a tray coming her way. On it was a beaker of lemonade, a plastic key ring and a boiled sweet.

A few hours later, the plane touched down in Xian. Instead of driving straight to the hotel, the driver took them to a local market.

"Hallo, hallo," a chorus of ragged children called out. "We hungry. We hungry!"

Whichever way the group turned, a market vendor or a beggar would be in their face. The group fled to the coach and ate their pre-packed lunches.

"Eh, what else can we do?" Norman remarked.

The driver started up the engine and moved the coach out of the market place. Mr Wu adjusted his megaphone. "Our next destination is the Terracotta Army. For more than two thousand years, children have listened to stories about a great army made out of clay by order of the first emperor of China, Qin Shi Huang Di, and of a burial tomb filled with jewels, where a hundred rivers of mercury flow out to the sea. The terracotta figures, which represent individual warriors, are placed in pits according to rank and duty. Each warrior is dressed according to rank. However, the spears, bows and arrows have disintegrated over time. Pit One is estimated to contain six thousand warriors."

An hour or so later, the driver stopped outside of the museum. It reminded Jolienta of an air-raid shelter. The group wound their way down a pathway. Illuminated underground pits came into view. The army was magnificent, frightening. The faces of the warriors.

Qin Shi Huang Di was a mean man, who consigned his workers to a cruel death. Jolienta tried to imagine what their last days would have been like once they'd realized they were to be sealed inside forever. There would be immediate horror, fear, rage, and indignation too—after all they were skilled craftsmen, the best in the land. They would have tried to put their heads together to figure a way out. Hysteria would have led to acceptance, then physical weakness, and then grief as each worker bade his kith and kin goodbye. For two to three weeks, maybe longer, it would be a case of survival of the fittest.

If dear Camilla had been one of the workers, she'd have initiated cannibalism. No problem.

*   *   *

Next stop: Shanghai by train.

The seats decorated with antimacassars were designed to swivel both ways depending on whether the foreign devils wanted to face each other or not. Inflexible hard seats were for locals. The carriage windows had original brass fastenings and lace curtains. On the hour, a stocky woman in uniform patrolled the aisles of the train with an enormous pot of Green Dragon Tea. Paddy-fields, terraced land, mountains and forest flashed by. The group entertained themselves with board games, cards, and the correct way to use chopsticks. The men drank beer and gossiped. One of the brothers began to scribble down verse:

> There was a young woman called Jolienta,
> Who resembled a plump slice of Polenta
> With the face of a panda
> And the breathe of a monkey,
> We wander, if lucky, without her!

> There was a Madame called Thierry,
> Who liked to travel by ferry.
> One day she declared, "I cannot hear,
> No beer, I fear, I prefer a bin liner
> Washed down with a bucket of sherry.

Mr Wu, not a speck of grease or fluff on his suit, he was clearly enjoying the journey. He began to reminisce, which was very unusual for him; he was normally on guard twenty-four seven. He was talking about the Xian Incident of nineteen thirty-six.

"The Kuomintang and Communist Party formed a truce in order to concentrate on fighting the Japanese perpetrators. Xi'an was far inland. Japanese carried out air attacks. Xi'an impacted minimal destruction . . ."

Everyone was fast asleep. Except for Jolienta.

Mr Wu, he has a golden face.

The train chugged on. The woman with big thighs carried the teapot up and down the aisles. Dinnertime. Smartly dressed waiters appeared out of nowhere with platters of bird's nest soup and chao-fan. The smell soon roused the group. Outside, the landscape was giving in to night. Lynn and Mr Wu had omitted to tell the group that the journey would take sixteen hours, but Jolienta had known all along and had made a point of walking up and down the carriages to keep her muscles loose.

Sixteen hours later, the train slithered into Shanghai. Jolienta tried to straighten up. Sally jumped up and down on the platform while her husband looked on. Lynn looked depressed. Mr Wu re-invoked his contempt for the foreign devil. Suitcases were shot-putted into a coach hold.

The driver crossed over the Wusong River. The scenery was enchanting. He stopped outside the Ritz-Carlton Hotel, which was next to The Temple of the Jade Buddha. The group scurried into the lobby and waited for their cases to be hurled to the floor.

Say it now for God's sake, Jolienta, she said to herself. Say it now. You want a room on your own—no more Madame Thierry, thank you very much.

She braced herself.

"The hotel staff don't like it when we make last minute changes, Jolienta," Lynn said.

"But, Lynn . . ."

Lynn's face was set in stone. "Not another word."

"Why, Jolie can share my room, Lynn. No problem."

It was one of the Americans—Peggy.

Problem solved.

Madame Thierry pretended to be pleased. "Ah, zat is a good arrangement for us."

Peggy took Jolienta up to her room. It was the most sumptuous suite that she had ever been in.

"Peggy, this is amazing."

"Yes, it's OK, don't ya think? One thing, Jolie, I don't like noise, in the night or early morning. By the way—no charge. The room's already paid for."

"Oh, Peggy, Madame Thierry was always cross with me, because I talk and move about quietly. And with my bad back and after a day out, I just want to lie down and be quiet. You won't have any problems with me."

Peggy smiled. She was in her seventies and had a perfect hairdo and manicure.

"I'm not happy about you not taking any money for the room though, Peggy."

"Ha, you ain't getting anywhere with that."

The next morning, they got up, took turns to use the bathroom, dressed, and found their habits to be compatible. They hugged, and she found herself confiding in Peggy. "Madame Thierry tried to push me into a lake. Madame Thierry cries a lot. Madame Thierry snored and made unreasonable demands upon me." It was good to get it off her chest.

"You stick with us," Peggy said.

*   *   *

Shanghai, full of rivers, canals, streams and lakes, is a peninsula defined by the Yangtze River and Hangzhou Bay and faces the East China Sea. It is equidistant to Beijing, Hong Kong and

Macau—an auspicious sign. The driver stopped. Lynn switched on the megaphone. Her voice was hoarse and scratchy. "If anyone is a minute late, we'll leave without you."

One minute? Jolienta thought. One minute?

The group dispersed. She was alone again and in the middle of Shanghai. A pain curved around her, not the physical kind, the kind that warps the soul and leaves you bereft.

I have wanted to travel across China for so many years; I have wanted to get in touch with my roots for as long as I can remember. Here I am.

A cacophony of bells iced the air. Hordes of cyclists dominated the road. It was the most crowded place she'd ever been in in the whole of her life. The city was stuffed with people, stuffed with black hair, golden skin, and stuffed with the greens and blues of their clothing, all squashed down under an oppressive sky.

She threaded her way through the crowd. People parted before the foreign devil.

How puzzling. I thought Shanghai was international. Anyone would think I was contagious. She lowered her head and kept her gaze on the ground.

We British, we plundered your country, and one day, who knows, maybe you'll plunder ours. If so, I hope you'll be kinder to us than we were to you.

We Portuguese, we bucked the trend of plunder and oppression. We were mainly interested in spices and set up ports along the coastlines. We weren't interested in exploiting your country's interior. That is what the history books say.

We Macanese, we bridged the gap between the British and the Chinese. We flew the Portuguese flag over Macau. We spoke and wrote in English, Chinese and Portuguese. We had our own patois. *Cheena pobre* or not, we've gone down in history. We led a unique life, and after the War, we dispersed and set up home in countries all around the world. One day, we will no longer exist.

The street map led her away from the city centre. Now she was close to the Canidrome racetrack. The Communists had taken twenty four thousand Chinese there to meet their death: Kuomintang officials, teachers, Christian churchmen, non-Communist union leaders, property owners, newspaper workers, factory managers and students.

Jolienta turned into Huangpilu.

The sky clung. It was right on top of her.

At Sichuanzhonglu, sweat ran off her brow.

A woman of similar age was running towards her.

"Gee, you look like the archetypal tourist," the woman said cringing.

"And exactly what do you think you look like?" Jolienta replied.

The two women threw away their reserve, hurried along the road and sped into The Golden Crane. In the sanctity of its bistro, the American ordered coffee with cream. Jolienta preferred tea with milk. They ate scones with jam and cream. Afterwards, they set off in opposite directions, stabilized by their own brand of whiteness, never to meet again.

With renewed courage, Jolienta walked into the Hongkou district—the safe-haven for World War II Jewish refugees. The Bund gave way to the sea. The light was a bright grey over the estuary. Gulls circled junks and ships. Along the sidewalk, people played chess, dominoes and mahjong, and it was true—people did take birds out for a walk in cages.

She looked over the bay and up into the grey sky. A man, a giant of a man, stepped out from behind a hedge.

"Hello. You American," the man said as if stating a fact.

"Bu shi meigou ren. Shi ying gou ren."

"Ahh, shou. Shou zhong gou ren ma?"

"Shou yidiar."

"I live in building over there," the man said. He pointed at a solitary tenement in the distance.

She located it and nodded.

"No good. No toilet," he continued. "Open pit in basement. Many fly."

"No toilet?"

"What is your name?" the man said, enunciating each word with care. "Ah, teeth very white. You big and strong."

He grinned. "You marry me. I go England."

"Excuse me. I must go now."

Jolienta hurried back along the roads and streets. The coach was in the same spot. The driver was clutching the wheel and staring into space. Jolienta walked along the gangway and smiled. No one responded. The engine started up. Mr Wu was absorbed with the view from his window. Lynn was writing in her diary.

How unresponsive everyone is.

"You kept the whole coach waiting," the nearest brother said from under his Panama. "Your appalling manners. You selfish, bad-mannered young woman."

"I do apologize, Benjamin. I don't have a watch."

"Buy one then, you ignorant twit." The brother crammed his handkerchief into his jacket pocket.

Jolienta stumbled into her seat. "Peggy, what time is it?"

"Three thirty-four."

"You mean he's yelling at me because of four minutes?"

"Yep."

"Just who do you think you are, talking to me like that? What makes you think you can insult me over four goddamn minutes? You stuck up piece of . . ."

She stood up. Benjamin's eyes widened. Her left fist was bunched up. He ducked.

"Shit. Oh Peggy, he was wearing a priest's collar."

"There you go," said Peggy, "stick with us Yanks."

In Hong Kong, they . . .

JOLIENTA PEERED OUT OF THE CABIN WINDOW; the plane was leaving the mainland and heading for Hong Kong. A wistfulness came over her. Guilin had been the most beautiful of all. She had been left speechless by the limestone peaks rising from the waters, children wading in the river, shouting, *Hallo, hallo, you buy*, cormorants perched on the edges of boats ready to please their masters, and butterflies had floated on the scent of camphor under a turquoise sky. Everything had glowed. In Hangzhou, she had hidden in a forest of bamboo and witnessed a rare sight—Chinese men laughing with abandon, playing musical instruments and practicing archery. Jolienta suddenly realized that she was afraid of what she might find when the plane reached its destination.

The plane climbed down, curved over tin shacks and mammoth tenements and dipped for Kai Tak Airport. It lowered its wheels onto a single strip jutting out into a bay and halted at the water's edge, in front of sampans, boats, ferries and skyscrapers. A new driver arrived and drove the group to the hotel, the last on the itinerary. Mr Wu, Lynn and the Americans said goodbye in the lobby and left. The remainder of the group found their luggage and disappeared into lifts and air-conditioned corridors.

No more complaints about split suitcases then. No more petty squabbles, or excessive banquets, for the foreign devil. No more panoramas of elegant pagodas or doting families of one child with rosy-red cheeks—no Peggy either. I will miss the Americans.

She gathered up her luggage. An extra thirty-five dollars had paid for a single room, Room forty-seven. Anything to avoid another encounter with Madame Thierry.

Here it is. No frills.

She lay down on the bed and touched the headboard with the tips of her fingers. A trick of the mind defied loneliness as it coiled around her bones. A net curtain waved towards the heat and traffic of Nathan Road.

"Nathan Rd? Isn't that where Mother spotted her dentist? He was marching along the road—she saw him—started jumping up and down and yelling at the top of her voice, *Mr Yamazaki! Mr Yamazaki!* She was too young to understand that the Japanese were invading Kowloon and her dentist was armed with a rifle and bayonet."

Jolienta closed her eyes and tried to concentrate. "Tomorrow morning, the group will be gone and I will find budget accommodation, acclimatize, and I will find Peace Avenue—to look for, to hope for, to find any remnant of Alvege.

"There's nothing wrong with talking to yourself, you know," she said to the room. "Besides the English didn't want to communicate with me and Lynn lost her voice trying to answer their endless questions.

"And Mr Wu walked off with his presents.

"I hope I see the Americans again.

"I hope I made the right decision, travelling the length of China, adjusting to the country and the culture before arriving at the place of my forebears. Or maybe I'm a coward, afraid I won't find anything at Peace Avenue, and in fact, I've been delaying the inevitable.

"Well, it seemed the right thing to do.

"Better than parachuting my way in like some numbskull tourist."

Jolienta rolled off the bed and straightened up. "Someone's at the door."

Three women were waiting in the corridor—the headmistress with the inflamed nose, a teacher with a helmet of white hair who never responded to friendly overtures, and a third woman, a woman who reminded her of a cigarette.

The trio filed in, arranged themselves at the end of the bed and waited for their elected speaker to begin. Jolienta ignored the pre-amble, puffed up her pillows and lay back. Here we go, she thought, should be interesting.

"We wanted to say, er, maybe we misjudged you, Coleen," the headmistress said, folding her arms. "Perhaps we were a bit hard on you."

Jolienta gazed at the woman's red swollen nose.

"Mind you, you should know better than to travel with a bad back, shouldn't you?" the headmistress added.

"And what with all that extra padding you carry," the cigarette woman chimed.

The cigarette woman patted her polyester midriff with a series of light taps and invited Jolienta to look down at her own belly. Jolienta obliged; if the cigarette woman was right, gravity had kindly flattened her stomach to disprove the woman's assessment.

"We wish you well in your search for roots," the helmet-clad woman said. "We really do hope you find your ancestral home."

Jolienta sighed.

"We do hope you find your ancestral home," the women echoed.

The three women waited for forgiveness.

They said goodbye and filed out of the room.

Jolienta sprang to the floor and issued a high-kick.

The sun baked on the pavements below. Office workers were out and about for a dim sum lunch. Nathan Road, known as the Golden Mile for its ability to suck money out of tourists, was crammed with hotels, bars, nightclubs, restaurants and shops selling watches and hi-fi goods.

The heat.

The humidity.

The heat.

She lay on the bed. The crane strutted out from beneath its leafy canopy, and sang, sang out to the heavens. Jolienta flew through the window and over Nine Dragon Hills, sped back along Nathan Road to the tip of the peninsula, hovered over Victoria Harbour with its pod of pink dolphins bobbing in the water, floated over bird colonies, floated over Stonecutter's Island. The noonday gun boomed. On the Peak, hibiscus grew in abundance. Over Stanley, she scoured the terrain for any remains of Valda, sailed over more islands, swooped high and low, flipped upside down and turned upright again.

On Lamma Island, sea turtles bred. Kau Yi Chau was deserted. Sunshine Island was once a refuge for opium addicts, and Hei Ling Chau had once been a leper colony. Cheung Chau was all pretty lanes and fishing boats. Lantau was mountains, monasteries and temples.

The crane descended and scuttled into the shade. Jolienta slept through the day and into the night.

Ten-thirty a.m. The net curtain was limp. No breeze. There was a note on the carpet, a goodbye limerick from one of the brothers. Jolienta grinned; the spat in Shanghai had been laid to rest.

"It's too late for breakfast now," she decided. "The group will have gone to catch the flight back to London. The yellow and magenta blouse will do."

She tied both ends around the waist and into a bow.

Nathan Road was hot hot hot.

The guidebook said: 'Chungking Mansions, dirt-cheap legendary haunt for backpackers. Mixed dorm. Beds for as little as ten dollars a night. A high-rise block of low-budget motels, shops and curry houses situated in Nathan Road, and if you are strapped for cash, you can always audition for a Kung Fu movie.'

"Excuse me, mister, which way to Chungking Mansions?"

"Keep walkin'. Ya'll see it on the same side."

The backpacker pointed.

"When ya go in, ya'll see a couple of lifts marked A and E. Ya want A Block. Don't get in the wrong lift now; the place is a goddamn labyrinth. Watch out for the bedbugs. They bite."

The man strode away, rucksack on his shoulders.

Oh, to be a seasoned traveller, big, burly and unafraid.

He's right. Chungking Mansions is on the same side. See its frontage, the row of Chinese and English letters. CHUNGKING MANSIONS the words say, as bold as brass. What was it he said? *When ya go in, ya'll see a couple of lifts marked A and E. Ya want A Block. Don't get in the wrong lift now or ya'll get eaten by bugs.*

Jolienta climbed the steps into the building and was confronted by a vast interior of stalls, vendors and shoppers layered up to the sky. A glance to the left found travellers waiting in a square vestibule of four lifts. Instructions on the wall listed thousands of businesses. She heard some travellers mumble "A block" and shuffled in behind them.

They were on the eleventh floor.

"Bed twelve dollars," a Chinese receptionist said.

Dirt cheap. The guidebook wasn't lying.

I can tell you, it's a relief to have secured a low-cost bed.

Not as bad as I expected either. The showers and toilets are revolting; muddy shoeprints everywhere. The walls and sinks have matted hair on them. I won't wash. That's all there is to it. I'll brush my teeth and get by with toiletries. The dorm itself is OK. These sheets are clean.

If I stuff my pillow under the top sheet, everyone will know the bunk is taken.

My stomach's churning.

The canteen was one floor down. Moisture trickled down the walls of the canteen and circumnavigated specks of mould. Postcards of people looking for travelling companions or fast ways to earn a dollar, or offers of massage and quests to reunite, were pinned to a cork notice board. Behind the food counter, grey gruel, as well egg and bacon, was on offer.

A couple of guys laughed. "Go for the coffee and biscuit. They aren't congealed."

"I will. Thanks. I'll be over to join you in a moment." Oh, they're Canadian. The pin in their sweatshirts.

An Italian woman pulled up a chair and lit a cigarette.

They're talking about going to one of the floating restaurants one evening, this evening or the next, and would I like to come too? Jolienta gulped at the coffee. "I'm in. Count me in," she said.

A few lone travellers were sat with their heads buried inside newspapers—young men in their thirties, deep in thought. It was obvious they wanted to set themselves apart. Keep-away-from-me was the message they sent out. One of them was very handsome, which reminded her of Polish Stan and of Peckham and of Tom and Kris. He was fair-haired with bristles on his chin. He suddenly got up, banged his chair on the floor and stomped out. The Canadians and the Italian woman snorted into their mugs. Puzzled by him, Jolienta said goodbye to her companions and left for Nathan Road.

The park on the other side was Kowloon Tsui Park and would take her away from Alvege, and from there, a side road would take her even further away and into Canton Road. I can't go straight there, can I? Do I really want all of my hopes and dreams crushed on my first day here?

Canton Road led to Yau Ma Tei, a typhoon anchorage crammed

with sampans and fishing boats. Immaculate children in white shirts ran along the gangways, shouting "Yum cha!"

They must be boat people, she thought. Hakka or Tanka, but I'm not going to go up to them and ask, am I? The smell is dense. Sandalwood and rotting meat? Burnt oil. Garbage and pollution.

Eyes were drilling into her. She turned. Laan jai flexed their tattoos and stared at the kwai loh. Sunglasses masked their eyes, but not their intentions. Beyond them, a thousand squares of laundry flapped in the breeze. A cha chaan teng was close by, had customers outside under green parasols. She sat down and ordered bean curd soup. Safe again.

The waiter appeared surprised at her choice of menu. She could understand why—the cubes of curd kept slipping through her chopsticks and splashed back into the bowl. An old woman chuckled with delight, held her bowl up to her gummy mouth, and began to shovel curd in. To finish, the old lady tipped the bowl into her face and drank the remaining liquid.

Jolienta followed the example and when she'd eaten enough, dried her blouse with a napkin, bade the woman farewell, and squinted at the sun. It was as hot as the previous day.

The guidebook indicated that Peace Avenue was parallel to the Kowloon Canton Railway and was close to the hotel she and the group had stayed in the night before. What are the chances of that? she wondered. So close? Chung-king Mansions is close by too.

She arrived at the corner of Peace Avenue and Waterloo Avenue, the place of her forebears, stopped at a crumbling step, and waited for the beat of her heart to slow down. An empty rickshaw was being pulled along the road. The thud of her heart quickened. After an eternity of not knowing about the past, she needed to collect herself, prepare herself, prepare herself for nothing, prepare herself for nothing more than a deep-seated wish generated by a stupid stupid artist with a fanciful disposition and the nose of a collie dog. She could hear her mother now . . . *Whuhaha, whuhaha. Stupid Jolly. Run over in Peckham. Spent the money on nothing. Whuhaha. Stupid Jolly. Nose like a collie dog.* The step embraced her. Her hands cupped her face and allowed her eyes to explore.

The avenues were on a pillow of land, home to a line of Portuguese villas—grand houses with open verandahs of decorative arches and twisting pillars. Palm trees. Elegant. At one end of the pillow, steps had been carved out of a chalk hillside. She climbed them and stopped at the nearest villa. The door's nameplate said Five and the word *Alvege* was engraved on it in thin curly letters.

That's impossible.

Suddenly, she felt afraid and dithered. She jumped down onto a neat lawn and began to scour the premises—guava tree with fruit rotting on the ground—dilapidated carnival horse on hind legs, pole coming out of the spine, palm trees and potted plants, the sound of children.

She had to follow the happy voices and saw an elderly man surrounded by young children. He was dressed completely in white except for a bowtie, which was black, and he was holding onto a lively toddler. The left side of his body sagged. A stroke perhaps, which might account for the severe expression he wore on his face. The children, six in all, were dark-skinned, dressed in white, some in nappies, and they were trying to leapfrog each other. The sound of a tennis ball being hit, voices in English, and voices in another language, floated over the roof. Jolienta turned to the children. They'd gone. The old man had gone too. The lawn was devoid of life.

She ran down the chalk steps and looked up at Five Peace Avenue. Three nuns clad in white floated along the verandah, shooing a line of schoolchildren. White sun danced on her eyelids. A shadow moved across, removed the hot sun and replaced it with a chill and wetness. She opened her eyes. The crumbling step had gone. An old man was hosing down concrete steps behind her. She stood up; the place she was in—air conditioners, bamboo scaffolding, buckled pipes, alien contraptions, flaked window frames, washing lines and balconies, rose into a steep dank alleyway. Crates and bags of fermenting garbage were wedged between a lamppost and a wall.

The old man banged his trolley down the steps and was almost upon her. She ran into the sun and could not believe what was before her: a modern thoroughfare. A doctor's surgery was next to Modification Specialists: Honda, Toyota. The Kowloon Canton Railway had gone from humble grassy verge, wire fence and track, to smart green elevations for commuters, parking restrictions, bus stops and parked cars; people were going about their day walking past the Eternal Rich Property and the Hong Kong Doggie House.

*   *   *

The gangway was lowered, ropes were secured, the bell was rung, the gate opened and passengers swarmed onto the ferry—fifty cents lower deck, seventy cents upper deck. The sea of dark hair and dark skin reminded her of Shanghai. The western clothes and blasé attitude did not. International cruise-liners, pleasure launches, green and cream ferries and barges jostled in the waters of Victoria Harbour.

Cheeki said the climate was cooler on the Peak and that it had been the place to live ever since the British moved in and Tai-Pans built summerhouses. Dear Cheeki—she enjoyed going to the one and only café at the top to drink milky coffee and watch humming birds collect nectar.

Four dollars each way. The Peak Tram started out from behind the Hilton and crept up the hillside. The café was there, a small red café defying time. Jolienta positioned herself among the flowers, sipped a café au lait and watched the birds, green and blue. They hovered over the hibiscus and pink orchids. The nearest bird wasn't afraid. It continued to hum, pretended to be a big fat bee. In fact, it was showing off. Its tongue was long and grooved; bushy hairs extracted sugary foam from the stamens.

Now to find the highest spot.

Here it is, one thousand three hundred feet above sea level. When the plane landed, I didn't realize Kowloon was a peninsula separate from Hong Kong or that Hong Kong was an island. And I didn't know Macau was forty-five miles across the South China Sea. I imagined these places as one piece of land easy to get to.

The Japs marched into Kowloon. The British, Canadians and the Indians were outnumbered and the Brits surrendered on Christmas Day. The Sino-Japanese War had already sent mainland Chinese spilling into Macau. On the day of the Japanese invasion, who knows what the residents felt—the symbol of the red sun buzzing in the sky, bombs dropping past their windows? The Macanese were spared the worst of it, except there were plenty of unlucky ones like Valda.

The tram crept down the shadowy hill. King Prawn in Ginger and Garlic beckoned. The waiter, neat in black and white attire, smirked at the British woman dining alone.

*   *   *

Someone had responded to her postcard on the canteen notice board—*Travelling companion for a weekend in Macau? Count me in, slut-face.* The day slowed down. Late night dinner with strangers on a floating restaurant no longer seemed like a good idea. She brushed her teeth and crushed a cockroach. A man stepped up to a urinal. She hurried out, put earrings and dollars under her pillow, unfastened her sandals and pulled the bed sheet up to her chin.

Mixed dorm?

I'm not taking my clothes off.

No, thank you.

Ten o' clock and Hong Kong danced on the walls. Jolienta turned away from the flickering lights. An insect crawled by. Blood pumped up and down its cellophane body. It was about the same size as a British earwig, but jellybean in shape. She buttoned up her blouse to keep the marauder at bay and tucked the ends into her jeans. She pulled the sheet over her ears.

Someone switched the dorm light on—and then off again. Time to sleep. The door opened and the light was switched back on. Awake again. It was the Mexican, a street-wise man with shoulder-length black hair. Very handsome.

He unbuttoned his check shirt and brazenly invited her to inspect his torso. She turned over to hide her face. His jeans fell to the floor. Coins fell out, clattered and rolled across the floor. He turned the light off, clambered into bed and sent his bunk clanking into hers.

Jolienta grabbed at the cotton sheet. It held her ears, her eyes and her breath, and it was stifling. Love . . . when will I find Love? When will I find it? she asked herself.

She tried to push the question away. She tried to be rid of the bugs, bugs crawling over her body, hot and sweaty, sucking at blood and nestling in the folds of her clothes. She begged the crane to appear. The Mother Crane strode through wetland, came up close, its red crown and snowy white feathers tipped in black. It fixed a yellow eye on her, lowered its gaze and began to pick out the insects. The Mother Crane moved closer and closer, drowning her in the yellow of its iris. Safe. Safe. Jolienta pushed downward and began to stroke, stroke methodically. Her body arched and sank.

The Mexican jolted upright and twisted his neck. The sheet blocked out his angry face.

Dawn. The noises of Nathan Road started up. The door handle

rattled. She dared to look. The Mexican was standing there simmering. He was fiddling with the door handle, rattling it impatiently. He stared at her, pretended to close the door and glowered at her. He was waiting for her to follow him.

He wants me to follow him.

The Mexican glared until the whites of his eyes protruded. He let go of the door and sloped off.

He's waiting for me in the shower! Her heart pounded. She got up and emptied her locker. Fucked and throttled in the shower? Left for dead among the footprints? No, thank you.

*　　*　　*

The YMCA was supposed to be clean and not claustrophobic like Chungking Mansions. Dorms were separate sex and cost twenty-five dollars. Jolienta locked the tartan case away, happy to have overcome the latest problem, and decided a celebration was in order—street food. She hoped and prayed that the haam sup lo's snake soup and lotus seed bun did not result in a loose stomach. In fact, the broth, served with lime leaves and slithers of mushroom in a plastic beaker, tasted of chicken and ginger, and resulted in no adverse effects. The bun was stuffed with a salty egg yolk and tasted of caramel. Delicious.

A stroll in an easterly direction passed The Peninsular Hotel, a queue of Rolls-Royces and an arcade of Gucci. Chatham Road led to Tsimshatsui East and more hotels and more office blocks. Back in Canton Road, jade sellers spread their wares over the pavements.

Later, at the YMCA, Jolienta discovered the dorm was booked out to one other female only, a young woman called Homani, who was completely at ease with her wit and sense of self. The young woman said she lived in Pimlico by the Tate Gallery and had begun a romance with an Englishman on the way to Hong Kong.

"He's mad about me, but he doesn't realize it yet," she said.

The Bela Vista

FANCY FINDING ALVEGE LIKE THAT and my great grandfather too. I wonder who the children were? Jolienta closed her eyes and turned on the shower. A large pool of water gathered at her feet. It became a large pond, a small lake. Ripples eddied to the edges of the pond. Chimps scooped up water and sipped. Larger chimps gathered around, drank the water or waded in. Apes appeared, groomed each other, drank, splashed, played. A bright light shone; a deity rose from the waters to greet all living creatures.

The next morning, after coffee and a bread roll with apricot jam in the canteen, it was time to go search of a ticket for Macau. She had been fretting over the arrangements for weeks due to the weight and significance of the visit and was armed with pataca, worth less than the Hong Kong dollar.

Passport? Yes. Money? In two currencies. Sketch book, one dress, underwear, earrings, necklaces, toiletries, guidebook.

The hydrofoil hummed into docking position. She folded her jacket into a neat shape and watched with interest. The entrance opened. The Keep-away-from-me Man from Chungking Mansions sped past and settled himself at the far end of the vessel. She tried not to look. His presence made her tremble. His stance spoke of business—odd, because he was dressed in jeans and T-shirt, and they clashed with his smart leather shoes.

The hydrofoil rumbled across the sea. The horizon was clear.

The guidebook recommended the Bela Vista. It looked excellent in the book. The Bela Vista was over a hundred years old and had started out under French and then British management, and by the nineteen-forties, it had become a centre for Hong Kong and Kowloon Portuguese refugees. In the fifties, the hotel was sold on to three Chinese women. One of them, Paulo Chung, disappeared during the Cultural Revolution, and another manager, Adriao Pinto Marques, died in his rocking chair on the verandah.

The hydrofoil bumped into the Macau terminal. The Keep-away-from-me Man catapulted through the gate and became a pinprick on the horizon. The seafront, coated in a haze, was heavenly—she had expected hordes of tourists, not a vista of sea and palm trees.

The hotel could be seen straightaway from the promenade, and as the guidebook said, had *a faded air of colonial decadence* about it. From the outside, it was a pleasing sandy yellow with wooden shutters at each window and each balcony had an ornamental parapet painted cream.

A man and woman were walking towards her. "Darling, the doors jam, the shower dribbles. You may as well give up. Thank heavens, the loo flushes."

"Never mind, Honeybun, we're here for the casinos, remember? We'll get dressed up. You can wear your jewellery. After that, we'll have champagne and gaze at the stars."

He put his arm around her. Jolienta walked into the hotel. The interior was decorated with rows of China elephants and the dining room doors were wide open with some forty people banging on the table demanding "more wine" to accompany their "roast suckling pig". Some broke out into song.

Jolienta pretended to look at newspapers in a display rack. One side of the room was belting out *America, the Beautiful.* The other side responded with *O Canada.* Another table replied with a rendition of *A Portuguêsa.* A couple, in crumpled linen sang, *God*

Save the Queen and everyone stood to attention. Finally, they lifted up their glasses and roared, "Yum Sing!"

The proprietor appeared and explained it was a Macanese encontro, a new annual event. He promised to find her a room with a view. "You are British," he said.

"Will the Macanese be here again tomorrow, sir?"

"I don't know. Senhorita dos Remédios? Your face and passport say British, you have the face of an English rose, but you have a traditional Portuguese name."

"My mother's Portuguese. She was brought up in Hong Kong and Macau."

"Ah, I see it around the eyes . . . green, and you have sparkling white teeth. Beautiful. What a beautiful smile. Breakfast is a buffet between six and nine o'clock. Senhorita may come across the Macanese again tomorrow. They are very happy to be here. Senhorita, I trust your stay will be pleasant."

The room and view were wonderful, the right atmosphere for romance, or even a slutty weekend. She unpacked and washed the white dress and hung it over a chair on the balcony. By coincidence, the Keep-away-from-me Man was sitting on a sea wall, exchanging items with another man. He lit a cigarette and stalked off.

Jolienta retraced her steps to where he had been sitting and continued along Rua de Raia do Bom Parto. This took her to Avenida de Almeida Ribeiro, which led to the Camoes Gardens. A few men were playing checkers in the shade. Nearby, the ruins of Sao Paulo stood. She'd seen photographs of the ruins and knew what to expect. The cafés sold Portuguese as well as Chinese food. It was different to Hong Kong. More Mediterranean.

Uncle Fufu said there was a family shrine in Macau and that we were all entitled to be buried there. Exactly where to look was the problem. The closest church was Saint Anthony's. If she explored the churches in a logical way, Saint Michael's was next, followed by Saint Dominic, San Domingos, Saint Augustine, Saint Joseph's and finally the Church of Saint Lawrence. Gravestones, such as—

> CAPTAIN SIR HUMPHREY LE
> FLEMING SENHOUSE SENIOR
> OFFICER IN COMMAND OF THE
> BRITISH FLEET IN THE CHINA
> SEAS. DIED ON BOARD H.M.S.
> BLENHEIM ON THE 13TH JUNE
> 1841 FROM THE EFFECTS OF
> FEVER CONTRACTED DURING THE
> ZEALOUS PERFORMANCE OF HIS
> ARDUOUS DUTIES AT THE CAPTURE
> OF THE HEIGHTS OF CANTON,
> MAY 1841

paid heed to the Opium Wars. There were gravestones of Dutch Captains too—from earlier years—DENG APRIL 1767, OVERLEEDEN MACAO, DEN 22 JULY 1821. The Dutch navy had tried to take on the British and grab what the Portuguese had such was the importance of Macau at the mouth of the Pearl River. There were Chinese graves too, of faded pinks and whites—small white lockers with photographs of the deceased and a thin vase for flowers. The result was a wall of poetry as to the ephemera of life.

The churches of Macau were not yielding any clues. The name 'Dos Remédios' cropped up on the front of lockers, but none had a first name she recognized. Dos Remédios was a traditional name as the proprietor had said, and it was also a popular one.

Jolienta went back to the hotel and set the alarm clock for nine o'clock. She may as well have a siesta and try out one of the casinos in the evening. In thirty-six hours, she would leave Macau and Hong Kong forever. The likelihood of returning to south China was remote. Why she felt this way and with such certainty, was a peculiarity. Jolienta lay down and stared at the sky through the open balcony doors and tried to figure it all out.

Dreamtime arrived, a welcome companion.

"Fufu, you look well-fed?"

Fufu stopped in his tracks.

'I chose the wrong route,' he said catching sight of his aunt. He straightened his tie and stood to attention.

Cheeki took a swipe at him.

"Yes, Aunty?" he said obediently.

"I haven't seen you for weeks. Been getting drunk? Gambling?"

"No Aunty."

He blinked and held his breath—a line of thin figures, armed with bowls and pans, were waiting for the priests to open up. 'No children in sight. I am no longer a child. One day, I will have to make my own way in the world.'

A white dove started in the sky.

"How we would run and throw up firecrackers, and POW, Daddy would shoot down the doves. 'What fun. I miss him.'

"Fufu!" Cheeki barked, arms on hips in polka dot dress with silver belt, "is it true you went gambling at Happy Valley?"

'No, Aunty, it's not. But they can't keep us cooped up in Macau forever. Eventually the status quo will return and we'll be able to eat in any restaurant once again."

"Ahhh, pig's trotter, hot and spicy. Wah, mangoes from Manila," Cheeki said.

"Stop it, Aunty."

The line of thin figures was staring at Cheeki, but Aunty didn't give a damn about what anyone else thought; she hadn't been put on the planet to worry about riff-raff.

'Tomorrow, the casino, to increase my winnings,' Fufu decided. 'Then I will leave this nightmare behind and travel the world.'

Jolienta woke up, showered and put on the white dress. It was still damp. She added the faithful black jacket, remarkably pristine considering the travel it had endured. She clipped on fake pearl earrings, added lipstick, mascara, perfume and put on the coral necklace.

The guidebook had described a number of casinos in Macau. The Macau Palace Casino was a floating barge adjacent to a walkway not far from the Bela Vista. Its proximity to the ferry terminal made it convenient for a last minute run at the tables before the last ferry returned to Hong Kong.

She made the walk to the casino. The sky and sea were beautiful. A muscular doorman ran his eyes over her as she entered the premises. Inside, couples in evening dress were floating up and down a spiral staircase of plush red carpet. The ceiling bore giant chandeliers. Jolienta wondered if there was a grand piano anywhere with a pianist in pyjamas at the keyboard, waggling his toes.

The main casino was on the second floor. On one side of the room were baccarat tables, three unused, two blackjack game tables, one dai-siu table and rows of slot machines. The Keep-away-from-me Man, dressed in tuxedo, placed a bet and looked right through Jolienta. A blonde woman sidled up to him and planted a magenta lipstick kiss on his cheek. Jolienta blushed and hid behind an elderly couple. She hurried out; he made her tremble every time she saw him.

The next morning, she paid the bill. The proprietor was nowhere to be seen and the dining room was empty. No Macanese people. Tinned grapefruit. Toast and scrambled eggs with a slice of grilled bacon and buttered mushrooms. Coffee with cream.

The hydrofoil left on time.

No sign of Homani in the dorm or in the canteen. Jolienta hurried to the Hong Kong Records Office in Tsui Ping Road. Talk about cutting it fine, she thought, leaving it to the last minute.

Mrs McKeever, in cashmere twinset and a thin row of pearls, led Jolienta to a young Chinese man, who showed her how to magnify paper clippings and view them on a screen. Jolienta searched for 'Alvege', 'Peace Avenue', 'School in Peace Avenue', and scanned for 'Dos Remédios'. Nothing showed up.

Well, that's it then. I failed. Well, half failed. Well, what did I expect anyway? I'll go and see Mrs McKeever on the way out.

"Mrs McKeever, I wasn't able to find anything about Five Peace Avenue. It's a shame. I fly back tomorrow. My mother has never been able to talk about the past. I so wanted to find out something about Alvege, and how it came to be a school after the War."

"Interesting. Number Five Peace Avenue was situated in Ho Mun Tin," Mrs McKeever said, "a substantial plot of land was originally purchased in the early nineteen hundreds by a Portuguese man called Francisco Paulo de Vasconcelos Soares, Miss Dos Remedios. He was a prominent local bill and bullion broker. At the time of the purchase, the area was mainly paddy-fields and considered too remote for settlement, but eventually he developed the land and became known as the Father of Ho Mun Tin. In fact, the avenues were named by him; Soares, Emma and Julia Avenue were named after his own family. He was a great lover of plants and flowers, and introduced many plants from other parts of the world.

"From nineteen thirty-seven to the end of the Pacific War, hc undertook the difficult role of honorary consul of Portugal in Hong Kong. In fact, he is said to have offered up his Kowloon home to shelter stranded Macanese and interceded with the Japanese regarding food, shelter and travel documents."

"Mrs McKeever, one of my great aunts, Valda, must have got stranded, because she died in Stanley Prison, alone, cut off from the rest of the family. I find it confusing. My cousin said the Macanese had it easy, but Valda died in dreadful circumstances."

"Dreadful indeed. A dreadful time you refer to. Some Macanese were caught up in prisoner of war camps set aside for the British and other soldiers such as the Canadians and Indians."

"My mother said she was in a POW camp. I didn't believe her. She's the only one in the family to have said that. I thought she was exaggerating, but after what you say, well, you've got me thinking."

Mrs McKeever held her tongue. Seven thousand British soldiers and civilians had been put into prisoner-of-war or internment camps at Sham Sui Po and Stanley Internment Camp. Famine, malnutrition and sickness had been rampant. Rape too. A lot of rape. The Chinese were beheaded and used as bayonette-practice by the Japanese. This Valda could easily have become ill, been raped, or starved to death. Or all three. Being Macanese was never a guarantee of survival. Accounts of people selling their children and even cannibalism! Macau's streets were littered with bodies. There were mass burials on Taipa, up to four hundred bodies a day.

Jolienta picked up Mrs McKeever's thoughts: *Sham Sui Po and Stanley Internment Camp?* She wanted to scream. Valda had been exposed to all of the worst dangers.

Valda were you raped? Cheeki said you were of a delicate disposition. In the photo she gave me, you clutched a doll and wore a bow in your hair. Did you die of a heart attack? Did that save you from worse happenings?

Mass burials on Taipa? No wonder no one could find you.

'The poor dear looks miserable,' Mrs McKeever said to herself.

Mrs McKeever, you are a kind woman. *The poor dear looks miserable.*

"Francisco is buried at a catholic cemetery in Happy Valley."

"Really?"

"Which part of the UK are you from, dear?"

"I'm from the north originally, but live in London now. It's the only place to be if you're an artist. I should have moved out years ago. It's been awful."

Mrs McKeever tilted her head to the side in a show of sympathy. "The north, you say?"

Jolienta squirmed. Mrs McKeever already knew her origins, what with her singsong voice, up and down, up and down; a cross between John Lennon and Minnie Mouse is what Kris used to say.

"I'm from the Wirral, Miss Dos Remedios. Would you believe that? Wait a moment; I have something for you."

Mrs McKeever disappeared. She reappeared and thrust sheets of paper into her hands. "I'm not allowed to do this," she whispered, "however, these photocopies represent the original mortgage deeds to Five Peace Avenue . . . the place you call 'Alvege'.

Jolienta looked at the papers. They were dated the twenty-second of December nineteen-nineteen. Curly black-inked entries, dates, and signatures, had been added by the Land Officer and overseen by Solicitors, Deacon Looker Deacon & Harston of Hong Kong. The words were also typeset in Chinese. The first page said:

FURTHER CHARGE
CECILIA MARIA DOS REMÉDIOS
—to—
THE CHINA PROVIDENT LOAN AND MORTGAGE
COMPANY LIMITED
MORTGAGE
—of—
Kowloon Inland lots Nos.1336 and 1337
situate at Ho Mun Tin in the Dependency
of Kowloon and colony of Hong Kong to
secure $16,000.00 and interest.

Registered at the Land Office by
Memorial No: *70145* on *Wednesday*
the *twentyfourth* day of *December* 1919 at *3 PM.*

The second and third page was an Indenture and contained lengthy paragraphs of legal information.

"This is incredible, Mrs McKeever. I will treasure these. I'll frame them."

"Miss Dos Remedios, you might also read City of Broken Promises by Austin Coates. It will give you a wider understanding of early Macau. Most of the big bookstores in Hong Kong have it. Coates—an interesting man—a British civil servant and connected to the East through his service to the Royal Air Force Intelligence during the Second World War. He went on to work for the Hong Kong Government in the New Territories. Later as a magistrate, he gained insight into Chinese customs and character, and applied Chinese law to solve many cases. Eventually, he settled in Hong Kong and was the guest of many a prominent Asian including Mahatma Gandhi.

"At one time, City of Broken Promises was staged in Hong Kong and San Diego. I recommend the book. Not a literary masterpiece, but insightful and enjoyable.

"You say you stayed at the Bela Vista Hotel. Did you know that during the war it was a center for Macanese refugees? It had well-equipped kitchens, you see, and meals from the Bela Vista were distributed to smaller centres around Macau."

Leytonstone

'I'M GONNA DO ME GARDEN UP LIKE SHE 'AS IT. I'm gonna put cornices on the walls under me ceiling, I'm gonna save me money up, bit-by-bit, ta-give-ta my boy, Johnny. It cracks me up that that bleedin' bitch—the effing ex—won't let me see 'im. She won't 'ave nuffin to do wiv me. Bitch. An' that bleedin' cow upstairs. Stupid cow. Always polite. What's her effing name again? Makes me sick, lookin' down 'er nose at me as she walks in and out. She can't wait to get through the bleedin' door an' shut me out.

'She knows—yer know.

'I'd fack 'er if I 'ad 'arf the chance.

'Nice lookin'. Nice tits.

'A good arse to grab 'old of. Yearse.'

He looked out of his bay window and into the front garden, an orchestra of pinks, purples and blues against a backdrop of white bell-shaped flowers. "Bleedin' cow. Mine's all weeds, nettles an' all. Even if I 'ad a lawnmower . . . I went an' landscaped it weird, didant I? A bleedin' 'elter-skelter of a hill is what I made. Didant I!"

Rain touched the window. The garden below was blooming. Her routine was back to normal. Jolienta ignored the rant, ignored the rage filtering through the floorboards. Since connecting with Cheeki and visiting China, she felt more whole and more real, more and more, and that was all that mattered—

228

and the pursuit of art. Her mission statement was shaping up nicely too—her infallible theory was being rolled out.

"I'd fack yer if I 'ad 'arf the chance," Bert yelled.

"I know," Jolienta replied.

An image needed to be spilled out. Something big. Something meaningful. She positioned a length of canvas over a stretcher, injected a staple halfway along the side of it pinning the canvas to it, took care to pull the material on either side of the staple to keep the centre of it almost taut but not too tight. Her hands worked their way towards each corner.

Is the canvas smooth? Good. No creases. Keep the corners tidy. No bulges. Ready for a coat of primer. If I'm going to use expensive colours then I must avoid putting pressure in the middle with my clumsy brush strokes. I don't want an imprint of the bar in the middle.

The canvas, four foot high by five foot six, was left to dry. A second coat of primer was applied, thicker than the first coat, and brushed on in the opposite direction.

"Been on a slow boat to effing China, Chinky Chungking?" Bert shouted up to his ceiling.

China? Chungking Mansions? How does he know that?

The canvas lay on the floor. The primer was left to dry.

The Coldharbour Lane etching and the tyre shop painting will be my guide.

Dilute vermillion was poured onto the dry canvas. A puddle of red was brushed out to each corner. A clean rag and deft of hand produced an outline of figures, architectural detail and shadows—a trick courtesy of Courbet, who often began with a dark wash of colour, wiped in his composition and then worked his way up to lighter colours.

The figures will be half-way whole, half-way real, Jolienta decided. Dilute viridian green picked out shadows and gave an outline to the mother and child. The child developed blonde hair.

229

The woman grew armour. The reds became more and more sonorous. Jolienta stopped to catch her breath—painting downward on the floor over such a size was strenuous; her arms ached.

"I'm gowin' orf me bleedin' 'ead down 'ere," Bert screamed. "That tart down the road. That blonde tart, she's always knockin' on the bleedin' door asking for a fag, an' 'arf the time she's pissed out of her bleedin' 'ead. Mind you, they're best when they're a bit mental, because you've got more chance of getting yer bleedin' leg over!"

He ran up and down his corridor. He banged an object against the walls. A frying pan?

She returned to the painting.

Bert attacked the ceiling with a frying pan. Bish! Bash!

Jolienta increased the volume on her cassette player. Spanish guitar drowned out the volume of his voice, but not the resonance of his anxieties.

"It's hard getting' back on yer feet," he cried.

She tried not to listen, tried to concentrate on the mother and child.

"I wanna show my sun I lav him. I lav him."

She shook her head to shake the sound of him out.

"I wanna real relationship. I wanna be happy like every other bleedin' body else.

"FACK!"

He rolled tobacco and lit it. He made a cup of tea with three sugars and pulled out a large brown envelope. It contained letters and photos of a Russian lonely heart searching for love in the UK. Her name was Olga and she was pretty, far too good for him—a skinny, short, bald, jobless, ignorant bastard without a penny in the bank. 'I'm still gonna meet her though,' he told himself. 'You never know, she might be bleedin' blind, an'—I can always grow a fackin' beard an' 'ide 'arf me fackin' face!'

Jolienta chuckled. He wasn't shouting anymore, he was thinking. Unfortunately, she could hear every thought.

The layers of paint bonded and were ready for more. She loaded a brush with a mix of crimson, burnt sienna and the tiniest hint of Prussian blue, and began to block in more shadows, allowing minute pinpricks of underlying colour to remain; colour which held the luminosity of the primed canvas.

The shadows echoed existing circular shapes and went round and round like the passage of time. Like the inside of a juggernaut tyre. Like a mother and child embracing. Like the bullet holes in a brick wall.

She sat back and tried to summarize her progress. The composition would certainly attract criticism.

Why are the figures cut off from below the waist? No one does that, an imaginary art critic said.

"Well, she's half-way whole, half-way real. Besides, I wanted to create a unique composition. And no one has painted such a composition before."

But you have given equal importance to cornices, windows and bricks, the art critic said.

"People and places . . . they have a bond."

Why are the colours tropical?

"The original source, the Coldharbour Tyre Shop, was a violent red and my ancestral roots come from hotter climes."

The mother embraced the child and stretched out an arm in a gesture of welcome. Either she was offering the child safe passage into the life ahead, or it was a greeting for others to join them on the journey. Jolienta didn't know which and applied swathes of orange, more yellow ochre and splashes of thick gluey pigment.

Sometimes, you just don't know what you're doing. You just try your best. And hope for the best. I couldn't keep the juggernaut tyre in. I couldn't keep Hopper in me. He left a while ago, but I'm more whole and more real now.

I'm going to make this painting work if it kills me.

The next day, Bert was in the vestibule.

Damn. It's a liability this vestibule. He wants to talk. Of course.

She looked at him quizzically. He was the new owner of a beard tinged with flecks of white, which gave him an air of dignity and subdued the mad glint in his eye.

"Well, 'Alenter," Bert began, "this Olga's coming over from Russia for two weeks, so I'd better get me fackin' garden done and finish the decoratin'.

"Fack me," he continued, "'ow am I gonna take the woman out on dole money?" His eyebrows met in the middle.

How I hate this. I hate it when he confides in me. It implies we are friends, and we aren't. The worse thing is, it's impossible not to feel some sympathy. I'm always trying to reinforce boundaries. We are neighbours. Nothing more.

I'm too tired to stop and talk in the vestibule. How about that? Has that ever occurred to him? Am I allowed to be tired? How dare I be tired?

I am afraid. Afraid that one day he will erupt, totally erupt and blame *me* for all of the wrongs in *his* life.

Bert bounded along his corridor. She peered down into his flat and watched him bounce up and down in his back garden.

God, he looks like a dog about to ejaculate.

His eyeballs were spinning in their sockets, round and round.

He looked at his weeds in dismay. "Can I 'ave some cuttin's from yer garden, 'Alenter?" he yelled, holding the precious Olga in mind and bounding towards the vestibule.

He was right next to her. He looked sort of vulnerable.

"You're welcome. Help yourself. I'm no expert. I don't know how to do take cuttings. They'll just die if I do it for you."

Bert looked at the plants, was confusion and retreated into his flat. She returned to the painting.

Is the girl, a girl, or is 'she' a boy? Not that it matters. Why should it matter? Both have the same value. She or he looks mean . . . sinister and has developed an enormous ear. The mother holds an arm out to show the way. The mother's face is a mask.

The hair, the art critic said, *resembles a warrior's helmet. Did you intend that?*

"No, I didn't. I hadn't seen it that way at all. I'm shocked at what you say."

The brick wall behind the mother and the child spoke of the years gone by: the rising of the sun each day, the wind and the rain, the traffic fumes that collect in the nicks of mortar, the capture of voices in the brick, the hub of feelings and ideas, the urination of pets, and even the faint residue of spiders who have never done anything dishonest in the whole of their lives. The cornice hung down. Tick-tock. Tick-tock. The window vanished. Its history, evidenced by the remaining windowsill, and the reflections on panels of glass, no longer existed. A solitary cup stood on the windowsill; it's shadow spilling onto brick.

The phone rang. It was Cheeki.

"Jolly the Sisters of Nazareth have given you permission to stay for free. Told ya."

"Wow. And you know what Cheeks, I'm not going to worry about the cost of the plane ticket. I'll sell artwork. I'll have a studio sale."

"Yes Jolly. Selling art is better than being run over by icecream van in Peckham."

Three weeks later the studio was opened and Jolienta plied neighbours with wine and hummus and pitta bread, olives, red peppers and salsa, mushroom and green bean risotto, roasted wedges of potato sprinkled with spices, and crispy corn chips and guacamole. Three paintings and several drawings were sold. The drawings went for modest amounts of money, which was annoying, but the overall sum was enough for a return flight to

L.A. She was on her way, and this time she would have the legendary Great Aunty Cheeki all to herself.

*   *   *

The sun shone between skyscraper, liquor store and palm tree; I was in red sleeveless top, skintight black leggings and red pointed leather shoes. I climbed over the crash barriers and waited for a break in the traffic. Ah, Los Angeles and its humungous roads. How could I forget?

Cars flashed by on either side of the metal barriers. It was a balancing act. I leapt and ran. Drivers blasted their horns at me and whizzed past.

On the corner of Melton and Ryan, the lights turned red— I was in the middle of the road when the lights switched back to green. A shuddering wall of cars was ready to release itself. I charged full speed to the far far side. Closer in, palm trees and blue sky peeped out over high high walls. Long shadows cast triangles of black across the hot midday. The crisp thwack of a tennis ball confirmed a sedate area at the height of summer. Closer in, more palm trees led to the entrance of The Sisters of Nazareth. The vestibule was cool and led directly to the sacred chapel.

Holy water fonts stood at intervals along the corridors, promising instant absolution. There was also, according to my great aunt, an air-conditioned restaurant and independent living quarters for each boarder.

I entered the chapel. It smelt nice. Incense. Sunday lunch. Etching. Rembrandt. Cheeki was kneeling down in the front pew praying.

"Jolly," she whispered, "you look gorgeous. You look like a ballerina."

I kissed my great aunt on the forehead and knelt beside her to pray.

*   *   *

California sun streamed through the window. The bathroom door was wide open. Cheeki was on the toilet, legs apart, stockings dangling around her ankles like bracelets, pushing out yesterday's sustenance.

Now you might find that shocking, I said to the art critic, with one arm dangling out of my sleeping bag, Well, I'd say, you've led a sheltered life, you silly art critic. These are the events that make life endearing. Make it real.

Shit represents many things:

—A love token trapped in a Knight's silver locket;

—A bygone gift from a Chinese relative;

—Essential nightsoil for crops in countries such as China, Japan, India and Tanzania.

"Jolly, blueberry muffin for breakfast?" Cheeki said, emerging from the toilet.

"How about wholemeal toast with jam and a cup of fresh coffee, Aunty Cheeks? I'm getting up now."

"Wah, wholemeal? What is this wholemeal? Jolly I don't know how to use percolator. I make tea."

"I need wholemeal to start my day, Aunty Cheeks. After all, you did say I was hefty the first time we met."

"Oh Jolly I was rude to one of your cousins the other day. I said she had big hips. But you are gorgeous. A beautiful ballerina. You walk like a ballerina, hee, hee. Look at you . . . tippetty-toe, tippetty-toe."

"Ha ha."

Cheeki gave me a mug of tea.

"Can I tell you about China, Aunty? I haven't had the chance to tell you yet. You keep getting visitors."

"Tell me now."

"I started out in Beijing, where I ended up in a police cell. I'll tell you that one later. Oops, I didn't mean to mention that one."

"Oh Jolly. You tease!"

"Travelled north to see the Great Wall of China, but I missed out on seeing the Wall itself because I pulled my back out really badly. I was at a right-angle. Like this." I got out of my sleeping bag and gave a demonstration.

"Jolly!"

"I flew to Xian in a rickety Russian plane to see the terracotta warriors. The airhostess said *Would you like champagne?* Unfortunately, it was fizzy lemonade. Arrgh. I travelled to Hangzhou and Guilin, both exceptionally beautiful. See these photographs. These are limestone peaks. The cormorants. The children. I bought one of those white hats that spring open."

"Wah!"

"Kunming Market sold desiccated cockroach for dinner and everyone crowded around us to see our big noses. Finally, I reached Hong Kong and Macau, the place of our forebears."

"Oh Jolly. You are intrepid."

"When you get off the plane at Kai Tak Airport, the heat and humidity hits you like a wet towel."

"Wah! You can do all that."

"But you know, since I've been back in London, just now and then, I've felt like an imposter. I've felt like I'm not real. But when I see you, I feel OK and then whole trip across China becomes relevant again."

"Oh Jolly, why is this?"

"I don't know. I seem to waiver in and out. One minute solid, and the next, I'm kinda two-dimensional like one of my paintings. Mind you, I learnt a lot about China and Kowloon. The history. I'm glad. The Opium Wars, Hong Kong and Macau, the Macanese people. Picture postcard territory everywhere I went. I told you about what happened in Peace Avenue in my letters. I saw your Daddy in a bowtie. I wonder if you were there too? The one in the nappy. I have a copy of the mortgage deeds, Cheeki."

"Jolly we talk about something else. I like to go to corner shops off Manning Avenue like you do. I envy your strength. That way goes straight into the Santa Monica Freeway. Impossible for me. The fucking traffic. The lights change too quickly."

"Oh Cheeki, I'm a fit woman in my thirties and even I have to run like hell to get to the other side of the road. You have to be an Olympian over here."

"I'm going outside to have a fag Jolly. Fucking nuns will go crazy if they see me. Hee hee."

We walked out onto the porch. Cheeki sat in the rocking chair, the one from Chanera Avenue. I leaned on the balustrade overlooking the gardens.

The feeling this tiny event evoked in me was indescribable. She made me feel relevant. She made me laugh, and as a consequence, out there on the porch, years of neglect got washed away . . . or blown away . . . on a puff of American tobacco.

We said Grace in the restaurant. Other residents and a Sister stopped to say Hello. The food was excellent, but three courses for lunch? And three meals of three courses per day? Yikes.

"Jolly, this is where I fight Mrs Wallace."

"Out here?"

"She in a wheel chair now and tries to run at me. I whack her with my stick. I look forward to it. She can make as many complaints as she wants."

After lunch, we watched TV in her rooms, talked and dunked doughnuts in our coffee. When evening came, Cheeki decided she was going to cook for me rather than take me back to the nun's restaurant.

"Jolly, no one cooks for themselves here, but I try. It's nice to eat exactly what I want, when I want. My choice. I make dinner."

Cheeki set a tin opener against the top of a can. It slid off. She tried again.

Cheeki's knuckles were swollen. "Let me do that for you."

"Thank you Jolly."

"I'll investigate tin openers as soon as I get back. I wish I had the money to buy you a mobility scooter. You don't see them over here, do you?"

"No Jolly. Not safe. Tell me Jolly. Things better with Mummy?"

"Nah. She lives in a world of her own."

"What about your uncles? Fufu is the one. We had to eat the pet dog while he went travelling round the world."

"I know. Last winter, I went to visit Uncle Rico in his bedsit. I'm not sure why I went. I suppose I felt sorry for him. What actually happened when I got there was: he appeared to be drunk, he knelt on the floor and slowly, very slowly he placed his hand on my knee and began to slide his hand up my skirt. I wanted to throw up. I was paralysed. It was like watching a horror movie."

"Oh Jolly."

"I hope my telling you doesn't shock you. I told my sisters. For what that was worth. They said I was "uncharitable". I haven't seen them since and I'm not going to see them again either. Not for as long as I live. What did they want me to do? Open my legs? *Ey up, Uncle, would you like to have a go? Here's my vagina.* Enough is enough and when you consider my father's behaviour.

"Now I understand why my oldest sister despises me, why she was never there for me. It doesn't explain why they both used to lock me up and hide away the key. What ever happened to them, they didn't need to take it out on me, did they? I was the youngest."

"Oh Jolly!" Cheeki switched TV channels. "What about your career? That go very well. Yes?"

"It's tough. I'll give you an example. Some dealer—quite well known in the West End—he came to a group exhibition I'd organized in north London and snapped up one of the artists—a woman who has a natural capacity to churn out images, and the dealer, Jeremy Westcliffe, invited me to bring some of my own work to his gallery. Well, Aunty, you can't go on the Underground with enormous works of art, so that meant hiring a van. Now we're talking about money to pay the driver. We packed the van, found a parking meter, pumped money into it, off loaded the van in Saville Row, and arranged my work on the gallery floor. Don't ask me what was going on, the dealer immediately went on the offensive. He was horrible to me in front of the driver. I was humiliated. Minutes later, he had me remove the work. His receptionist was embarrassed as well. The irony is, on the way home the police stopped the van to alert us about the roof rack. One of my pictures had snapped in half and was dangling precariously. On top of that, none of the artists in the group exhibition I organized ever returned the compliment of my efforts, the woman, who got taken on by Jeremy thanks to me, blanks me now. I'm insignificant."

"Oh Jolly. What about Santa Monica?"

"Yes. The gallery owner was very nice to me and she took some lithographs, but sadly, she died of cancer. The husband sent them back and closed the gallery down. I remember thinking that she looked uncommonly white. Poor thing."

"Look Jolly. Look. See how unlined my arms are . . . just like a young lady." Cheeki pulled up her nightdress to show off floppy breasts and a stomach ringed with shingles. Her arms were a lovely honey-dew in tone.

Great Aunty Cheeki cleared the dining table and climbed onto an egg-crate of foam designed for sore bones, said Goodnight, turned onto her side and pulled a quilt over her body. I got into the sleeping bag on the floor next to her. Outside, it seemed to me that stars were twinkling in the blue-black sky of the City of Angels, holding me, telling me everything would be all right.

Downey

JUST FOR ONCE, I'D LIKE BERT not to jettison into the vestibule like a crazy man and demand my attention as soon he hears my key in the goddamn lock. Talk about a rude awakening. You are back home. If he's opened my letters, I don't know what I'll do. He already plucked a cheque from out of my letterbox and held onto it for maximum inconvenience. As if it isn't hard enough getting paid in the first place and then he goes and hides it. It's enough to make me want to commit murder.

Jolienta unlocked the door and avoided the temptation of glancing in the direction of Bert's bay window. She put the key in. The door jammed.

Don't tell me it's him, ready to pounce.

Leaflets and junk mail blocked the way.

Bert. I knew going on strike wouldn't make any difference. He hasn't lifted a finger to clean the vestibule in months. Jolienta shouldered her way into the vestibule and stepped over the pile.

Days and evenings were spent working on the mother and child. The canvas was full of the sun. The mother's second hand, a new addition, touched the child gently at the side. The woman developed the features of a Macanese woman. The child was no longer evil and listened to the woman with curiosity. On either side of the figures, a palm tree and other tropical plants flourished. The woman's fingers were substantial and heavenly.

They were the hands of an angel on the ceiling of the Sistine Chapel.

*   *   *

Sometimes, Jolienta phoned Great Aunty Cheeki up, eager to connect. Sometimes, Cheeki was delighted. Sometimes Cheeki said, "Jolly why you call me? I old lady."

*   *   *

She was going to Los Angeles once again. She was going to visit Cheeki's grave. First of all, she needed to make a souvenir befitting the occasion. Jolienta poured plaster into a mould, let it dry out in part and began to carve flowers and Cheeki's name into the moist oblong with a curved rasp.

"Jane, no one seems to know where Cheeki is buried. Typical. I expected that, you know. Of course, nobody knows. Of course, no one will tell me. I will get there though. The nuns will tell me where it is. They can't deny me the information."

"This is really beautiful, Jola." Jane turned the block over and admired each side of it.

"The tulips. Reminds me of the William Morris Museum. Yes," Jane said, "the nuns can't deny you the info."

"Thanks for that."

"Jola, I promise to look after the flat while you're away and promise to water the garden. And I promise not to let Bert into the flat."

"If you let him in, he'll be snooping around, weighing me up, what I'm worth, how he can take advantage of me, and it'll be a case of What can I steal?

"You can do whatever you like while you're in the flat, Jane. Throw a party. Have company. But please don't smoke in the studio. There are inflammables in there. Don't put the central heating on in the studio either. I'm on a tight budget."

241

"Don't worry about a thing, Jola."

"Bert's fixated on me, Jane, and he's becoming stranger and stranger. I can't emphasize enough what a nuisance he is. He terrifies me. He follows me down the road and breathes on my neck.

"You don't have to live here, Jane. You don't get the measure of him—experience the verbal abuse, the threats, the banging on my door and the walls and the ceiling in the early hours. He steals my post from the letterbox."

"OK, OK! I said I promise not to let him over the threshold. I *promise* not to get friendly with him. I did get friendly with him once. I thought he was a good bloke. Hope the trip goes well. Hope you find out where your great aunt is buried."

*   *   *

Everything looked the same. Palm trees lined the drive-in and the vestibule was tranquil with its marble holy water fonts placed at intervals. I rang the bell. Sister Teresa appeared and invited me in with a puzzled expression written across her face.

"Sister, I wrote to you recently and telephoned you about my Great Aunty Cheeki—Ermina Dos Remédios. You said you'd be happy to disclose where she was buried and that we could talk about her last moments. As you know, I've flown in from London. Here I am. I was very, very fond of her. I stayed here one summer, and you were very hospitable to me."

This seemed to reassure Sister Teresa, who was sitting at her desk surrounded by religious souvenirs, on the walls and on the mantelpiece. "Of course my dear. I'd be happy to tell you anything you want to know."

"Can you tell me where she's buried? That's the most important thing."

Sister Teresa opened the window.

"First of all, let me tell you about the history of our order."

242

Sister sat down and rolled up her sleeves. "In nineteen twenty-six, religious persecution ran rampant throughout Mexico. Many priests and nuns tried to escape torture by fleeing to the United States. Reverend Mother Matilda made a decision to send a group of five Religious to a Franciscan Convent in Santa Barbara. The Bishop then enquired at different parishes to see who would accept them. A response came from Reverend Father Emmanuel, the Pastor at St John's. With the help of the Sisters of St John, a small home was prepared for them on Green Street. Soon, Father Emmanuel realized that the little house could no longer accommodate the Sisters as three more arrived from Mexico. He obtained a larger house in Gardena, where they stayed for three years. The Divine Providence that always watched over His beloved daughters was manifested in an admirable manner, because when the benefactors realized the number of staff had grown, they made larger donations.

"In June, nineteen forty-two, our Superior General Maria Conchita Fernandez took the first steps in obtaining the Archbishop's authorization for the addition of a room to be used as a Chapel. And on the fifth of October nineteen forty-two, Mrs Custer came to ask the Mother Superior for two Religious to help care for some aged ladies. This home was named Mater Benefiscio and Holy Mass was celebrated there once a week at the same time as the Holy Hour.

"Praise be to God!" Sister raised her arms up to the ceiling.

"The home that served as a convent for the Religious was on loan from the Chancery. Acting on the permission of the Superior General and the Council, it was decided to buy the home in installments. The three Sisters paid for the home with the salary they received from Mrs Custer. In October nineteen forty-three, Mother Mary Judy was brought in to replace Mother Guillerma Velasquez, and realizing that the work of these Religious was not sufficiently enumerated, the Superior decided to make an application to begin working on their own.

"Next to the convent, there was a small home that was used to begin their work. They received a County License on February the twenty-forth nineteen forty-four, and in September of that year, payment was completed on the Santa Maria Convent. The first aged lady to come to us was Mrs Nape. Three months later, more began to arrive and on November the fifth of the same year, two rooms were added to the home. The funds came from a drama festival staged by Catechism students."

Sister Teresa glowed with rapture.

"On December the twelfth, nineteen forty-five," she continued, "The County gave us a license for the care of twelve aged women. One day, a Fire Department Inspector arrived unexpectedly to check the home's condition, and seeing that the home did not meet the necessary requirements—gave the order that it be closed within three months. We went to the Municipal Office that had issued the license to see Dr Brown, who had already given medical attention to our aged women. The Municipality spoke with the Fire Department assuming responsibility for the Home, as did Dr Brown, and thanks be to God, we were permitted to continue our work, although the Inspector told us our case would have to go before the State.

"Although, we were saddened by this, we trusted in the Sacred Heart of Jesus. We began a novena of confidence with the certainty that the Inspector would permit us to continue in our small home while the larger one was being built. After a few months, the State Inspector came. He examined the home and said—"I am a Third Order Franciscan and I know the Franciscans are poor. Don't be afraid, I won't close the home. I'm going to permit you to continue your good work with these aged women. But try to realize your plans as soon as possible." We were very pleased and we tried everything we could."

Sister took a deep breath and began with increased vigour.

"In February nineteen forty-six, Reverend Mother Romana became ill. It was discovered she had tuberculosis. On August thirty-first, Reverend Mother gave up her soul to God. Her dreams and sacrifices in helping our beloved Community were like a constant prayer. There is no doubt her prayers were heard.

"In nineteen forty-eight, we found out that some wooden buildings, previously mess halls for soldiers, were up for sale. Two of our Religious went to the government office to inquire, but were told that they had all been purchased. We contacted the official there and told him of our plans. One day, he asked how much money we had, and we told him we had three thousand dollars. For this sum, the building was purchased.

"Soon the building had been converted into a comfortable home for twenty-five aged women, meeting all the state's requirements. All of this we owe, first of all, to God, and then to the generosity and interest of the Monsignor and Mr Upton, who did not hesitate to make sacrifices, and did everything possible to see the building completed. The first part of the rest home was blessed on March the nineteenth. The active life of the Religious in their work for the good of the aged continued. Meanwhile, many applicants were awaiting their turn, causing us to plan on enlarging the building. With the co-operation of the Monsignor, Archbishop Lloyd and our Superior General, a study was made to plan for the second part of the home.

"Many became aware of our existence, and like swarming bees, many aged women in search of love and compassion, began arriving. For this reason, we asked permission, again, for a loan to build a larger Chapel, in order to accommodate a hundred persons, plus a convent for the Sisters. At first it was denied. We then informed the Archbishop that we had use of only one dormitory while the patio was our dining room."

"Sister . . ."

"The first planned fundraiser was a chicken dinner," Sister

Teresa continued. "Chickens were donated alive and the Sisters had quite a job of killing them and cleaning them. The event was hard work, but a great success. Next came successful hamburger dinners followed by spaghetti dinners. The entertainment for these events never failed, because Sister Celia had an ability to entertain as only she knows how!

"In recent years, we have been provided with a new fire alarm system, extensive air conditioning, dishwashers, fire sprinklers, a new buzzer system, surplus quality mattresses and many luxuries like solar fountains."

I sighed.

"Blessed be the past fifty years with the undoubted sacrifices of all our dear Sisters, the Priests and Bishops, the generous support of our many benefactors and the continued work and support of the Guild. We recognize and appreciate our Sisters' dedication to the resident's care, the aid of our employees, the outstanding directives of our Superiors, and the perseverance of the Guild and benefactors to which we owe this celebration of fifty years of loving service."

"Please can you tell me where Cheeki is buried, Sister?"

"Of course, my dear, let me write down the details for you on a piece of paper."

Sister Teresa leaned over her table and began to write.

"Sister, you said on the phone that you were with my great aunt when she passed away. Can you tell me . . . did she mention my name to you? Did she leave any message for me? Was she in pain, or afraid, in the moments before her death?"

Sister considered the questions carefully. "Hmm. I do not recollect the name Jolienta. No. She never mentioned you. She didn't mention you. Sweet Mother of Joseph, be sure about this, she died peacefully and I was with her to the end."

Outside, the salty Pacific washed over, trickled down the sides of my nose. Leafy branches, happy to hang over the high high walls, brushed against my face offering comfort. Comfort. Both legs moved along moved along the wide pavement sifting grains of sand from one vestibule to the other. One minute I was weighty, the next I was defying gravity.

Of course, she loved me, I told myself. Of course, she did.

Where is that piece of paper the Sister gave me? It would be like me to come all this way and lose it.

It's in my hand.

The scrap of paper contained the words *Row H* and *Downey Cemetery* in black biro and the writing slanted to the left and slanted to the right.

"Downey Cemetery?" I opened my rucksack. The map was falling apart at the folds. Downey was at least twenty miles away from the rest home and southeast of Downtown L.A. The route was accessible via the Santa Monica Freeway. If I walked the length of Manning Avenue I'd probably be able to catch a bus and get off at Lakewood for Firestone.

Along Lakewood Boulevard, I passed companies, stores, and places of residence. At Firestone, there was a McDonald's with a Harvey's Broiler sign, a picture of a porky boy dressed up as a sailor and holding a triple burger.

Downey Cemetery at last.

Tall metal gateway. Gold letters against black:

> No Pets Allowed.
> No Flowers Allowed.
> Any Ornaments / Statuettes left on or
> by the gravestones will be disposed of.
> No Litter or Eating on the Premises.
> This Cemetery will close promptly at
> 5.30 p.m. Daily.

No ornamentation? I searched for the block of plaster in my rucksack. It was wrapped inside a tea towel, unharmed by the journey and waiting for its final resting place. Opposite the gate was a building. Inside, the reception counter could have been that of any council department in the UK.

"Yes," a man said. He was reading a newspaper.

"Hello. I'm here to visit a grave. The name is Ermina dos Remédios. The site of the grave is written here."

The man went away and came back with a receipt. He pointed at a diagram and began to fan his face with the newspaper.

The sound of an electric lawnmower shattered the stillness of the cemetery. The grass was perfect, cropped to the edge of each tombstone. No room for irregular shapes. No room for ornamentation.

There it is: a black shiny tombstone.

I put the carving on top of the stone to acquaint it with its new home, pulled out a knife and began to cut through the turf. Nearby, a funeral was taking place. Rows of gold-lacquered chairs had been placed in neat rows and a smart white coffin with gold hinges, gold brackets and gold handles was being hoisting by crane into a hole. Mourners were sitting on the front row facing the priest and someone had brought along a yapping white poodle. Hymns emanated from loudspeakers. I couldn't figure out where the speakers were, and when everyone had gone, a bulldozer drowned out the religious treacle by shoving dirt into the hole.

I removed a piece of turf, exchanged the knife for a fork and began to dig. When there was enough space and I was sure nobody was watching, I dropped the carving in and put the turf back.

The vestibule

WHO ELSE WOULD BE IN THE GODDAMN VESTIBULE in the middle of the night?

She could hear him—"That fackin' bitch."

Don't tell me he's going to push the door in.

Jolienta flung back the bed cover and crept across the landing. Some of the steps creaked. The thud in her chest was immense. She sat on the last step.

He is behind my door, facing me, breathing into it.

Did I double-lock it?

She gripped the stair carpet.

These altercations always occur when I'm concentrating on something important such as enlarging the painting of the mother and child. The woman no longer works. She needs legs and feet.

Jolienta faced the door. Thin white plywood. She sat and thought, sat and waited for the next outburst.

Bert punched the door. The door shuddered. The lock held.

Bert, he invades every part of my life now. I creep from room to room while he bashes the ceiling with a frying pan. He has to jump up to reach it. What a madman. And so he won't know which room I'm in, I tiptoe from room to room and slip quietly into bed at night so that he won't know exactly when I'm asleep— then he can't delight in waking me up. I leave the radio on low when I'm in the kitchen. I try to confuse him about which room I'm in.

He still goes on three a.m. jaunts looking for houses to burgle, and when he gets back, he goes right on and slams the doors on his way out and slams them again on his way back in.

If *I* want to go out, I wait until he's gone, or I make a dash for it. Coming back home is always the worst, because all he's got to do is look up from his settee and he'll see me on the garden path. I've spoken to the housing officer. They may be the largest housing association in east London, but the housing officer is a disinterested, harsh woman, who despises my white face, and all white faces of all white people. But she doesn't know me. She doesn't know the life I've led or what my beliefs are.

I've called the police. Tried to explain my fear. They told me to keep a diary with dates and times. The housing officer didn't tell me to do that. The police said that until an act of violence occurs, or I get myself a third party witness, they're unable to act on my behalf. That's the problem. I live alone. No witnesses. That's why he gets away with it. And Jane won't admit it, but she likes him, that's why she won't be a witness.

Let me return to my painting. Let me walk right back up these stairs. I will creep up them slowly. Slowly.

Shhh! You almost made a sound. Shhh.

Jolienta looked at the canvas on the studio floor.

It's a ridiculous idea what I intend to do, but I'll do it anyway.

She unstapled the canvas from the stretcher, pulled it clean away, and began to sew on an additional length of canvas with a large darning needle. Enough space for the legs and feet.

The needle was unwieldy in her hands. A sturdy thimble helped to push the needle into the material.

Two sections of canvas, one heavily painted, and the lower half blank, lay on the floor sewn together as one.

Jolienta knocked the stretcher apart with light taps and measured out lengths of wood. The shortest side needed to double in length.

The joints are fiddly. When the glue is dry and I've added some screws and corner backing, I'll re-staple the painting and prime the lower half of the canvas.

Who is going to buy a painting with a seam running along its centre? the art critic said.

You expect me to exhibit a painting with a seam running along its centre? the gallery dealer said.

After a second coat of primer, water was applied to the lower portion of the canvas. The enlarged painting was left to lean on a chair opposite a calour gas heater. The lower portion of canvas quivered dry. The crevasse created by the seam was filled in with melted beeswax.

Tomorrow will be different, she told herself. She slipped into bed. "Jane's coming for brunch, and in the afternoon, Kris and Alison are coming for a picnic, and whenever I get visitors, Bert leaves me alone.

"The extra space on the canvas is reserved for a pot of snakes, and the mother's hand will rest there too. The mother will protect the child, whose head is twisted in an impossible fashion, about to break. The child will have a blue skirt. The mother will have a breast, be proud of her nakedness, and to balance out the palm tree, I'll add an African lily with leaves of orange. An opaque orange. It will sit in the corner."

The alarm clock rang at seven o'clock. Jolienta hurried to dress and get out of the house. At the corner of her eye, and behind the clump of irises, she noticed Bert's window was open. She smelt cigarette smoke and heard the sound of his radio.

Damn.

His eyes stayed on her as she opened the garden gate. He patrolled the movement of the top of her head as it glided past the hedge. She heard him as clear as the morning: "Shall I stampede the bitch when she gets back? Ha, ha, ha!"

He closed his eyes.

"Nah, carnt be bovverrred."

His cigarette dropped onto the carpet.

He began to snore and twitch.

He dreamt about winning the lottery and what he'd do, what he would change.

The key was being turned in the latch. Alenter's footsteps were in the vestibule. She brushed against the door. The keys jangled.

"Ya stupid bitch!" Bert screamed.

There. Now, there's no need for me to even move me arse, 'cos I've terrified the bleedin' life out of 'er.

"Fack me. That fackin' cow's in the paper again!" he hissed. Bert grabbed the Walthamstow Recorder lying on the coffee table, snarled at his yellow-stained walls, shuffled through the pages and narrowed in on the photograph of Jolienta dos Remédios surrounded by paintings. An assault on his senses, a "downright aggravation".

In the photograph, Jolienta wore large hooped earrings, the size of curtain rings, and was leaning forward to provide the reader with a view of four paintings. One of the paintings was of a naked woman dancing barefoot in a moonlit jungle.

"Fack me," Bert said, "she's called it *Warrior Woman*."

He sprang to his feet and switched the kettle on.

"Goin' to a bleedin' rainforest?" he spat. "A bleedin' rainforest? Gawd help me."

The last paragraph of the article stated, The work of Jolienta dos Remédios is currently appearing alongside the work of Picasso and Titian in the exhibition, 'The Nude, a New Perspective' at The Victoria & Albert Museum.

He crushed the out-of-date newspaper in his hand. "She must be bleedin' loaded!" He tore the page out. "I know. I'll poison 'er fackin' plants!"

She was at the top of the stairs, listening, shaking. "Two hours to go. Jane will be here and Kris and Alison will be along later."

*   *   *

She and Jane sat down to a cheesy omelette with organic red peppers. "Thanks for looking after the flat, Jane. How did you get on while I was away?" The telephone bill had arrived and Jane must have phoned every person on the planet while looking after the flat.

"Oh, I really enjoyed being here. I loved it. Nice area. Cows walk up and down the road. I got such a shock. I didn't believe you. Epping Forest cattle have the right of way."

"What did you get up to while I was away?"

"I just took it easy."

"I was wondering why the table was pulled away from the wall in the studio."

"Oh, the radiator leaked. I had to pull it away."

"Really? That's odd. It's never leaked before and to tell you the truth, I've never switched that radiator on since I moved here. You know . . . the bills and all that."

"Oh. I switched all the radiators on," Jane said, munching.

"Really? Even when I asked you not to put any heating on in that room?"

"Sorry."

"Katy next door said you threw a party. No problem with that. In fact, I suggested it. Have a good time, I said, but I did ask you not to put the radiators on in that one room, my studio space, to keep the cost down."

"Sorry."

"And most of all, because of the inflammables."

Jane lowered her head.

"You know, I asked you not to let anyone smoke in that room due to the amount of turpentine, white spirit and methylated spirits. It's a cocktail waiting to go off. I found stubs and ash on the floor."

Jane's face reddened.

"And why did you rearrange my furniture and my bathroom? I like my flat the way it is and I had to put everything back."

253

"Sorry."

"Anything else I should know about? Don't tell me you let Bert into the flat?"

Jane's lips tightened into a thin line. She looked at the table.

*　　*　　*

The rugs were on the lawn ready for a picnic. Soon Bert would see that she had more than one friend.

Kris and Alison smiled and opened the gate. Kris was holding the baby in his arms and looked very happy.

"Hey, Jol, this is great," he boomed glancing at the paper plates, the salad niçoise and homemade apple pie.

"We love our double portrait, Jolienta."

*　　*　　*

Dissatisfied with the mother and child painting, which dominated the whole of the studio floor, Jolienta photographed it, took the film to be developed at a local supermarket, and four hours later scanned the prints, printed the images off on an A3 printer and examined the results.

"It's the woman's legs. I need to move the woman's hand. The biggest problem is exactly what to do with the right leg. The breast looks great. The effort of standing naked for hours in front of a mirror with a piece of charcoal in my hand was worth it.

"If I play around with Photoshop . . . try out different saturations, different hues? I have to admit the only part of the painting that works is the African lily.

A bang echoed from in the vestibule.

"Yer fackin' shit bastard!" nicotine-fingered Bert yelled.

Thump. Bang. Wallop.

The peephole view showed two men fighting. Bert and another man were in an angry clinch, bouncing off the vestibule walls. They crashed into his living room. A windowpane shattered.

"Yer fackin' bastard," Bert yelled.

"If only the other man was stronger," Jolienta cried.

Now the other man was being rolled around the front garden and punched in the stomach. He was losing.

Bert might kill the man and no one would ever know. I'd better call the police. I'm not doing it here though where I'm alone.

Jolienta flung the door open and ran through the vestibule. The men were tumbling on the lawn and squashing the flowers. She scurried over the road and ran to the opposite house. "Hello, is Mandy in, please?"

"No, she isn't. What's up?" Mandy's husband looked bored.

"Can I use your phone to call the police? Bert's beating up some bloke in the garden."

"Oh, all right. Take it in the living room."

The police arrived and disappeared up the garden pathway. Ten minutes later, they re-emerged. Jolienta hurried out and stayed in the middle of the road so that she could run away if she needed to.

"Oh, hello Miss, it's you. Don't worry," the officer said. "I think they've both worn each other out. Mr Cornipple sends his apologises to you."

Jolienta stared at the officers, beseeched them, begged them.

"Come on, Miss, it'll be OK. You can always ring us again."

After upturned plant pots had been put back, Jolienta hurried through the vestibule and double-locked the door. She sensed she would be left in peace for a while.

"It is hard to concentrate. The Millennium is looming and I want to portray the landmasses of the world, the cracked earth, and I want to make a holistic landscape where every person and creature is equal. I want to capture the rainforest. Much work needs to be done and so little time to do it in. So little time."

The mother and child stared back. Their half-baked features and parts of their anatomy just didn't work.

"Yer fackin' slut. Yer fackin' whore. I'm gonna grass you up! I'm gonna get you good an' praper!" Bert hissed in the vestibule.

Jolienta crept down the stairs. She was becoming adept at avoiding creaking panels of wood.

Damn, I'm trembling again. I can't switch the tape recorder on. If I click it on, he'll here the click.

She clicked it on. Did he hear the click?

Bert's fists pummelled the door. He began to kick at the door.

She pushed an eye up to the peephole. Her eye closed in on the lens. Her eye closed in on the aperture and her heart missed a beat. It was a horrible sight—Bert's white, bulging eyeball squashed against the peephole, assaulting her with a balloon of blood-shot jeering madness.

"Oh," Bert said in that sneer he reserved for her and her alone, "Have you got your eye against the peep-hole? You stu-pid fackin' tart!" he shouted. "Well, I'm gon-na get yer. I'm gon-na get yer. You'll see!"

The bell rang. It was Johnny.

Bert let him into the vestibule.

They began to whisper.

"Money saved up . . . that tart upstairs . . . should have had kids years ago . . . I'm gonna grass 'er up . . . "

"Is that so, Dad? Me Ma said . . . OK. I'll see you next . . . "

Johnny said goodbye.

"Boo-hoo-hoo," Bert said. "Boo-hoo-hoo. Are we cry-in', are we? Yer stu-pid bitch!" he bellowed into the peephole.

At that moment, Jolienta sensed something else, something truly, truly terrifying. Bert had been rifling through her dustbin. It had been going on for months—him rifling through her garbage and private information. She focused on the interior of his home. She saw his kitchen. It was a shrine. Dedicated to her. A shrine. She could see it all—an old red bra dangled from a hook on the wall, her letters and old drawings that didn't work were stuck to his fridge, and notes she'd made were on his table, and in big bold red letters he'd scrawled across his kitchen wall:

GONE TO CHINA? NOT BLOODY LIKELY!

GOING TO THE RAINFOREST? YOU MUST BE BLEEDIN' JOKING

COLLECTED BY THE VICTORIA & ALBERT MUSEUM? HA HA

I'M GONNA GRASS YOU UP. YOU'RE GONNA GET IT.

She ran into the kitchen. She was blubbering, choking on her own saliva.

Bert attacked the ceiling. Bish! Bash!

"Oh Jolly," a ghostly Cheeki hovered over the fridge.

"Aunty, tell me what to do."

"Jolly, face your fear. I will be near."

"What? Go down there and face Bert?"

"Yes, Jolly. We are the Dos Remédios clan and we are fearless."

Jolienta gulped.

Cheeki shooed her on. She staggered down the stairs and wrenched the door open. Bert fell into the hallway and wrapped both hands around her neck. His hands were tight; she couldn't breathe.

I'm on the brink, the brink.

I am on the brink. The brink.

*   *   *

Catching the train from Euston Station to the north of England is an easy feat. It's one of those things you do if you want to survive. But first of all, you think about the possessions you've accumulated: framed oil paintings, drawings that are beginning to fox and need to be treated with chamomile tea. There are crumpled etchings that need to be re-flattened, outdoor and indoor plants that beg for a lasting home, nice furniture, pretty rugs, rickety pans and chipped dishes, an impeccable fridge, a washing machine, lovely table lamps, a bed with plenty of matching bedding and feather pillows, a black angora jumper with a sunflower design that's falling apart, wardrobes, a mobile phone, a laptop, a printer / copier / scanner, electric and manual tools from the days of when you were a professional artist, maps galore for when you go to Malacca to continue your investigations of Portuguese trading posts, and of course, the treasured photographs of your forebears, who lived in Kowloon.

You'll have to transport the pet dog, Sausage, and the cat, Winnipeg, in advance. Unfortunately, there isn't a single friend to stay in touch with. It has been one l—o—n—g nightmare—your life—initially alleviated by the presence of Edward Hopper, and then endured, while you sought to understand the past.

You can't put everything on a train—as much as you would like to do this. You'll have to hire a truck. Will the driver be willing to listen to me? Can I make sure nothing gets broken, stomped on, thrown to the ground, or stolen?

Is it too late for me to start all over again?

Begin a new life?

Will I make friends?

Once I move into my new home, I'll be stranded in a new town, and something tells me, maybe it's my age, but this is my last chance. My heart will go pitter-patter pitter-patter, *Please let me have a life before it's too late!* and my foot will slip off the kerb and I'll break a leg. I've seen it happen. Now I'm in crutches.

"Oh, Jolienta dos Remédios," she stared at the reflection in the living room window—white lined forehead indicating an inquisitive nature, black hair well-styled and greying at the temples, red lips waiting for that one kiss, "if that happens to me, if I break a leg, I'll pick myself up and start all over again. AM I NOT A GOOD PERSON? AM I NOT WORTH TREASURING? AM I NOT TO BE APPRECIATED?"

I twist my neck searching for something to extinguish my fear. I feel hysterical. I smile. I put the percolator on the hotplate. My mind chugs along and brings with it a sense of adventure. I add a dab of romance and imagine hedges, trees and bridges flying by. My mind cradles me with its movement and hum. I am on the brink of life. I am speeding to the north of England. I am on the brink of all hopes and dreams.

Jolienta dos Remédios, you will relax.

I'm on the brink!

Jolienta dos Remédios . . .

I'm on the brink!

"Jolienta, my darling, come closer and let me hold you. What have you been thinking about? I've been watching your reflection contort in the window. Are you worried? There's no need. I should think the two of us will cover everything that's needed, and the insurance policy will cover any possible damage that incurs during the move. We can take Sausage and Winnipeg and the fragiles by car. Let me hold you. Let me kiss those red lips."

END OF PART ONE

In memory

Before my dream ended, I peered into the drawer of a magnificent mahogany desk. Inside, an atlas of the world lay wrapped in tissue paper. It told the story of Portuguese trading posts on exotic coastlines, including Macau, the place of my forebears.

Other drawers began to open of their own accord. A butterfly from Hangzhou fluttered out bringing with it the smell of camphor wood. A Chengdu panda lay curled up in another dozing quietly, while to the right, a dugong from Malacca raised its wet head for a kiss. I put my arms around it squeezing its salty mass.

Another drawer shuddered open, full of travel. I reached inside and found a blue envelope postmarked Los Angeles. It was waiting to be read one more time:

> *My dear dear Jolly,*
>
> *It made me happy to get your phone call. You will be glad to know a new pill is working wonders at ninety years of age. I have no fear of death in fact will welcome it. Weather here turned cold. Thinking of going to Vancouver in March, the month I can eat mangoes from Manila.*
>
> *Jolly, there has never been a doubt in my mind that one day you will be a famous artist.*
> *Cheeki*

Cheeki, you have gone back as dust to the earth, but I will remember you and the Macanese people.

Author biography

Yolanda Christian graduated with a first class honours degree in Fine Art and went on to complete postgraduate printmaking at The Slade School of Art, London. After that, she went on to teach in adult education and was Visiting Lecturer at various Faculties of Art, including Cardiff and Newport in Wales.

During the 80s, Yolanda travelled across China to research her family tree. This resulted in a UK solo-touring exhibition called *Taking Root*. Around this period of time, Yolanda's work was purchased by museum collectors such as The Victoria & Albert Museum.

From the 90s onwards, Yolanda was commissioned to write in art magazines and began to freelance within publication teams as designer, proof-reader, sub editor and editorial executive.

Yolanda says she has always been fascinated by books and as a youngster would happily walk from Lark Lane to Liverpool City Centre to buy the latest Thames & Hudson.

"Although being a writer is not an easy lifestyle, I'm happy working with the written word and enjoy the world of writing and its power."

Praise for The Girl in Peckham & Kowloon:

"After the end of Portuguese Macau all the memories start fading and each time an old person dies is a moment of no return. That's why your interpretation is so valid and useful."

Dr. Jorge Forjaz, author of *Familias Macaenses*

Longlisted by the Mslexia Novel competition

If you would like to give the author feedback, please post a review on Amazon or eyeofanartist.blogspot.com. Thank you for reading this book.

Printed in Poland
by Amazon Fulfillment
Poland Sp. z o.o., Wrocław